The Marines

Giles Bishop

Alpha Editions

This edition published in 2022

ISBN : 9789356786158

Design and Setting By
Alpha Editions
www.alphaedis.com
Email - info@alphaedis.com

Contents

INTRODUCTION

How many of our boys, in times past, while glancing through the morning paper have read the following statement: "The United States Marines have landed and have the situation well in hand." The cable message may have come at any date, and from any part of the world. If those words caused any comment on the part of the young American, it was probably a mild wonder as to just who the marines were. Sometimes he may have asked his father for enlightenment, and the parent, being no better informed than the son but feeling a reply was necessary, would say in an off-hand manner, "Oh, they are just a lot of sailors from one of our battleships, that's all," and there the subject rested.

It is the author's desire in this volume to explain just who the marines are, what they do, where they go, so as to make every red-blooded American boy familiar with the services rendered by the United States Marine Corps to the nation in peace and war. And if in this endeavor you suspect me of exaggeration I ask that you will get the first real marine you meet to tell you where he has been and what he has done. Then, if at the end of a half hour you are not convinced that the adventures of Dick Comstock, in this and the books to follow, are modest in comparison, I shall most humbly apologize.

THE AUTHOR.

CHAPTER I

A BITTER DISAPPOINTMENT

"Dick Comstock, you've been fighting! What will Mother and Father say when they see your black eye?" and Ursula Comstock looked with mingled pity and consternation at her brother, who, at the moment, cautiously entered the cheery living-room.

"And to-day of all days in the year to have such a thing happen," she continued. "Everyone in town will see it to-night when you deliver your oration. I do think, Dick, if you had to fight, you might have waited until to-morrow, at least."

"It couldn't be helped, Sister, so stop scolding, and get me a raw steak or something to put on my eye," answered her brother, ruefully. "I know it's going to mortify Mother fearfully that her 'handsome son' is so badly banged up, but necessity knows no law, in war anyway. Now be a good sister and help me. Maybe by to-night it won't look so bad, and if you are as clever painting my face as you are your canvases it may not even be noticed."

"How did it happen?" inquired Ursula a little later, after first aid had been applied to the injured eye.

"Oh! It wasn't anything really of any account. I had to teach 'Reddy' Doyle a lesson he has been needing for a long time, that's all," answered Dick, bending over a basin of hot water while the tall, lithe girl, one year his junior, handed him steaming hot compresses.

"Tell me about it," demanded the girl, for between Richard and herself there were few secrets, and a more devoted brother and sister would be hard to find in all New England.

"Well, you see, Doyle and I never have been good friends in all the years we've been classmates at school. He goes with a gang I never cared for and he has always been inclined to bully. We've often had little tussles, but nothing that amounted to a great deal. You know he's a dandy athlete and I couldn't afford, half of the time, to have trouble with him. He is just cranky enough to have resigned from the school teams, and he's really too valuable a fellow to lose, consequently I've so often swallowed my pride in order to humor him that he began to believe I was afraid of him, I guess.

"But he has one mean trait I simply can't endure, and that is the torturing of dumb animals. I often heard from the other fellows of his tricks in that line. To-day I witnessed one, and--well--I've a black eye to pay for my meddling."

"That is not all the story, and you know it, Dick, so you may as well tell me now, for I shall get it sooner or later. What did he do that caused you to take such chances on this day of all days?"

"I didn't happen to think much about the day," grinned Dick, "but I do guess I'm a sight. Dad won't care; yet, as I said, I do feel sorry on Mother's account."

"Richard Comstock, if you do not stop this evasion and tell me at once what occurred, fully and finally, I'll refuse to help you another single bit. Now talk."

While Ursula was speaking she unconsciously shook a piece of very raw, red beef at her brother in such an energetic manner that he feared it might land in any but the place for which it was intended unless he obeyed without further delay.

A final rehearsal for the high school graduating exercises which was scheduled to take place in the evening had been held in the theatre, and after dismissal, as a number of the boys were going along Broad Street, a poor, emaciated cat ran frantically across the road towards them and climbed a small tree just in time to escape the lathering jaws of a closely pursuing bulldog. Percy Doyle, the red-haired owner of the dog, not satisfied with witnessing the poor feline barely escape his pet, ran quickly to the tree, grasped the cat by the neck and threw it to the eager brute. Almost instantly the powerful animal had shaken the cat to death.

This cold-blooded act was more than the good-natured Dick could stand and with a warning cry of anger and indignation he called upon Doyle to defend himself. Then there followed a royal combat, for these two lads were strong for their age and their years of activity in all kinds of sports had made them no mean antagonists.

In the end Doyle was beaten, but the victor had by no means escaped unscathed.

By the time Dick finished his recital the raw beef was properly bound over his eye and the grime of battle washed from his face by his gentle nurse, who completed her task by kissing him as she exclaimed with enthusiasm:

"Good for you, Dick, I hope you thrashed him well while you were about it, for he certainly deserved a beating. Now run along and get a bath and clean up properly before Mother comes home. She has gone to the station to meet Father. You have no time to spare; the New York express is about due," and with the words she shoved him towards the doorway leading to the hall.

"Call me when you are ready, and I'll come and paint you up like an Indian," she added as he disappeared up the stairs.

A half hour later when Dick appeared in the living-room and greeted his parents, Ursula's efforts at facial decoration proved so successful that no one other than his fond and adoring mother discovered the deception. Her searching eye was not to be deceived, however, and once again Dick was obliged to recount the details of his afternoon's experience.

"No one will notice my black eye, Mother, and if so half of the audience will have heard how I got it, so you need not worry."

Dick's father said nothing, but the look of pride and approbation in his eyes was enough to quiet any qualms as to his father's attitude.

John Comstock, having laid aside the evening paper he was reading when his son entered, now began searching through its pages, speaking as he did so:

"Have you seen to-night's paper, Dick?"

"No, Dad. Why, is there anything of particular interest in it--that is aside from the announcements of the big event being staged at the theatre?" inquired Dick.

"Unfortunately, yes," replied his father. "When I left home last week I told you I would see Senator Kenyon while in Washington and try to get him to give you that appointment to the Naval Academy we all have been hoping for and which we believed as good as settled in your favor until a few weeks ago."

"Did you see him? What did he say?" asked Dick in one breath, his face lighting up with excitement.

"Yes, I saw him, but my visit was fruitless. He politely but firmly told me he could not give it to you; and he would not tell me at the time who was to be the lucky boy. In to-night's paper I have just read that the selection has been made."

The look of disappointment which came over Dick's countenance was reflected in the faces of both his mother and sister. He gulped once or twice before he finally mustered up courage to reach out his hand for the paper, and the tears blinded his eyes while he read the brief article which so certainly delayed if it did not entirely destroy his boyhood's dream.

For a few moments silence reigned in the little group, and Ursula, rising quietly, walked to her brother and placed an affectionate, consoling arm over his dejectedly drooping shoulders.

"Never mind, Dick, the appointee may not pass the exams, and then possibly you will get your chance after all," she said consolingly.

"There's no hope he won't pass," answered Dick dolefully, and then more bravely, "neither would you nor I wish him such bad luck."

"Is it anyone we know?" now inquired Mrs. Comstock.

"I should say we do. It's one of my best friends;--it's Gordon Graham, our class valedictorian."

"Gordon Graham!" exclaimed Ursula, a slight flush tinging the peachy contour of her cheek, "Gordon Graham! Why, I never knew he even wanted to go to Annapolis!"

"He doesn't," answered Dick ruefully, "but his father does want him to go, and now Gordon has no choice."

"Mr. Graham is a rich man, and a politician. I suppose he wields such an influence in this district that Senator Kenyon could not afford to go against his wishes in the matter," said Dick's father, "and unfortunately I am not wealthy, and have always kept out of politics. Consequently, my boy, you may blame your father for this miscarriage of our plans. With the election so near, a senator has to look to his fences," he added as they arose to answer the summons to the evening repast.

"Our Policy in the West Indies and the Caribbean," was the subject of Richard's salutatory address in the crowded theatre that evening at the graduation exercises of the Bankley High School. To his friends it seemed something more than the average boyish ebullition. At any rate, Dick was a thoughtful lad and had expended his best efforts in the preparation of his oration. During its composition he had even looked into the future and in the measures he advanced as necessary for the military, naval and commercial integrity of the nation, he had always liked to think of himself as a possible factor.

To-night he experienced his first bitter disappointment, and instead of "Admiral Richard Comstock" being an actor in the stirring events that some day indubitably would occur, he saw his more fortunate chum, Gordon Graham, writing history on the pages of his country's record.

After the exercises he met Gordon, and the two boys walked home together along the lofty, elm-arched streets.

"Naturally I'm fearfully disappointed," said Dick, having first congratulated Gordon on his good fortune, "but I'm not churlish about the matter, and I guess the chief reason is because you got it. I'm mighty glad for you, Gordon."

"It is too bad, old man," Gordon replied feelingly, "because I know how you have looked forward to being appointed, and you know, Dick, I never was anxious for it. If it was not for frustrating my father's wishes, I should almost be inclined to flunk the examinations. In fact I may be unable to get by anyway, for they are very difficult."

"You'd never do that, Gordon! You couldn't afford to do such a thing-- humble your pride in that manner. That wouldn't be helping me and you'd only injure yourself and hurt your father beyond measure," said Dick bravely.

"Oh, I suppose I shall have to go, and I will do my best, Dick; only I do wish we both were going. It is beastly to think of separating after all these years we have been together."

"We have a few days left yet before you leave, so cheer up," answered Dick, "and suppose we make the best of them. What do you say to a swim and row to Black Ledge to-morrow morning?"

"Good! I will meet you at eight o'clock. Bring along your tackle, for we may get some bass or black-fish, and we will make a day of it," responded Gordon enthusiastically, as they parted at the corner.

On entering the house Dick immediately sought his father.

"Father," he said, "what do you propose for me now that the Annapolis appointment is closed?"

"I have been thinking over the question for weeks," answered Mr. Comstock, leaning back wearily in his chair. "I counted on the Naval Academy more than you did, I might say; for, Dick, things have not been going well in the business, and the family exchequer is at a very low point, so low in fact I hardly know just how things will end."

Dick, immersed in his own selfish thoughts, for the first time realized how worried and care-worn his father appeared.

"What is the trouble, Dad?" he asked with a world of solicitude and tenderness in his voice.

"To tell you the truth, Dick, I cannot afford to send you to college. I am afraid that unless I can recoup my recent losses I shall be unable even to allow your sister to finish her art studies after her graduation next year, as we had planned. My boy, I have very little left."

He stopped for a moment and his hand visibly shook as he passed it over his troubled brow.

"I broke the news to your mother some time ago, and my visit to Washington was in the hope of recovering something from the wreck, but it looks dark. Also while there, beside seeing Senator Kenyon, I tried my best to get you into West Point. But that, too, was a failure."

"Dad, don't worry about me," said the boy, rising and going to stand by his father's side; "I'll get along all right, and between us we will fasten on something I can turn my hand to. I have had a mighty easy time of it for seventeen years, nearly, and I'm only too glad to pitch in and help out."

"The situation is not so bad as all that, Richard," answered Mr. Comstock, gazing at his manly boy with a proud look. "You do not have to strike out for yourself for a good while yet. I even thought another year at Bankley, taking the post-graduate course, would be the best plan for the present. In the meantime you have a whole summer's vacation ahead of you, which your good work at school richly deserves."

"No, I've finished with Bankley," said Dick with finality in his tone.

"Well! Well! We must talk about the matter some other time, my son, and if you intend to go to Black Ledge to-morrow morning with Gordon, you had best be getting under the covers."

Whereupon Dick said "Good-night" and slowly climbed the stairs to his bedroom.

Before Dick succeeded in getting to sleep he firmly resolved to relieve his father's shoulders of some of the burden by shifting for himself, but just how he proposed to go about it was even to his own active mind an enigma.

CHAPTER II

"THE OLDEST BRANCH OF THE SERVICE"

When Dick ran down the wharf the next morning he found Gordon and several other boys there already. He was later than he had intended; unless an early start was made their sport would be spoiled. Black-fish bite well only on the flood tide, and the row to Black Ledge, situated at the mouth of the broad river, near the entrance to the spacious harbor, was a distance of at least four miles.

In order to better their time Dick and Gordon invited Donald Barry and Robert Meade, two boys of their own age, to join them and help man the oars, while Tommy Turner, a freshman at Bankley, was impressed as coxswain of the crew.

Lusty strokes soon carried them away from the landing out into the sparkling waters of the river. Tommy Turner, though not a "big boy," knew his duties as coxswain, so he set his course diagonally for the opposite bank. Already the tide had turned, and to go directly down-stream would have meant loss of more time, while under the shelter of the left bank of the river the current and wind were not so strong as out in mid-channel.

With expertness born of much experience he guided the little round-bottomed craft in and out amidst the river traffic. The swell from an outward-bound excursion steamer caused the rowboat to rock and toss, but not a single "crab" or unnecessary splash did the rowers make as they bent their backs gladly to their task.

"Those farmers from up state on board the *Sunshine* thought we would all be swamped sure," remarked Tommy, laughingly. "I'd like to bet that half of them never saw blue water before in their lives."

Dick, stroking the crew, only grinned appreciatively at Tommy's sally, but Donald Barry called out from his place as bow oar:

"Don't get too cocky, Tommy, for if they knew you had never learned to swim, they might well have felt uneasy about you."

"I'll learn some day, fast enough," answered Tommy, slightly chagrined at Donald's remark, "but in the meantime, Don, if you would feather your oar better maybe the wind against it wouldn't be holding us back so much."

Tommy Turner was always ready with a "come back," as the boys expressed it, and for a while nothing more was said. Suddenly the coxswain, who had been gazing fixedly ahead for some time, gave a loud shout.

"Say, fellows, the fleet is coming in! I thought I couldn't be mistaken when I saw all that smoke way out there, and now it's a sure thing."

By common consent the rowers ceased their exertions and looked in the direction indicated by Tommy. Far out over the white-capped waves of the Sound could be seen against the deep blue sky, dark, low-lying clouds of black smoke, while just becoming distinguishable to the naked eye the huge hulks of several battleships could be discerned.

"This sure is luck," exclaimed Robert Meade. "I've often wanted to see a lot of battleships come to anchor together, but never have been on the spot at the right moment."

"Let's call off the fishing and row out to their anchorage; it's only a little over a mile farther out. What do you all say?" asked Donald, appealing to the others.

"Yes,--let's!" spoke up the ubiquitous Tommy. "We can go after the fish later if we like."

"You would not be so much in favor of that extra mile or two if you were pulling on an oar, kid," vouchsafed Gordon rather grimly, for the sight of the ships brought to his mind that sooner or later he might be passing his days on one of those very vessels.

"Right you are, sir, Admiral Graham, sir," quickly retorted the coxswain, and even Dick joined in the laughter now turned on Gordon.

How differently he gazed at the ships to-day from what he would have done a few days since. Then they would have meant so much to him, while now he seemed to resent their very presence in the harbor.

The rowers had resumed their work and without further words Tommy changed the boat's course.

By the time the five boys in their tiny craft reached the vicinity the great vessels were steaming in column towards the harbor entrance. On the fresh morning breeze was borne the sound of many bugles, the shrill notes of the boatswain's pipes calling the crew on deck, and the crashings of many bands.

The boys resting on their oars drank in the beauty and majesty of the scene with sighs of complete satisfaction while they interestedly watched every maneuver of the approaching ships. The powerful dreadnaught in the lead flew the blue flag with two white stars of a rear admiral. From the caged mainmast and from the signal yard on the foremast strings of gaily-colored flags were continually being run up or down, and sailors standing in the rigging were waving small hand flags to and fro with lightning rapidity.

"Those colored and fancy flags make the outfit look like a circus parade," remarked Tommy, lolling back in the stern sheets with the tiller ropes lying idly in his hands.

"That's the way the Admiral gives his orders to the other ships," volunteered Dick. "You'll notice they run up every set of flags first on the flagship, then the ships behind follow suit, finally when the order is understood by them all and it comes time to do that which the Admiral wants done, down they all go together."

"Jinks! I'd think it a pretty tedious way of sending messages," remarked Donald Barry, watching the gay flags go fluttering upwards in the breeze; "just imagine spelling out all those words. I'd think that sometimes they'd all go ashore or run into each other or something before they half finished what they wanted to say."

Dick, having spent considerable of his spare moments in reading up about naval matters, smiled at Donald and continued his explanation.

"It isn't necessary to spell out the words. Each group of flags means some special command, and all you have to do is to look it up in the signal book as you would a word in the dictionary. Most of the commoner signals become so well known after a little experience that it is only a matter of seconds to catch the meaning."

"I wish we could go on board one of the ships, don't you, fellows?" mused Robert rather irrelevantly. He was generally the silent one of the party, but the lads agreed with him that his wish was a good one. Yet such luck was hardly to be expected.

The flagship was passing but a few yards away, and the watchers could readily see the sailors on her decks all dressed in white working clothes, while on the broad quarter-deck a line of men, uniformed in khaki and armed with rifles, were drawn up in two straight military rows. Near these men glistened the instruments of the ship's band as they stood playing a lively march.

Suddenly the boys heard a sharp command wafted to them over the water. "Haul down!" were the words, and simultaneously from every ship in the column the lines of flags were hauled down to the signal bridges. Then came the splash of anchors, the churning of reversed propellers, the smoke and dust of anchor chains paying out through hawse pipes, and the fleet had come to anchor. Hardly had the great anchors touched the water when long booms swung out from the ships' sides, gangways were lowered, and from their cradles swift launches with steam already up were dropped into the water by huge electric cranes.

"What is the blue flag with all the stars they hoisted at their bows when they stopped?" questioned Donald, turning to Dick as being the best informed member of the party.

"That is the Union Jack," Dick replied, "and they fly that from the jack staff only when a ship is in dock, tied up to a wharf or at anchor; and also, if you noticed, they pulled down the National Ensign from the gaff on the mainmast and hauled another up on the flagstaff astern at the same time. When the flag flies from the gaff it means the ship is under way."

"It certainly is a shame, Dick, you cannot go to Annapolis in my place," remarked Gordon, regretfully; "you already know more than all of us combined about the Navy. But do you know, seeing these ships to-day and the businesslike way they do things has stirred my blood. It is just wonderful! But for the life of me I cannot see how a chap can learn all there is to know about them in only four years. I rather think I shall have to do some pretty hard digging if I ever expect to be a naval officer."

"Keep your ship afloat, Admiral Graham, and hard digging won't be necessary," interposed Tommy, and a roar of laughter followed his quip, as was usually the case.

The boys now began rowing towards the flagship, which in anchoring had gone several hundred yards beyond them. Nearing her, the strains of a lively march were heard, and an officer in cocked hat, gold lace and epaulettes, went down the gangway into a waiting motor boat. No sooner had the officer stepped into the boat than she scurried away for the shore landing. Again the boys stopped to watch proceedings. When the motor boat started from the gangway one of the sailors on deck blew a shrill call on a pipe and the khaki-clad line of men, who had been standing immovably with their rifles at the position of "present arms," brought them to the deck as if actuated by a single lever, and a moment later they were marched away.

"Those soldiers are marines, aren't they?" asked Robert. "Anyway, they are dressed the same as the marines up at the Navy Yard."

"Sure they are marines," answered Tommy; "I know all about 'em, for my Uncle Fred was a marine officer once. He swears by 'em, and says they are the best fighters in the world."

This was Robert Meade's first year at Bankley High School, having spent all his life previously in an up-state town, and the soldier element on board ship was not clear in his mind.

"I always used to think that the marine was a sailor," said he. "At least, most of the papers half the time must be wrong, for you see pictures supposed to be marines landing at this or that place and they are almost always dressed as sailors."

"That's because the papers don't know anything," commented Tommy indignantly. "Why, the marines are the oldest branch of the service; older than the Navy or the Army. Aren't they, Dick?"

"Well, to tell the truth," Dick answered, "I'm a bit hazy about marines myself. Of course I've seen them around town and on the ships all my life, off and on, but I've been so much more interested in the work of a sailor that I haven't paid much attention to the military end of it."

"The marine is 'soldier and sailor too,'" said Tommy, sententiously. "That English poet, Kipling, says he can do any darned thing under the sun; and if all my uncle tells me is true, it must be so. He was a volunteer officer of marines in the war with Spain and fought in Cuba with them."

"Well, if they are soldiers also, why don't they stay ashore with the army?" persevered Robert, wishing to understand more about the men who had excited his interest.

"It's a pretty long story to tell you in a minute," answered Tommy; "besides, I may not get it all straight."

"That will be all right, Tommy," Gordon called out. "I do not know anything about them, either, and I suppose I had better learn everything I can about the Navy now. I've made up my mind, boys, that I do want to be an officer on one of these ships, and I am going to tell my father so to-night, as I know it will please him. So, Tommy, I propose that when we start for the boat-house, as you will have nothing else to do but steer, you tell us all you know about these 'Sea Soldiers.' Is my motion seconded?"

As Gordon finished speaking they were lying a little off the starboard quarter of the flagship, idly tossing in the short choppy sea that the breeze from the Sound had stirred up. A whistle from the deck now attracting their attention, the boys looked up in time to see a small marine with a bugle in his hand run along the deck and, after saluting the naval officer who had summoned him by the shrill blast, receive some instructions from the officer. After giving another salute to the officer, a second or two later the little trumpeter blew a call, the meaning of which was unknown to the silently attentive lads in the rowboat.

All the boys had some remark to make at this.

"Hello, look at Tom Thumb blowing the bugle," called Tommy, and he added, "If all the marines are his size, I should think someone had been robbing a nursery."

"Wonder what all the excitement means, anyway?" inquired Donald, as he saw various persons on the ship running about, evidently in answer to the summons of the bugle.

"You know all the bugle calls, Dick, because you were the best bugler in the Boy Scouts when we belonged; what was the call?" Gordon asked.

"You've sure got me buffaloed," answered Dick. "I learned every call in the Instruction Book for Boy Scouts, and I know every army call, but that one wasn't among them."

During this time their little boat was drifting slowly astern again when suddenly a long heavy motor boat rounded the battleship, just clearing her, and at terrific speed bore down on the drifting rowboat.

Instinctively the occupants of the rowboat sprang into action.

A warning cry was shouted to them through a megaphone from the deck of the battleship, the coxswain of the fast flying motor boat sounded two short blasts on his whistle, threw his helm hard over, and the crew shouted loudly. Tommy Turner in the excitement of the moment mixed his tiller ropes and sent his frail craft directly across the sharp bow of the approaching vessel.

With a smashing and crashing of wood the heavy motor boat practically cut the rowboat in two, forcing it beneath the surface and passing over it, and more quickly than it has taken to relate it the five boys were thrown into the sea.

*　　*　　*　　*　　*　　*　　*　　*　　*

How the accident occurred

- 13 -

How the accident occurred

1. B is the position of the rowboat when the motor boat A came under the stern along dotted line, heading directly at rowboat. Tommy pulled on wrong rope and sent his boat in direction of B'. It can be seen the coxswain steered in the same direction and the boats smashed at the point B'. The motor boat stopped about A'.

2. The diagram illustrates also the manner of designating the directions of objects from the ship by lookouts. Example: A sailboat at "C." The lookout would call out "Sailboat, Broad on Port Bow" or he might say "Four Points on Port Bow."

*　　*　　*　　*　　*　　*　　*　　*　　*

Dick Comstock, coming first to the surface, looked about him for his companions. The motor boat was now about fifty yards away; her engine had stopped and her crew were looking anxiously towards the spot where the accident had taken place.

As Dick shook the water from his eyes and ears, he heard the voice of the coxswain answering a question apparently addressed him by someone from the deck of the flagship.

"I can't reverse my engines, sir. Something fouling the propellor," he called out.

By this time Dick saw the bobbing heads of Robert, Donald and Gordon not far from him.

"Where's Tommy?" called Dick, anxiously, trying to rise from the water as far as possible in his endeavor to sight the missing boy.

To these four lads the choppy sea meant nothing, in spite of the fact they were fully clothed when so suddenly upset. But in Tommy's case it was a far different matter, for, as has been stated, Tommy, though a plucky little fellow, was unable to swim.

The wrecked rowboat had floated some distance away and with one accord the four boys swam rapidly towards it in the hope that Tommy might be found clinging to the débris.

Meanwhile on the deck of the battleship there was great excitement. A life-boat was being quickly lowered from its davits and active sailors were piling into it. The starboard life-lines of the quarter-deck were lined with men in white uniforms and dungarees, for many of the engine room force had been attracted to the deck to witness the episode though they were not allowed there on ordinary occasions in that attire, and also there was a sprinkling of marines in khaki. Shouts, signals and directions were coming from all sides, while two of the motor boat's crew were already in the water swimming back towards the boys to lend them aid if necessary.

On reaching the wreck, Dick, who was first to arrive, half pulled himself out on the upturned bottom in order to search to better advantage. Discovering with sinking heart that Tommy was not there, without a moment's hesitation he disappeared beneath the boat searching with wide open eyes for his little friend, nor was he alone in his quest, for each of the boys in turn dove under the boat on arrival. Staying as long under water as he possibly could Dick came to the surface to free his lungs of the foul air with which they were now filled. Again his anxious eyes swept the roughened water in eager survey and then with a loud cry of gladness he was going hand over hand in the famous Australian crawl, but this time away from the boat and towards the ship.

In that momentary glance he saw an arm and hand emerge from the waves, the clenched fist still holding fast to a piece of tiller rope. It had shown but an instant above the surface and then disappeared. Could he reach the spot in time? Could he? He would--he must, and with head and face down his arms flew like flails beating the water past him as he surged forward.

On board the flagship, Sergeant Michael Dorlan, of the Marines, had been an eye-witness of the whole occurrence. For some time previous he had been watching the boys in the boat. The manner in which they handled their oars showed him they were no novices. He noted also that there were five occupants in the unlucky craft when she was struck. Calmly he counted the heads appearing in the water beneath.

"One," counted Dorlan aloud to himself as Dick's drenched head almost instantaneously bobbed up, "two, three," he continued in rapid succession, "four----," and then he waited, holding his breath, while his honest Irish heart beat faster beneath his woolen shirt.

"They kin all shwim," he muttered aloud as the four lads struck out vigorously in the water, "but, bedad, the fifth kid ain't up yet."

During all this time Dorlan was unlacing his shoes with rapidly moving fingers. His coat he unconsciously took off and threw to the deck and then he climbed to the top rail of the life-lines, steadying himself by holding to an awning stanchion. Never once did his sharp, gray-blue eyes leave the surface of the water. As Dick cried out and dashed through the waves towards the spot where he momentarily glimpsed the tightly clenched hand of Tom Turner, a brown streak appeared to shoot from the rail of the dreadnaught and with hardly a splash was lost and swallowed up in the sea.

Sergeant Michael Dorlan had also seen that for which he was looking and like a flash he had gone to the rescue. From the height of over twenty feet his body shot like a meteor in the direction of the drowning boy. To the officers and crew on board the flagship it seemed an eternity before a commotion below them and a spurning and churning of the water announced his reappearance. And Dorlan did not come to the surface alone, for it was seen that he was supporting the form of the boy he had gone to rescue.

A great cheer filled the air as the crew of the ship spontaneously gave vent to their relief, and a few seconds later the unconscious lad was hurried up the gangway by willing hands, followed unassisted by his four drenched and solicitous comrades.

CHAPTER III

UNCLE SAM'S UNINVITED GUESTS

"Right down to the sick bay[#] with him," ordered an officer as Tommy was carried over the side in the strong arms of Sergeant Dorlan, who, on climbing up the gangway, had tenderly taken the boy from the sailor holding him. "Hurry along, Sergeant, the surgeon is already there waiting."

[#] Sick bay--The ship's hospital.

After giving these directions the officer turned to the four dripping lads and said:

"Are you boys injured in any way?"

"No," they replied as if with one breath.

"You look as though you had been struck in the eye pretty badly," said the officer, giving Dick's bruised cheek a close scrutiny, and for a moment the boy blushed as if caught in a misdemeanor.

"I was hit in the eye yesterday," he finally managed to stammer; "it wasn't caused by anything that happened to-day," and then to change the subject if possible, he inquired:

"May we have permission to go down where they have taken Tommy Turner? We are all mighty anxious about him."

"Don't you all want to get on some dry clothes first?" inquired the officer.

The boys preferred, however, to hear first the news as to their friend's condition; consequently they were taken below, where already the ship's surgeon and his assistants were working hard to restore life to the still unconscious Tommy.

Sitting on a mess bench which some men had placed for them, each boy wrapped in blankets furnished by other thoughtful members of the crew, they waited silently and with palpitating hearts while a long half hour slowly ticked away. Though many sailors were continually passing to and fro they were all careful not to disturb the four shipwrecked boys who sat there with eyes fastened in anxious hopefulness on the door to the "sick bay," as the hospital is called on shipboard.

After what seemed an eternity, the door opened and Sergeant Dorlan came out quietly, closing it behind him. Immediately the watchers jumped to their feet.

"Is he all right?" whispered Dick, plucking at Dorlan's wet sleeve. "Is he----"

"Lord love ye, me lads, he's as fit as a fiddle and will live to laugh at ye in yer old age," replied Dorlan, cheerfully, and it was with a mutual sigh of relief they heard the announcement. A messenger approaching at this moment, called to the boys:

"The Officer of the Deck says, seeing your friend's all right, that you are to follow me to the Junior Officers' Quarters, where you can get a bath and your clothes will be dried out for you."

"We'd like to see our friend first, if we might," suggested Dick.

"The little lad's asleep and old 'Saw Bones' wouldn't let ye in to disturb him for love nor money. Go ahead and get policed up," suggested the sergeant, turning aft towards the marines' compartment as he spoke.

"We do not know your name, Sergeant," spoke up Gordon, placing a detaining hand on the marine's arm, "but we all want to thank you for saving Tommy Turner's life. It was just too fine for words, and I for one should like to shake hands with you."

"It's all in the day's wurruk, me lad," said Dorlan, confused by this frank praise, "but it's happy I am to shake the hands of such plucky lads as ye are yersel's, so put her there," and he extended a brown horny hand which they all grasped simultaneously.

"When ye git all fixed up and dhried out, come on back here and it's proud I'll be to show ye about the old tub," with which remark he left them at liberty to follow the Officer of the Deck's messenger to the Junior Officers' Quarters.

Divesting themselves of their soaked garments on arrival there they were supplied with soap, towels and bath robes and were soon enjoying the bath. With spirits no longer depressed for fear of danger to their friend, the four lads were now beginning thoroughly to enjoy their novel experience.

"Which fellow said he wished he could visit a man-of-war?" questioned Donald from the confines of a little enclosure where the sound of splashing water announced he was already under the shower.

"It was the Sphinx," laughingly answered Gordon from his own particular cubby hole.

"I didn't want to come on board in quite the manner I did, though," called out Robert, "and furthermore, don't call me Sphinx in the future. If I'd had the sense of that old hunk of stone, I could have foreseen the danger and been able to avoid it."

"Hurry up, you fellows, and don't talk so much. Let me have a whack at one of those showers," called Dick, who had been forced to wait, there being not enough bathing places to allow all to indulge at the same time. "I want to hurry out of this and take a look around this ship before I go ashore."

"Speaking of leaving," remarked Gordon as he emerged for a rub down, "how do you suppose we are going to leave?"

"To tell the truth, I hadn't thought of that," Dick replied, "and how about your boat? It's all smashed up."

"She was about ready for the junk pile, anyway," said Gordon, "and I was going to give her to the boat club before I left for Annapolis next week."

"I wonder what Uncle Sam does when he smashes up your boats like that?" questioned Donald.

"In this case," Dick vouchsafed, "I rather guess 'Uncle Sam' will say it is altogether our own fault. Poor Tommy was so rattled that he pulled on the wrong rope and steered us right in front of the motor boat even after they had veered off to avoid hitting us."

"Well, if they permit us to take a look around the ship, I am willing to call it square," Gordon remarked philosophically.

A little later the boys were escorted to a vacant stateroom or cabin where they found their underwear already dry and waiting to be donned.

"I call that quick work," exclaimed Gordon, and while he was speaking a knock sounded at the door.

"Come in!" he called out, and a colored mess boy stuck his woolly head into the room.

"Yoh clo'es will be ready foh yoh all in jest a jiffy, sah. Here am yoh rubber shoes dry a'ready an' de tailor am a-pressing yoh pants and yoh coats, sah."

"Where did you find our coats?" inquired Dick. "They were in the rowboat the last I knew."

The colored boy grinned broadly, showing an expansive row of shining white teeth.

"Ah don't rightly know foh shu, boss, but Ah reckon dey foun' 'em floatin' on de water an' fetched 'em aboahd wid yoh boat, sah."

"You mean to say they have rescued the rowboat too and have it on board this ship?" asked Gordon incredulously.

"Shu as shootin', sah, an' Chips wid his little Chips is fixin' of her up good as new. Dey ain't nuthin' we cain't do on one ob Unc' Sam's ships, sah."

With which closing encomium the black face was withdrawn and the door closed.

"Wonder what he meant by his 'Chips wid his little Chips'?" laughingly questioned Robert Meade.

"You will have to ask Dick," answered Gordon rather enviously. For now that he had become so enthusiastic over his determination to follow his father's wishes and become a naval officer he felt he had neglected many past opportunities for learning about the service.

"He meant the Chief Carpenter and his helpers, I 'reckon. 'You see, 'Chips' is a nickname in the Navy for the man who handles the saw and hammer," Dick announced.

"When you boys are dressed come out into the mess room. Put on your bath robes till your clothes are ready for you," called a voice from the passageway outside their door and needing no second bidding they all walked out into the comfortable room where a number of junior officers were standing about.

"I am Ensign Whiting, and these are the junior officers of the ship," announced the officer who had previously called to them, and he introduced the lads to the others with an easy wave of his hand. "Sit down and tell us all about the accident. By the way, your friend Tommy is still sleeping, and as it is noon we should be very glad if you would accept our invitation to lunch. The Captain sent word he wishes to see you, but I told him you probably would eat with us, so, unless you are in a hurry to get away, you need not go up to see him till later."

The boys gladly accepted the kind invitation and as the meal was immediately announced they sat down in the places already provided and proceeded to enjoy thoroughly their first meal on board a battleship.

During the repast they related how the accident occurred, and all were high in praise of the marine sergeant who so promptly came to their rescue. They learned that their wrecked boat had been towed back to the ship and hauled out on board, and the damage to it was not so great but that the ship's carpenters could easily repair it.

"Mike Dorlan is a bit too fond of the firewater," volunteered one of the officers, "but when it comes to being the right man in the right place at the right time, it would be hard to find his equal."

"We tried to thank him for rescuing Tommy," said Gordon, "but we could not make him understand what a noble thing it was."

"That's Mike all over. He's a gruff old chap as a rule, and I suppose saving anyone in such an easy manner, as he would call it, doesn't seem much to him," remarked Ensign Whiting. "Mike already owns gold and silver life-saving medals presented to him by the Navy Department."

"I never knew that," said an officer who had been introduced to the boys as a Lieutenant of Marines. "He never wears them at inspection nor the ribbons for them at other times."

"Dorlan? Wear medals? Not that old leatherneck!"[#] exclaimed Whiting. "Yet I happen to know that he has several in his ditty box[#] and if you tackle him just right he will spin you some mighty interesting yarns. Why, he was all through the Spanish War, first on a ship and then ashore at Guantanamo; he fought in the Philippine Insurrection and was one of the first marines to enter Pekin during its relief at the Boxer uprising in 1900, and later he was in Cuba during the insurrection there in 1906, and I believe he has landed for one reason or another in about every place there ever was trouble brewing in the last fifteen years. To cap the climax he even has a medal of honor which he received for some wonderfully impossible stunt he did out in China. Ah! Old Mike is a wonder, all right!"

[#] Leatherneck--A sobriquet often applied to marines. Supposed to have originated from the leather collar which formed part of the uniform of marines in the early days of the last century.

[#] A small wooden box issued to the men in which they keep writing paper, ink, and odds and ends. It is fitted with a lock.

"Do you suppose we can see Sergeant Dorlan later?" asked Dick eagerly. "You see, he promised to show us over the ship, and this being the first time that any of us has ever been lucky enough to get on board a United States ship, we all want to make the best of fortunate misfortune, as you might say."

"Why, certainly: right after you see the Captain," replied Ensign Whiting, "and as your clothes are now ready, suppose you get into them at once and I will take you up above for your interview."

Captain Cameron, of the U.S.S. *Nantucket*, flagship of the Battleship Division of the Atlantic Fleet, was a big jovial man of ruddy complexion and his greeting of the shipwrecked boys who were ushered into his cabin by the marine orderly was hearty, and complimentary.

"It is a pleasure to meet you, young gentlemen," he said, shaking each of them by the hand. "I only regret your introduction on board my ship was attended by such an unhappy incident. However, it is to be hoped that you won't bear the Navy any grudge after I explain to you that we are doing our best to make full amend for the accident. Mr. Ennis, the ship's carpenter, reports that his men will soon have your boat in nearly perfect condition, and the surgeon states your young friend will have no ill effects from his experience. Please be seated and make yourselves at home, for I have a few questions to ask you."

It was indeed an interesting place to sit, being filled with curios which the Captain during his many years of service in the Navy had collected in nearly every corner of the world, and while he talked they found it difficult to keep their eyes from wandering about the room on cursory inspection of the idols, weapons, pictures and objects of art, attractively arranged on walls and tables.

"Now that we are all comfortable, suppose you tell me how the accident occurred," said their host, turning first to Dick, who was seated nearest him. Whereupon the boy told him the entire story and each of the others added the details that came to their minds.

"It is needless to say that I wish it had not happened," said he; "my coxswain was at fault for coming around so close under the stern of the ship, but I can see that you are inclined to place the blame on your own coxswain, who steered you across the bow of the motor boat after she had blown the proper whistles. However, I have endeavored to do the best I can by you. Your boat is nearly repaired; your oars and stretchers replaced, your clothes recovered, and though they may have suffered a little from their wetting I do not imagine any great harm has resulted. It is true you lost your lunches but I am inclined to believe you have not suffered on that account either, and even the box of fish lines was picked up. The only thing really worrying me is your friend Tommy, but even in his case nothing more than a slight bruise on the forehead has resulted. Now I want to know if there is anything else I can do to even up our account?"

"Well, sir," Richard answered, looking a little embarrassed while he turned the edge of a rug with the toe of his shoe, "there is one more thing you may do for us if you will."

Captain Cameron, believing he had already done more than he was called upon to do under the circumstances, was surprised at this reply.

"And what may that be?" he inquired rather sharply.

"If you would permit all of us to have a good look around your ship, sir, before we leave, it would be greatly appreciated and also, sir, we should like it very much if Sergeant Dorlan could act as the guide. You see, he offered to do it," and Richard ended his request by looking directly at his host.

"If that is all, my boys," said the Captain, once again his genial self, "I gladly grant it, and furthermore, during our stay in port I shall be happy to see you on board at any time outside of working hours."

Ringing a bell, the marine orderly answered the summons.

THE MARINE ORDERLY ANSWERED THE SUMMONS

THE MARINE ORDERLY ANSWERED THE SUMMONS

"Orderly, present my compliments to Captain Henderson and ask him to detail Sergeant Dorlan to accompany these young gentlemen on an inspection tour of the ship."

The marine snapped his hand to his cap in salute, and after his "Aye, aye, sir," which is the naval way of replying to an order, he turned and left the cabin, followed by the delighted youngsters.

Captain Kenneth Henderson, United States Marine Corps, was holding five-inch gun drill when the orderly found him. After receiving the message from his Commanding Officer he immediately called Sergeant Dorlan and gave him his instructions.

"Before you start out, Sergeant, you had better stop in the sick bay and pick up the other member of the party. When I came by there a while ago he was feeling fine and getting ready to dress. He of course will wish to go around with you."

Tommy was feeling perfectly well. A small blue mark still remained on his forehead showing where he had been hit by some part of the wreckage in the accident and knocked insensible. Being fully dressed when the others arrived, they all were soon investigating the wonderful battleship. For two full hours they pestered the patient Dorlan with more questions and inquiries than he could have answered in a lifetime. In the course of their personally conducted trip they were on a visit to the bridge when their attention was again attracted to the small bugler of marines who had been the innocent cause of their presence on board the flagship. He was again sounding the call which they had been discussing when the motor boat dashed under the stern of the vessel and crashed into them.

"What is the meaning of that call?" asked Dick of their guide.

"He's callin' away the motor sailer," replied Dorlan.

"Is he a marine--the little fellow blowing the bugle?" inquired Tommy.

"Surest thing ye know," was the answer.

"Why! He can't be as old as we are," remarked Dick; "how old do you have to be to enlist in the Marines?"

"Those kids sometimes come in at the age of fifteen," answered Dorlan; "they enlist as drummers and trumpeters and serve till they're twenty-one years old."

"May anyone enlist?" Dick asked.

"Sure, if yer old enough."

"And work your way up to a commission, as they do in the army?"

"Indeed ye can, if ye've got it in ye," replied the Sergeant; "Captain Henderson come up from the ranks, and a mighty good officer he is, too," he added.

After this talk Richard Comstock remained very thoughtful. A sudden idea had come to his mind, and he wanted to think it over. The sight of the neat-looking marines, their military bearing, smart uniforms and soldierly demeanor attracted him powerfully, and when he learned that enlisted men were afforded the opportunity to rise in rank to that of commissioned officer, he saw in this a means of following a career which, if not exactly the one he had always desired to pursue, was similar in many respects, at least.

A little later the boys were taken ashore in one of the flagship's steamers, first being assured that their own boat would be sent to the boat club in the morning.

CHAPTER IV

SEMPER FIDELIS--ALWAYS FAITHFUL

The actions of Dick Comstock for the next few days were clothed in mystery so far as his own immediate family was concerned, for he kept his own counsel as to his movements when away from home. Even his sister Ursula was not taken into his confidence. In the meantime the day of Gordon Graham's departure for Annapolis arrived, and his friends went to the station to give him a proper send-off.

Ursula and Dick were there, also Donald, Robert and Tommy Turner and many of Gordon's classmates, of whom Dick was the closest friend.

"I still wish you were going, Dick," said Gordon sadly when the express pulled in under the train shed. "It will be fearfully strange down there with none of the old crowd around. Have you made any plans yet regarding what you are going to do?"

"Not fully," answered Richard. "I expect to be leaving town in a day or two, though."

"Where are you going?" inquired Gordon in surprise. But Ursula approached them at that moment, and Dick gave a warning signal for silence which Gordon saw and understood.

"Good-bye, Gordon," she said prettily, and Gordon suddenly regretted that so many of the boys and girls were there to bid him farewell. He would have much preferred to say his adieus to Ursula with no others present. Strange he never before realized what a beautiful girl she had become, with her blue eyes looking straight out at one from under the black eyebrows and the hair blowing about her delicately tinted cheeks.

"A-l-l A-b-o-a-r-d!" rang the voice of the conductor, standing watch in hand ready to give the starting signal to the engineer. The porters were picking up their little steps and getting ready to depart.

"Good-bye, Ursula," said the lad simply, wringing her hand with a heavier clasp than he knew, and though he nearly crushed the bones, she never gave the least sign of the pain he was causing her; perhaps she did not really feel it.

"Kiss me, Gordon," cried his mother, as she threw her arms around him. "Don't forget to write immediately on arriving."

"Come on, my son, time to jump aboard," cautioned his father in a suspiciously gruff tone, and in a moment more Gordon mounted the steps where from the platform of the moving train he stood waving his hat in farewell.

"Give him the school yell, fellows," shouted Tommy Turner at the top of his lungs, and with that rousing cry ringing in his ears Gordon Graham started on life's real journey.

That same evening while Dick's father was engaged with some business papers, the boy came quietly into the room.

"Father, may I interrupt your work for a little while?" he inquired.

"Nothing important, Dick, my boy," answered Mr. Comstock, laying aside the document he was reading; "what can I do for you?"

"Mother has just told me you are going to New York to-morrow; is that so?"

"Yes, I have business there for the firm. Why?"

"I was hoping I might go along with you," returned the boy.

Dick's father scrutinized his son's face for a moment, wondering what was behind the quiet glance and serious manner of the lad.

"What is the big idea?" questioned Mr. Comstock. "Want to spend a week or two with Cousin Ella Harris?"

"No," replied Dick slowly, "I have something else in mind, but I don't want to tell you what it is until we get on the train. It's a matter I have been thinking over for some time and--well, you will know all about it to-morrow, if I may go with you."

"Very well," replied his father, turning again to his work; "pack up and be ready to leave in the morning. We'll take the ten o'clock express."

"Good-night, Dad, and thank you," said Dick simply.

"Good-night, Dick," answered Mr. Comstock, without looking up, consequently he failed to see the lingering look the boy gave the familiar scene before him, as if bidding it a silent last "good-night." For Dick was drinking in each detail of the room as if trying to fix its every feature indelibly in his memory.

At breakfast next morning he was more quiet than his mother had ever known him, and both she and his sister Ursula were surprised to see the tears fill his eyes when he kissed them.

"I never knew you to be such a big baby, Dick," said Ursula. "If you feel so bad about leaving us why did you ask Father to take you on for a visit with Cousin Ella?" Although Dick had not said that this was his object in going away, it was a natural inference on Ursula's part, and as he vouchsafed no reply to the contrary she consequently watched him depart with a light heart.

In the crowded train Mr. Comstock and Richard succeeded finally in getting a seat to themselves, and while his father finished reading the morning paper, Dick spent his time in looking out the car window at the familiar sights along the road. But before long he was talking earnestly.

"Dad, I've decided what I want to do," he began, "but I can't do it unless I get your consent."

"What's on your mind, son?" said Mr. Comstock, folding his paper and smiling at the boy beside him. "Go ahead and I will pay close attention."

"If I went to Annapolis," Dick observed, "I'd finish my course there at the age of twenty-one, shouldn't I?"

"Yes, the course is four years at the Naval Academy."

"It would be the same if I went to West Point. In other words, by the time I was twenty-one years old I would, if successful at either institution, be either an ensign or a second lieutenant, as the case might be!"

"Quite true," remarked Mr. Comstock, still unable to comprehend where this preliminary fencing was leading.

"Have you ever heard of the United States Marine Corps?" asked Dick after the silence of a second or two.

"Most certainly I have," was the reply. "The marines figure in nearly every move our country makes in one way or another. They are always busy somewhere, though they get but little credit from the general public for their excellent work. I am not as familiar with their history as I should be--as every good American who has his country's welfare at heart should be, I might add, though perhaps I know a little more about them than a vast majority. Were it not for the marines our firm would have lost thousands of dollars some years ago when the revolutionists started burning up the sugar mills and the cane fields in Cuba. Our government sent a few hundred marines down there in a rush and they put a stop to all the depredations in a most efficient manner. The presence on the premises saved our mill beyond a doubt. But, how do the marines figure in this discussion? You don't mean----"

"Well, you see, it's this way," said the boy, and now his words no longer came slowly and haltingly, "I've made up my mind to become a Marine Officer, and if I can't do it by the time I'm twenty-one, then my name isn't Richard Comstock."

"Bless me! How do you propose going about it, Dick? As I have told you, there is no chance of going to the Naval Academy this year, and I understand that all marine officers are appointed to the Corps from among Annapolis graduates. For that reason I do not believe you have----"

"Excuse me, Dad, but that's just where you are mistaken. All the marine officers don't go through the Naval Academy. Some of them enlist and go up from the ranks. They win their shoulder straps on their own merit. That's what I expect to do if you will only give me the chance. And you will, won't you, Dad?" Dick's voice trembled with eagerness as he put the momentous question.

A few moments elapsed before his father answered and when he began speaking he reached out and gently placed his hand over that of his son.

"Evidently you have been looking into this matter thoroughly. I know now what has been keeping you so silent these last few days. I suspected you were grieving over your disappointment at my inability to send you to the Naval School or possibly over the departure of your chum, Graham, but I might have known my boy was using his time to better advantage than 'crying over spilled milk.'"

Mr. Comstock paused a moment and then continued:

"I know how your mind is wrapped up in a military career, Dick. Ever since you were a little shaver you have played at military and naval mimic warfare. You love it, and I believe you would become a good officer some day with proper training. Anything I may honorably do for the attainment of your desires and your advancement I am but too willing to undertake. But, my boy, I am not sure of the advisability of permitting you to become an ordinary enlisted man with that uncertainty of ever gaining your point--I imagine it is a more or less uncertain proposition. Besides, Dick, you are pretty young to be allowed to start out on such a hard life. The career of an enlisted man is not a bed of roses--full of trials and temptations of all kinds. At West Point or Annapolis you will be given kind treatment and be under careful surveillance for four years and not subjected to the roughness and uncouthness which must attend a start in the ranks. In another year there may be an opening for you at either place. However, I will not deny your request until I have looked further into the case. I am afraid your mother would never hear of such a thing for her only boy. Why not wait and consult her regarding it?"

"I'll tell you why, Dad," began Dick, launching again into his subject at once so as to press home the slight advantage he believed he had gained, "on the Fourth of July I'll be seventeen years of age. Mother didn't happen to think of that, or she would have made me wait a few days before going to Cousin Ella's, where she believes I have gone. You know, Dad, that for years I've been able to blow a bugle and handle the drumsticks better than any other boy in town. Well, last week, when we were on board the *Nantucket*, I saw some young boys belonging to the Marine guard of the ship, and I found out all about them. Why, they were smaller than Tommy Turner!

"It appears that there is a school for musics[#] at the Marine Barracks in Washington, D.C., where boys between the ages of fifteen and seventeen are given training. They enlist to serve until majority, but often after they have served a short time as drummer or trumpeter they get permission to change their rank and become privates. This puts them in line for promotion to the rank of corporal and sergeant. I've been talking with Tommy's uncle, and he was kind enough to have me meet an officer of Marines stationed at the Navy Yard back home, who recently came from recruiting duty. That officer, Lieutenant Stanton is his name, told me that the Corps is filled up just now, and all enlisting stopped, so that my only chance to get in right away would be in this school for musics. In two days more I'll be too old to get in. I knew if I proposed the subject at home, Mother would offer such objections that I just couldn't refuse to do as she wished. Therefore I've packed up and left home for good. Dad, you--you won't stop me, will you? You'll give me this chance? I've set my heart on it so much!"

[#] In the Army and Marine Corps drummers and trumpeters are generally called "musics." On board ship the sailor man who blows the trumpet is called a "bugler." The school for Marine Corps musics is now located at Paris Island, S.C. (1919)

Dick stopped talking. It was the longest extemporaneous speech he ever had made in his life, and as he watched his father's face, he wondered if he had said too much or not enough!

Once again a long silence ensued, while Mr. Comstock reviewed all the boy had said. What should he do? To deny Dick's request might be the very worst step he possibly could take, for he knew the process of reasoning by which this purposeful, upright son of his arrived at his conclusions. He believed thoroughly in his son, and wanted to make no mistake in his decision.

"Let us go in to luncheon, Dick, and give me a little time to think this over. It is a little sudden, you know, and should not be gone into unwisely."

During the meal John Comstock questioned Dick closely regarding this subject uppermost in the minds of both. He saw that the lad was bent upon carrying out his project; that the boy had given it careful thought; that he had weighed its advantages and disadvantages with more acumen than most boys of his age.

Richard was a good student, and not for a moment did the father doubt that his son if given the opportunity would win his commission.

"Was it your idea to go to the New York recruiting station to-day on our arrival?" asked Mr. Comstock, when they resumed their seat in the day coach.

"Yes, Dad, for if I enlist in New York the government sends me to Washington and pays my way there."

"I have a better plan than that," said his father. "I will let my business in New York wait on my return, and we will both go to Washington this afternoon, and spend the night in a comfortable hotel. To-morrow I will go to the Commandant of the Marine Corps with you, armed with a letter of introduction, and we will talk it over with him. In this way I shall have a much clearer and more authoritative view of your prospects. Then if you get by the physical examination and are accepted I shall be able to see for myself how and where you will be fixed."

"Then I may go? You will allow me?" cried Richard, almost jumping out of his seat in his enthusiasm. "You are just the finest Dad in the world! And what is best of all about your plan is that Mother will be less worried if you are able to tell her everything as you see it."

"That is one of my chief reasons for going about it in this way," quietly remarked his father. "I know she will be heart-broken at first, and probably will accuse me of being an unworthy parent; so, my boy, it is a case of how you manage your future, which must prove to her that we both acted for your best interests."

"I'll work hard; I don't need to tell you that, Father," Dick replied.

On arriving in New York they hastened across the city, luckily making good connections for Washington, and the following morning the schedule as planned was begun.

It was Richard's first visit to the capital, and consequently everything he saw interested him. The wonderful dome of the Capitol building; the tall white shaft of Washington Monument, the imposing architecture of the State, War and Navy Departments, the broad streets, the beautiful parks and circles with their many statues, all claimed his attention.

After securing the letter of introduction, Mr. Comstock first took Richard to the Navy Department where, on inquiry, they found that Marine Corps Headquarters was in a near-by office building. The original structure built for the Navy was even then getting too small for the business of its many bureaus. The building they sought was but a few steps away, and their route led them directly past the White House, the official residence of the President of the United States.

While on their journey they saw but few persons in uniform. Even in the Navy Building there was a decided absence of officers or men in the dress of their calling. This seemed very odd to the boy, as he always pictured in his imagination the "seat of the nation" was gay with uniformed officials of his own and other countries.

"Why is it, Father, you see so few uniforms in the capital?" he inquired.

"I am not positive I am right," replied Mr. Comstock, "but the American officers, soldiers and sailors object to wearing their military clothes except when they are actually required to do so.[#] Our nation is so democratic that they believe it makes them appear conspicuous. Furthermore, in uniform they are often discriminated against, particularly in the case of enlisted men. This is one of the reasons why a better class of men do not go into the service--they consider the wearing of a uniform belittles them in the eyes of the public."

[#] Previous to the war with Germany officers of the United States services were not required to wear uniforms when off duty and outside their ship or station. Enlisted men were also permitted to wear civilian clothing while on liberty, under certain restrictions. Civilian clothing was generally called "cits" by those in service.

"I think a uniform is the best kind of clothing a fellow can wear. I'll be mighty proud of mine, and never will be ashamed of it."

"In Europe," continued Dick's father, "a soldier is looked upon in a different light, depending to a great extent in what country he serves. They are honored and usually given every consideration, or at least the officers are, and particularly in Germany, where militarism is the first word in culture. The United States, on the other hand, maintains such a small and inadequate army and navy that our men in uniform are really more like curiosities to the people than anything else."

"But there are a lot of men in uniform back home," Dick remarked.

"Yes, enlisted men, seldom officers. The reason is, the proximity of several army forts, a navy yard and the frequent visits of the men-of-war in our harbor. So we at home are familiar with the different branches of the service; but it is far from being the case in most cities of our republic," answered Mr. Comstock.

They were now approaching the building wherein the headquarters of the Marine Corps were located, when Dick exclaimed:

"Look, Father! There are some marines now; aren't they simply great?"

Two stalwart men in uniform were crossing the street just ahead of the speaker. In their dark blue coats piped in red, with the five shiny brass buttons down the front and yellow and red chevrons on the arms, trousers adorned with bright red stripes and blue caps surmounted by the Corps insignia over the black enameled vizors, they were indeed a most attractive sample of the Marine Corps non-commissioned officer at his best.

"It's their regular dress uniform," Dick announced, "and I think it's the best looking outfit I have ever seen, but, Dad, you should see the officers when they get into their full dress!"

"Where did you pick up all your knowledge of their uniforms, Dick?" asked his father curiously.

"Oh, Tommy Turner made his uncle show them all to us. You see, he stayed in the Corps for some years after the Spanish War, and he has always kept his uniforms. He believes that some day he may need them again if ever the United States gets into a big fight, and if that time comes he is going back into the marines."

Following the two non-commissioned officers into a tall structure, Mr. Comstock and Richard were whisked up several stories in an elevator and found themselves before an opened door upon which were the words, "Aide to the Commandant."

A young man in civilian dress rose as they entered and inquired their business, which Mr. Comstock quickly explained.

"Sit down, sir, if you please, and I will see if the General can talk with you," he said.

They did as directed, while the young man disappeared into an adjoining room. A few moments later he returned and motioned for them to follow him.

"What may I do for you, Mr. Comstock?" inquired a large, handsome, gray-haired gentleman standing behind the desk when they entered. He too was in civilian clothes, but despite the fact, looked every inch the soldier he was known to be.

Mr. Comstock introduced Richard to the General and then told him the reason of his visit.

"My boy is anxious to become a marine, and I have promised to look into the necessary preliminary steps. I understand that you are not recruiting just at present, but we were told that possibly my son would be taken into the Corps as a bugler or drummer."

"Yes, we do take boys in for training as field musics," said the General, glancing at Dick for a moment, "but your son, I fear, is too old; the ages for this class of enlistment are from fifteen to seventeen years, and judging by the lad's size he already passed the age limit."

"He is very nearly, but has yet a few hours of grace," replied Mr. Comstock. "He will be seventeen to-morrow, and I was hoping that you might enlist him to-day. My son's object in going into the Corps is to work for a commission. That is one of the inducements which I understand the Corps offers its enlisted personnel, is it not?"

"You are right, Mr. Comstock; at the present time our officers are taken from graduates of the Naval Academy or from the ranks. There have been times when civilian appointments were allowed, but the law has now been changed."

"In that case then, could you take my boy into your organization? He understands that his advancement depends entirely on his own merit, and he has taken a decided stand as to what he intends to do and has my full consent to try it."

"Does he also understand that the number of officers appointed from the ranks are few, and picked for their exceptionally good records and ability, and that he serves an apprenticeship until he is twenty-one years of age?" inquired the Commandant.

"Yes, sir," answered Richard, speaking for the first time.

"Why do you not enter the Naval Academy, young man, and after graduation come into the Corps?" asked the General, looking at Dick with his stern eyes.

"Well, sir, I failed to get the appointment at the last minute."

"Do you also realize there are many unpleasant things connected with the life of an enlisted man, and are you prepared to meet them?"

"Yes, sir, and I believe I can make good."

"I like your spirit, young man," said the General approvingly; "the motto of the Marine Corps is '*Semper Fidelis*--Always Faithful,' and to be a true marine you must bear that motto in mind at all times and under all conditions, if it is your hope to succeed in the service."

He now turned to Dick's father:

"Ordinarily, Mr. Comstock, our young men are held at the school for a few days before we complete their enlistment in order that they may get an idea of the life and duties to which they are about to bind themselves when taking the oath of allegiance. In your son's case, I believe he knows what he wants, and he is the kind of young man we wish to get. Were he compelled to wait according to our usual custom he would be past the age limit, consequently I will further your desires and arrange to have him sworn into service immediately, providing he passes the surgeon's examination. I will give you an order to the Commanding Officer of the Marine Barracks which will answer your purpose."

Saying this he gave the necessary directions to the aide, who had remained standing near by, and a little later Dick and his father were on a street car bound for the barracks, where the School for Musics was located. Arriving there they soon found themselves in the presence of the colonel commanding the post, who, on reading the instructions of the Commandant, looked the boy over with an approving eye.

"I reckon you will be about the tallest apprentice we have here," he said, and calling an orderly directed him to escort Dick to the examining surgeon, and invited Mr. Comstock to sit and await the result.

The Marine Corps is primarily organized for service with the Navy, though this has by no means been its only function in the past, nor likely to be in the future. On many occasions the Corps has acted independently and also with the Army, which is provided for in the statutes. Being attached to the Navy and operating with it at Navy Yards, Naval Stations and on board ship its medical officers are supplied by the Navy, for the Corps maintains no sanitary service of its own.

The Navy surgeon gave the lad a very thorough examination, one even more thorough than usual, and after Dick had been passed and departed he remarked to his assistant:

"That boy is one of the finest specimens of the American youth I have ever examined. He is so clean limbed and perfectly muscled that it was a joy to look at him."

After this visit, Dick, with the attendant orderly, returned to the office of the Commanding Officer.

"Well, the surgeon states you are all right," said Colonel Waverly, having glanced at the slip of paper the orderly handed him; "you are quite positive that you wish to undertake the obligation, young man?"

"Quite, sir," was Dick's laconic response.

"Very well," and the Colonel then called loudly for the Sergeant Major. "Sergeant Major, this young man is to be enlisted as an apprentice at once. Make out the necessary papers."

Fifteen minutes later, with his right hand held high, his head proudly erect, Richard Comstock took the solemn oath of allegiance to his country, which so few young men seriously consider as they repeat its impressive vows, and with the final words he graduated to man's estate.

CHAPTER V

A DRUMMER IN THE U. S. MARINES

"Rise and shine! Come on, you kids, shake a leg and get up out of this!"

Dick Comstock sleepily rubbed his eyes for the fraction of a second and then sprang out of his comfortable bunk as the sergeant's voice bellowed through the room. In the long dormitory thirty-odd boys, their ages ranging from fifteen to Dick's own, were hurrying their preparations to get into uniform and down on the parade ground in time for reveille roll call. Another day in a marine's life had begun.

Out the doors and down the stairs clattered the noisy, boisterous throng, fastening last buttons as they emerged into the light of the midsummer rising sun.

August was half gone and Dick had now completed over a month and a half in Uncle Sam's *corps d'elite*, for such it was acknowledged to be by well informed military men of both continents. During that time he had not found the days hanging heavily on his hands. Being fortunate in knowing, before he came into the service, how to handle the ebony sticks and blow a bugle, he had escaped a good deal of the monotonous preliminary ground work which the boys in the "school for musics" were required to undergo. It is true that he first had to prove his ability to his drill masters, and having received no regular instruction previously, he made no mention of his accomplishments during his first few days at the school.

With the others he had gone each morning to the basement, where the drumming lessons were given; sat astride the wooden benches with his companions and lustily pounded out "Ma-ma, Dad-dy," till the very walls seemed to shake and tremble from the fearful racket.

The old retired drummer who called him up for his first lesson asked Dick no questions.

"Comstock!" he had called out, and Dick went modestly forward to receive his instructions from the old martinet, for such he was, and had to be with that mischievously inclined, irresponsible lot of young Americans. "I want you to start in practising this to-day--yes, that is right--you hold the sticks correctly! Now, make two strokes with the left hand,--slow, like this,--then two with the right. Now watch me," and the old fellow tapped the bench before him demonstrating his meaning.

With each two strokes of the left-hand stick he would say aloud, "Ma-ma," and with the right-hand strokes, "Dad-dy," slowly at first then more quickly, till finally the plank beneath gave forth the wonderful roll of sound never acquired except by long and faithful practise.

"Now you see how it should be done! At first you must only try to do it slowly, for unless you get this down thoroughly at the start you will never be a drummer. Next!" And Dick was moved along to practise in playing "Mama, Daddy," "Mama, Daddy," for the next hour.

It had been otherwise with the bugle instructor. He saw at once that the boy knew how to "tongue" the mouthpiece, and that his lip was in condition, and after trying him out the first day and finding him able to read notes, Dick was told to learn the calls with which he was unfamiliar and left to work out his own salvation.

In a little over a month he passed the required examination and was regularly appointed a drummer.

The prediction of Colonel Waverly that Dick would probably be the largest boy in the school proved nearly correct, there being but one other boy, Henry Clay Cabell, a Southerner, who approached him in size. "Hank" or "Daddy" Cabell, as he was called by the rest of the school until Dick's entrance, had been the oldest boy there; he was as tall as Richard, but did not have the weight nor strength. From their first meeting Dick and Henry formed a liking for each other which daily increased and strengthened. Henry confided to Dick that he hoped to work his way up to a commission, and they agreed to help each other with that end in view. At the same time Dick was graduated and made a drummer Henry Cabell was appointed a trumpeter, and it was their fondest desire to be detailed for duty at the same station if sent away in the near future, as was very likely to be the case.

On this particular August morning while the two walked back to their squad room after the regular physical drill which followed the reveille roll call, they were discussing this matter.

"I reckon it won't be long before we get our walking papers," said Henry in his deliberate Southern drawl, "now that we are no longer apprentices.

"I'll be glad to leave that crazy bunch, anyway," he continued as they stopped for a moment under the barracks arcade and watched the apprentices racing wildly across the parade ground after being dismissed from their drill. "I don't reckon they ever will learn anything. They are only mischief-making children, and seem to have no sense of responsibility at all. Sometimes I wonder why they take such babies into a crack organization like this. Do you reckon it ever pays in the long run? They try to fuss 'Old Grumpy' the entire time, and never make the least attempt to learn their lessons at school."

"I guess you've still a great deal to learn about the marines," remarked Dick drily. "In the first place, those boys seldom fool Gunnery Sergeant Miller with their tricks. He has been handling boys for such a long time in the capacity of 'N.C.O.[#] in Charge' that they have to get up pretty early in the morning to put one over on him. He has been through the mill himself, for he is a graduate from this very school. It's just because they are kids, that's all, and most of them have not had the advantages you and I have enjoyed, Hank, in the way of schooling and home training and associations. They get the spirit of the Corps sooner or later, I guess. You see, we were fortunate; we both went through high school, and that is why we were excused from taking the lessons those boys have to labor over. Some of those chaps never got beyond the primary schools till they came here."

[#] Non-commissioned officer.

"Where did you get all your dope, Dick?" inquired Henry, rather curious to know how his friend found out so many things.

"Well, you see, Hank, I'm in the Marine Corps to learn all I can about it. I want to be familiar with its history in every way, and I've had several talks with Miller and other N.C.O.'s about service things. In this way I get quite a little valuable information not put down in the rules and regulations; and it may come in handy some day."

"Oh yes, I reckon so, and you may be right; but for my part the N.C.O.'s are such an ignorant lot themselves, and more or less vulgar too, that I avoid all of them as much as possible. Until you came along, Dick, I hardly spoke to anyone in the barracks. It goes against the grain to have too close an intimacy with them."

"Henry, you are too good a fellow to hold such ideas; and besides, you are wrong about their being ignorant, or vulgar either. I am beginning to believe that every individual can teach us something which, if we use the knowledge properly, is bound to help us and make us better men. If you hope to become a successful officer you will have to know your men, how to treat them and to deal with them; you will have to make their interests your interests to a great extent; but if you despise your men because they all don't happen to measure up to your standard, socially, mentally and morally, I'll tell you right now you've got a hard row to travel ahead of you, old boy."

"Your argument doesn't appeal to me, Dick," responded Henry, with a little coolness in his voice. "I reckon I'll get along. So, as we can't agree on that point, let us cut out the discussion and get our quarters policed up. It is nearly time for mess call."

It was Saturday morning, and the quarters of the apprentices were due for an extra cleaning, for on this day of the week the Commanding Officer of the

Post held his weekly inspection, and woe betide any luckless youngster whose bunk was not properly made up, shoes not accurately lined and shined, or whose steel clothes locker was not in "apple pie order."

Each boy had his own work to do. The narrow aluminum painted bunks were carefully aligned along either wall of the long room. Folded back on the wire springs towards the head of the bed were the mattresses in their immaculate white covers; on top of each mattress were the folded sheets, their smooth edges to the front. Next came the pillow in its linen case; and finally surmounting these were the gray blankets with the initials "U.S.M.C." woven in dark blue lettering across their centers, while plainly in view were the owners' names in white stencil.

In the five-foot spaces between bunks were the dark, green-painted steel lockers in which were stored toilet articles, knickknacks, and wearing apparel. Each bit of clothing was laid with the folded edge outward and flush with the front of the locker shelves.

The hard-wood floors needed but a careful sweeping and dusting, for Friday is field day in every Marine Corps garrison, consequently the scrubbing and preliminary polishing had been previously attended to.

The work was barely completed when the blaring call of a bugle announced breakfast.

"Soupy, soupy, soupy,

The worst I 've ever seen:

Coffee, coffee, coffee,

Without a single bean:

Porky, porky, porky,

And not a streak of lean."

Thus sang the bugle!

Again the clattering down the stairs, as not only the music boys, but the entire garrison "fell in" under the arcade and were marched into the spotless mess hall to a breakfast of bacon and eggs, hot cakes and coffee. Then the clatter of heavy china dishes on the wooden mess tables, the noise of knife and fork and spoon, the clatter of voices filled the air. Messmen, who were themselves marines detailed for the duty, for which they received an extra compensation of five dollars pay per month, their uniforms covered with long white aprons, scurried to and from the galley, with steaming pitchers of hot coffee or large platters of golden-brown flapjacks, serving the hungry men at the tables.

In the middle of this tumult an officer entered, dressed in khaki, and wearing at his left side the famous "sword of the Mamelukes" in its glittering scabbard.

"'Ten--shun!"

The command rang out in stentorian tones through the room. Each man sat bolt upright in his place. The hustling messmen[#] stood halted in their tracks and instant silence reigned. Some N.C.O., catching sight of the Officer of the Day coming through the doorway to inspect the morning meal, called out the order, but only for a moment was the progress of the repast delayed; almost before the noise had ceased the O.D.'s command, "Carry On,"[#] was heard, and the din and clatter began with redoubled energy.

[#] By Navy Regulations one mess-man is allowed for every twenty men in the mess.

[#] A Navy and Marine Corps command, by voice or bugle, meaning for the men to continue work, drill, or occupation in which they were engaged when interrupted. This command has been in vogue for many years.

In and out among the tables walked the officer, asking this or that one questions about the food or calling the attention of the busy messmen to some trivial defect, then he disappeared in the direction of the galley to taste for himself the quality of the articles served. This routine was part of the O.D.'s duty.

In service, meals are quickly over, and no loitering is allowed at tables, especially on inspection day. Richard, having finished his rations with all the gusto of a healthy boy, strolled from the mess hall back to his squad room. The apprentices were supposed to have their quarters in proper "police" by mess call in the morning, and while they were engaged in filling their stomachs, the N.C.O. in charge, Gunnery Sergeant Miller, usually made his unofficial morning inspection in order to discover and correct any violations of requirements before the regular function by the O.D., or on Saturdays the Commanding Officer.

"Old Grumpy" knew boys from "A to Izzard," and though they were ever attempting to play all sorts of pranks on him it was seldom they succeeded. Tall, lean, gruff, the boys soon found he possessed a heart under the weather-beaten exterior, and honestly admired and respected him. He was never unjust, he gave them no work not necessary to their welfare. He heard their complaints, settled their disputes; or, if he believed these could be settled only by a fistic encounter, he arranged the match, and acted as referee, timekeeper and general adviser.

He also took charge of their scholastic career, so sadly neglected in many cases. It was called "Grammar" school, but its curriculum was little more than the "three R's." Besides being the drill instructor, Gunnery Sergeant Miller strove at all times to teach his young charges the manly virtues of honesty, courage, self-control, obedience, industry and clean living.

When Dick entered the squad room he thought at first it must have been occupied during his absence at breakfast by a menagerie of wild beasts. At the far end, where there happened to be a few empty bunks, a regular free-for-all fight seemed to be in progress. Shoes were flying about the room in all directions, boys wrestling on the floor, pulling at one another, yelling, laughing, punching, crawling. During "Old Grumpy's" inspection, while they were at mess, he had found several pairs of shoes unblackened, others not aligned, and still others poked away in improper places. So he gathered all the shoes in the room in a heap and left them for their owners to disentangle and set aright. It was not an easy job to find one's shoes when mixed up in a jumbled mass of over sixty pairs, and by the time the owners secured their rightful property, get them again cleaned (for the scrimmage had effectually destroyed any previous gloss), and aligned under the bunks, brass work of drum and bugle polished, leggins khaki-blancoed, clothing and equipment brushed and adjusted, guard mounting was over and first call for inspection sounded from the area of barracks.

At the sounding of assembly the lads formed in two ranks on their allotted parade ground, while the companies under arms and the band marched to their assigned places.

This was the first Saturday inspection for some of the apprentices recently arrived, so Gunnery Sergeant Miller took occasion to give them a few last cautions regarding their duties, and ended by addressing them as follows:

"I want to tell you boys that every time in the future I don't find your shoes properly policed at early inspection they all go into a pile as they did this morning. That means more work for all hands. I can't stop to pick out the few that are all right when so many are all wrong. Take the hint and all of you coöperate and save yourselves extra and useless work. That's all! At Ease!"

The strains of the band were now heard and the apprentices watched the movements of the companies as they went through the ceremony of inspection and review.

The United States Marine Corps band is one of the most famous organizations of its kind in the world. It is stationed at the Marine Barracks in Washington, D.C., and plays during all parades, guard mountings, and other like ceremonies. Once John Philip Sousa was its leader, and the band has always rendered his well-known march music to perfection. At this moment following the sounding of "Adjutant's Call," the space between the barrack buildings was filled with marching men forming in one long line with the band on its right, swords flashing, guns glinting in the sun, and the red, white and blue of the silken flag fluttering. It was indeed a martial and inspiring sight. Later, as the armed men passed in review before Colonel Waverly to the sound of the Marines' own march by Sousa--"Semper Fidelis"--every step and movement was in perfect unison.

"Any man whose feet don't just naturally keep in time to that music never will be a soldier if he lives to be as old as Methuselah," remarked Gunnery Sergeant Miller to the latest recruit near whom he was standing, "and when you get to blow the bugle like those musics in rear of the band, then you're a field music and no mistake."

Behind the band twelve boys, all recent graduates from the school, among them Richard Comstock and Henry Cabell, were adding volume to the music during certain parts of the march. It was then that the whole enclosure fairly vibrated with the soul-stirring strains.

The review ended: the extra musics fell out and joined their fellows under Miller, and the inspection of the troops began. During this function the band rendered various selections much to the delectation of many curious sightseers who had been admitted at the Main Gate to the barracks. Many of these people were music lovers and could be found seated on the same benches day after day, listening to the band.

"Do you see that pretty girl across the parade, Dick?" asked Henry. "No, not where you are looking, but the one standing near the bench under the trees--the girl looking this way."

Dick's eyes following the directions of his friend soon spied the girl referred to. How familiar she looked! She reminded him of--yes,--it was,--Ursula, his sister, and by her side stood his mother and father.

Forgetting he was no longer a free agent, Dick gave a wild "whoop" and started from the ranks. Just in the nick of time Henry caught him by the coat-tails and jerked him backward to his place in line.

"Watch yourself, Dick," muttered Henry between his teeth, "here comes the 'Old Man!'" His prompt action probably saved Dick a severe reprimand, if nothing worse.

Gunnery Sergeant Miller had whirled about on hearing the unaccustomed war whoop but he was not swift enough to catch the culprit. So he was forced to postpone further investigation of the untoward circumstance until another time, for Colonel Waverly was now but a few yards away, coming to inspect the apprentices.

"Attention! Prepare for inspection; Open--Ranks; March!"

The apprentices became a stiff line of human ramrods and at the command of execution--"March,"--the rear rank took three paces backward and halted, while in both lines heads and eyes were turned smartly to the right. Having verified the alignment of both ranks the Gunnery Sergeant stepped to the front and commanded:

"Front!"

Each head snapped to the front. The N.C.O. in charge then saluted the Commanding Officer by bringing the sword he carried up to a position in front of the center of his body, the right hand grasping the hilt a few inches from his chin, with the blade slanting upward and slightly outward. This part of the ceremony being over Colonel Waverly carefully inspected every boy in line. He examined their shoes, the fit of their clothing, their equipment, the cut of their hair and even, if truth must be told, their necks, to see if soap and water had been recently and properly applied.

All this time Dick was nearly bursting with impatience. He began to believe the Colonel never would finish. At last the ordeal was over and immediately on being dismissed he requested and received of "Old Grumpy" permission to speak to the Commanding Officer. Approaching him, Dick rendered his most military salute.

"What do you wish, Music?" questioned Colonel Waverly.

"Drummer Comstock would thank the Commanding Officer for permission to go to the visitors' benches and speak with his mother, father and sister. They have just arrived, and are over near the gate, sir."

"Granted, young man, and you are excused for the rest of the day."

Dick Comstock cannot recollect whether or not he saluted his colonel after a fervent "Thank you, sir," but he still remembers the feeling of those motherly arms about him and the sweet kisses on his lips as Mrs. Comstock gathered her stalwart drummer boy to her bosom,--drum, drumsticks and all.

CHAPTER VI

A QUEER CONVERSATION

"We were here all the time, Dick," said Ursula soon after the first outburst of joyful greeting had subsided, "and we all tried our level best to catch your eye but, goodness--you were so military you would look neither to the right nor left," and she straightened her back and puffed out her cheeks in comic imitation of her brother on parade.

"It is quite as well I didn't see you, for if I had, I'd have forgotten every bit of military discipline I've absorbed since being here," responded Dick, smiling good-naturedly at his sister's mockery; "as it was I came near making a break when Hank Cabell pointed you out to me; but fortunately he grabbed me and saved my reputation as a marine."

"Is 'Hank,' as you call him, the boy about whom you wrote to us--the Southerner?" inquired Dick's father.

"Yes, Dad, and I want you to meet him. He's a dandy chap and comes from a good family, though I believe they are very poor, and likewise very proud."

"Sometimes that combination isn't all that could be desired as an asset," drily remarked Mr. Comstock.

"But he is all right, Dad," said Dick, quickly coming to the defense of his friend against any possible insinuation. "There he is now. I'll get him to come over here."

Suiting actions to his words Richard presently returned with Henry, and the formality of introductions over, Mr. Comstock invited his son's friend to join them at luncheon and for the day. Henry's rather sombre face lighted up with pleasure.

"I should be very glad to go, sir, providing I can secure early liberty," he said.

"How about you, Dick, are you in the same boat as your friend Henry?" inquired his father.

"No, Dad; you see, when I told Colonel Waverly you were here he excused me for the rest of the day," replied Richard, and turning to Henry he said, "Suppose you hurry up and get permission, Hank, while I go and put away my implements of warfare."

"Implements of war, indeed!" laughed Ursula, pointing banteringly at the drum slung over her brother's shoulder, "and are your weapons as dangerous as my brother's?" asked she, turning her questioning eyes on Henry.

"Mine consists of a brass trumpet," replied the boy with a smile, "but it has one advantage over the drum as a weapon, for it makes a handy bludgeon in time of need."

"Run along, boys," cautioned Mrs. Comstock, "it is nearly noon and I for one am famished."

"I reckon it would be better for us to get permission to wear cits; it might be less embarrassing for you all," and Henry looked inquiringly at Richard's parents.

"Not for me," interposed Dick, with some emphasis; "I'm in uniform, and I'm proud of it, and so are my people."

"I didn't mean it in that light," Henry replied, flushing at the suggested rebuke. "I was merely thinking of your mother and sister and the possibility of saving them embarrassment. You may not know this, but enlisted men in uniform are not greeted cordially everywhere, even here in Washington."

"Excuse me, Henry, for being so hasty; I had not thought of that side of the question," said Dick frankly, and he turned red himself because of his readiness to find fault with his chum's remark.

"Yes, Henry was quite right in what he said," stated Mr. Comstock. "I read of many such incidents in the papers; but there are laws now which slowly but nevertheless surely are making people understand that the enlisted man in uniform may no longer be treated with disrespect. A better class of men seem to be joining the colors these days, and they are calling their defamers to a strict accounting. But this is not getting something to satisfy our appetites. You boys hurry up now and get yourselves ready."

After a bountiful luncheon at one of the best hotels in the city a tour of the capital was proposed and an enjoyable afternoon of sightseeing followed. In Dick's spare moments during his stay in Washington he had visited nearly every one of the public buildings and he took great pleasure in showing his sister about. The three young people even climbed the thousand steps of Washington Monument, scorning the slow-moving elevator which carried their elders up the five hundred feet which still left them fifty-five feet beneath the apex of the wonderful shaft.

Ursula was enchanted with this superb view of the "magic city," as she was pleased to call it, and for a long time they all enjoyed the panorama of land and water, field and forest, country and city, spread before them to the distant horizons.

After this they walked back to their hotel, and while Mrs. Comstock enjoyed a little rest before dinner and Mr. Comstock departed on a business engagement the trio of young people occupied themselves in animated conversation in one of the ornate reception rooms.

Feeling that Ursula and Richard might appreciate being alone together for a while, Henry excused himself, promising to return in time for the evening programme, which would not end until after the roof garden supper following the theatre.

After his departure Ursula and Dick strolled over to one of the low windows and pushing aside the long curtains which reached to the floor they stepped into the vacant space of a small narrow balconied window ledge and stood looking at the passing traffic. A group of palms, the half-closed blinds and the long curtains effectually concealed them from the view of people inside the room.

The mere fact of being together was happiness in itself for these two devoted young people and gradually a silence fell upon them as they stood absorbed in the scenes outside.

A subdued murmur of voices came from the room behind them, and Dick heard someone say:

"Here is a quiet place where we may talk freely."

Glancing over his shoulder the boy saw three men seating themselves and deliberately placing their chairs near the window where he and his sister were standing. He was wondering why they took such care with the chairs, when again the same voice gave him the reason.

"We can see from here whomever comes into the room, gentlemen, and it is well to observe caution while discussing this question."

"Shall we speak in German, Señor?" brusquely inquired a heavily built man whose blond hair stood up in short stiff bristles on his head.

"Si, Señor," deferentially replied the third member of the party, a slender, black-haired man whose dark skin announced him a resident of some Latin-American country, and from then on they spoke in the tongue agreed upon, and so quietly that Dick could not overhear. Knowing that he was an unintentional eavesdropper he turned back again to the street feeling it was unnecessary to move from the window, for unless he made an especial attempt the words of the speakers were inaudible to his ears. A little time passed in this way, when suddenly Dick placed his hand over Ursula's mouth, for she had turned, meaning to address him. At the same moment he motioned her to be silent.

To both Richard and Ursula Comstock the German spoken language was an open book, for Mrs. Comstock had employed German nursemaids to attend them when they were little tots, and until Ursula was twelve years of age she had had a German governess. Even the cook, a family retainer for years, was a native of Cologne. In consequence the loud remark which Dick heard from the room behind was as significant as if spoken in English. He knew that the big foreigner from across the ocean had uttered it. There was no mistaking the deep, abrupt, explosive voice.

"The United States can do nothing! Germany can whip her any day! Germany can whip the whole world; and some day she will!"

The speaker had risen and the others now pushed their chairs back and stood beside him. Their voices came distinctly to the ears of the boy and girl tensely listening in the shadow of the blind.

"Well, I should not go so far as that, you know!" protested the tall man who had led them to the window for their talk and whom Dick decided was an Englishman.

"Maybe you wouldn't, but it's so," reiterated the German, using his words as a ruffian would a cudgel. "Now, Señor, I must have your decision regarding this canal business at once, or it will be too late to be of any use to us. If your revolution in Nicaragua is a success, will the man you put in the presidential chair grant Germany the canal right-of-way or not?"

"I cannot tell you, Señor. It is a question which must be placed before the committee. I am only empowered to offer you the things already mentioned in return for financing our uprising. The United States has a concession, I believe--had it as far back as eighteen eighty-two. They would not permit us to agree to your proposal."

"I tell you that you are wrong. The United States never made any treaty with Nicaragua. Your government granted a concession to a private corporation in 1897 to build a canal, and they bluffed for a while at digging it on the Atlantic side. The United States also sent a commission down to Nicaragua several times, but nothing came of it. Then they forced Panama into revolt against the Colombian Government, and made her give them the present location. Therefore if you want our money and our secret aid your candidate must agree to Germany's terms."

"Suppose we give Señor Cabanas a few days to consult with his committee," suggested the Englishman in his mild voice.

"The committee knows it already," exclaimed the exasperated Teuton. "The subject was thrashed out in Leon while I was there six months ago. I tell you it is subterfuge, pure and simple. They know what we want, and they should have deputized their man to grant our demands."

"Pardon me again, Señor," came the suave voice of the little man, yet his eyes must have flashed ominously at the brutal pounding of the German's heavy voice, "I assure you that this is absolute news to me."

"It shouldn't be! Your committeemen are a set of vacillating fools; that is all, and the best I can say of them. Go back to them and arrange it; but I warn you--not a mark,--not a single mark, unless----"

"Be careful, Mein Herr, here comes the house detective--they are all secret service men in Washington. We had best postpone this and meet again."

It was the Englishman who gave the warning, and with the words the three conspirators moved towards the door leading to the hotel lobby.

Behind the curtains Richard and Ursula still stood, hardly daring to breathe for fear of disclosing their presence. Every word uttered by the plotters since Dick placed his hand over Ursula's lips had been distinctly heard and understood by both, and they realized the import of the information they had obtained so unintentionally.

Barely had the three men disappeared when Dick, exclaiming, "Wait for me here!" was running towards the door in pursuit.

Henry Cabell, returning from his self-imposed absence, came around the corner of the entrance at that identical moment, and the lads collided forcibly. The delay caused thereby was sufficient to enable the quarry to efface themselves and though Dick made a careful search his efforts were futile.

Returning, he found Ursula excitedly relating their experience to Henry. They both looked up expectantly at Dick's entrance.

"Did you catch them, Dick?" his sister inquired breathlessly. "Did you have them arrested?"

"No, I lost them," announced Dick in a disgusted tone; "I couldn't have them arrested anyway on the little we know; this is a free country. But I sure would have liked to see their faces. All the time they had their backs towards us, and I merely glanced at them when they first came in. I do wish I'd been more observing."

"What would you have done had you caught them?" asked Ursula.

"I'm sure I don't know; only I'd have pointed them out to that house detective, for one thing."

"Could you identify any of them if you saw them again?" asked Henry.

"I'd know that big brute of a German by his back, in a million, but I'm not sure of the others,--yes, I believe I could tell the Englishman too."

"I should know him if I ever saw him again," said Ursula. "I never should forget that peculiar suit of clothes he wore, nor----"

Both the boys broke into a shout of laughter at this remark and Dick said:

"That's like a woman; noticing the dress first of all."

"Oh, you need not laugh, Dickie dear; I do not doubt that he has other clothes, but the chief thing I should recognize him by was a peculiar patch of white hair on the right side of his head behind his ear, and also half the middle finger of his left hand was missing."

"We apologize most humbly for our premature expression of opinion regarding your powers of observation," said Dick, bowing low to Ursula with mock deference, "but now the question is,--what shall we do with this information we have acquired?"

"Here is Father; let us ask him," and Ursula ran to greet Mr. Comstock who at that moment approached them.

After hearing of the episode, Mr. Comstock advised Dick to write out all the details as he and Ursula remembered them, and he, Mr. Comstock, would see that the report was placed in proper hands.

"I believe you have discovered a very pretty plot, which would seriously damage us if carried to an ultimate conclusion," said Dick's father. "We all know that Germany is expanding her trade lines enormously and making greater strides in systematic foreign commercialism than any other nation, but I can hardly conceive she would dare to finance such a risky venture with the canal right-of-way as her only payment."

"Would Uncle Sam permit Germany or any other country to build a canal across Nicaragua now that the Panama Canal is almost completed?" asked Henry.

"I doubt it so much that I feel perfectly safe in saying, most emphatically,--No!"

"The United States would never allow any country to acquire territory in the Western Hemisphere--it would be contrary to the provisions of the Monroe Doctrine," said Dick. He leaned over and picked his campaign hat from the floor, then pointing to the small metal object thereon, he continued:

"This little insignia of the marines tells its own story; this is the Western Hemisphere; across it the anchor and above the eagle with spreading wings, holding a ribbon on which is inscribed the motto of our Corps. It is our part to look out for these little countries, and according to history the marines have been doing it mighty effectually since the United States became a nation. And I guess we can keep up the good work."

"With the able assistance of one Drummer Richard Comstock, U.S.M.C.!" slyly interposed Ursula, and Dick joined in the laughter which followed her remark.

"The thing I can't figure out," said Henry, "is what the Englishman is mixed up in it for! Do you reckon England is joining hands with Germany?"

"No, I doubt anything of that nature," answered Mr. Comstock. "The interests of England and the United States are too closely allied for her to risk rupturing them by any such hazardous undertaking."

"I would not trust an Englishman as far as I could see him! I cannot bear them!" exclaimed Ursula, vehemently.

"Why do you feel so bitter against our mother country?" asked Henry, who was surprised at her outburst. "Is that the general feeling up North? For I am quite certain it is not in the South."

"Ursula's feeling is largely due to local influences," answered her father. "In our home town the English have never been popular since the day during the Revolutionary War one of their officers, a major, after having received the surrender of our brave Colonel Ledyard at the Battle of Groton Heights, took that officer's proffered sword and ran him through the heart and then commanded his troops to massacre the surviving gallant defenders of the fort, who were drawn up, unarmed, in one of the bastions. That same day our city was burned to the ground by the traitor, Benedict Arnold."

"The brute! Why! I'd rather be Benedict Arnold than that Englishman," and Ursula's pretty face looked very stern and her hands clenched in anger.

"It was fortunate you both understood German," said Henry a little later in the evening. "I never could bear the study of languages, though I did struggle along for a year or two with Latin at school."

"We neither of us have studied German, merely picked it up as children, and we always use it talking to the cook. But I like French and had it three years at school, but really no practise in it," said Dick.

They were at the theatre and Dick sat next to his father, which afforded the two many opportunities to converse during the vaudeville acts.

"I am glad, Dick, that you keep writing to your mother regularly," said Mr. Comstock; "it is a fine habit to form and to stick to. If every boy wrote home at least once a week, I believe the world would be a better place. So many boys grow careless and after a while lose touch with the home ties and associations. Then, too, besides being a good thing for you personally, you have no idea what those letters mean to your mother."

"I like to get letters, and unless I wrote them on my part my mail would be pretty slim," replied Dick. "I have seen already how the men welcome the sight of the mail orderly, and some who never get mail envy those who do. Some of our boys never receive home news, and they must be homesick and heart-sick at times the way they sort of hang around and listen when some fellow happens to read out a few of the things that happen back in the home town. I know I'd be, were I in their place."

"You will never regret being thoughtful when it comes to giving your mother a little line or two of written happiness. But in your letters I have noticed an absence of complaints. Is it because you have none to make or that you didn't want us to feel bad by recounting them?"

"I haven't a single kick coming, Dad, for we are treated splendidly. Good food and well cooked, good clothes, fine beds and healthy work. I only wish it was more strenuous than it is. I spend a lot of time in the gym and playing ball. I did hope we musics would get more military drill than we do, but outside of a little marching and physical drills and a 'hike' across the river into Maryland, we do nothing of real soldiering. One of the privates has taught me the manual of arms and bayonet exercises, so I'm not wasting my opportunities. I think that in a year more I can get my rank changed to a private, then I shall be in line for promotion to corporal."

"Time enough, my boy. It is better to make haste slowly and thoroughly, for I don't doubt you will have to be very thorough if you are to succeed. Have you any idea what books you will require?"

"Well, I'm studying the U.S. Army Guard Manual, which the marines have adopted, and there is a book called 'Landing Force and Small Arms Instruction' for the Navy which is just filled with meat and will take some time to digest. I shall have no difficulty in getting the books as I need them, and my high school education was along the lines that would have helped me most at Annapolis--physics, chemistry, astronomy, surveying and so forth. All these are sure to be valuable, to say nothing of the mathematics up to trig."

"It pleases me to hear you like the life," said Dick's father. "That is more than half the battle always,--the interest and liking we have for the task at hand. No man ever became successful without being in perfect harmony with his work and his environments, no matter what his walk in life."

Richard's mother was more solicitous regarding her son's creature comforts, and the following day she insisted on making a visit to the barracks and seeing with her own eyes exactly how and where her boy lived. The manner of her request so enchanted Colonel Waverly when she asked to be taken around the post that he volunteered to act as her escort, nor was her New England sense of cleanliness and order once outraged with what she saw.

They visited the living quarters, offices, mess hall, auditorium, storerooms and galley, and she even tasted with approval the food in preparation for the noonday meal. A youthful Lieutenant of Marines, accompanying the party, insisted on presenting Ursula with several pairs of N.C.O. dress chevrons and trumpet cords from the Quartermaster's stores, with which she might decorate a sofa pillow, and not to be outdone in gallantry, Henry Cabell, on seeing these evidences of the officer's regard for the charming sister of his friend, made a dash for the post canteen before its closing hour and purchased for her a dainty little gold and silver pin, a miniature of the Marine Corps emblem, for which he required her to give him a copper in payment.

Dick and Henry had not been included in the inspection tour but they later accompanied their visitors to the train which carried them away that beautiful Sunday afternoon back to New England.

"These two days have been, sure enough, the happiest days I have spent since leaving home," remarked Henry as the boys retraced their way to the barracks. "I didn't half thank your folks for the great pleasure they have given me."

"It was fine, wasn't it?" said Dick simply, for his mind still dwelt on the last proud look his father had given him; the suspicion of tears bravely suppressed in Ursula's eyes and voice; and the never-to-be-forgotten good-bye kiss from his mother's trembling lips.

Yes, it was fine indeed!

And how fortunate this visit was, for two weeks later came orders sending aboard the cruiser *Denver* a detail of marines to replace men whose tour of sea-duty had expired, and with that detail went Richard Comstock and Henry Cabell, Drummer and Trumpeter.

CHAPTER VII

OFF FOR TREASURE ISLAND

The little detachment for the *Denver* were ordered to go on board fully equipped. This necessitated packing all personal belongings in the khaki-colored canvas knapsacks and haversacks.

Gunnery Sergeant Miller happening through the squad room found Dick and Henry thus engaged soon after they had been notified to be ready for departure in two hours' time.

"Want some help?" he questioned, stopping near their bunks.

And indeed they did want help, for though they had been taught how to make up their packs, they had never before been required to stow away every blessed thing they owned in one of the infernal things--this being about the way they expressed themselves in answer to his query.

"To begin with, you won't be allowed to have any cit clothing on shipboard," said the Sergeant. "The best thing to do, if you don't want to send them home, is to sell them to Ikie Cohen across the street, or if you choose, you can pack them up with the things you won't need and turn them over to the Police Sergeant for storage; then when you transfer to shore duty again have them sent to your new station."

Following this sound advice the boys proceeded to divide their possessions into two lots. Even then it did not seem possible to carry along everything laid out for their taking.

"Now dump the whole outfit on your bunk," directed Miller, "and first fold your blankets and clothing in the way you have been taught. The detachment will travel in blues, so before doing anything else run down to the Post Tailor and tell him to press them in a hurry and send them up. Here, Cabell, you take both uniforms with you and Comstock will help you on your return."

Henry picked up the new blue uniforms, which the boys had not worn as yet, and hurried to the Post Tailor. Then proceeding under his able instructor, Dick first packed his knapsack to its limit. Two blankets, three suits of khaki, two O.D. shirts, three suits of summer underwear, one pair of tan shoes, six pairs of socks, a towel or two, and his toilet articles, one by one disappeared into the enchanted bag. His overcoat, recently issued him, was rolled and tied in straps to the top of the pack after fastening down the flaps by means of the rawhide thongs. In the meantime Henry had returned.

"Put that extra pair of tan shoes in your haversack with all the rest of your odds and ends," advised their instructor. "You will wear leggins and campaign hats, though personally I think it a poor combination with blues, and you can hook your blue cap to the pack after you get it on."

"Sergeant, didn't you tell me that marines used to have dress coats with long skirts, black spiked helmets, white helmets and white uniforms?" asked Dick, while he stowed away a little pocket edition of the New Testament in his haversack as the final act of his work in hand.

"Yes, that's right," answered Miller.

"Well, for the love of Mike, how did you ever travel with all that junk and still always be the first to get there when there was trouble brewing?"

"Indeed it was a question in the old days," said Miller reminiscently, "but you must understand that when hurry-up orders came along we took what was needed for the work in hand and no extra stuff at all. When we made a permanent change of station then we hauled along our whole equipment, and what we could not carry on our backs was shipped to us by the Quartermaster."

"About how much do you reckon this knapsack weighs, Sergeant?" asked Henry.

"I should say at least sixty pounds--that means all your equipment, and it is about the weight you would carry on a regular hike, counting arms and ammunition and all that. Now when you boys come to leave ship and go to a shore station, you will be surprised to find how much more junk you will have to send ashore than you took on board. It's always the way. Things accumulate, and you never seem to know where they all come from. Many a souvenir and trinket I've left behind or lost in my time which I'd like to have right now. If you are able to, take my advice and send all your little keepsakes back to your home people. The day will come when you will have a heap of fun looking them over and living again the pleasure you experienced in acquiring them."

Word having been passed for the detachment to "fall in" for the O.D.'s final inspection, Dick and Henry struggled into their harness. Canteens and haversacks were slung by their leather straps over opposite shoulders and the galling heavy knapsacks adjusted as comfortably as possible. Besides these impedimenta each boy was armed with a web belt from which hung a forty-five calibre Colt's revolver in a fair leather holster, tightly strapped to the right leg to prevent swinging. Dick was also loaded down with his drum and sticks, and Henry carried his trumpet with the red trumpet cord attached. The other men of the detachment carried their Springfields--among the best military rifles in the world--and bayonets in leather scabbards.

The trip to Philadelphia and its Navy Yard, where the *Denver* was lying, occupied a little over three hours, so that the men from the Washington Barracks reported on board their future home in time for evening mess call.

First Sergeant Stephen Douglass, commanding the Marine Detachment of the U.S.S. *Denver*, a gray-haired, clean-shaven, wiry little man, was known throughout the service as a "sea-going marine." Never, if he could prevent it, would he serve at a barracks, and his length of service and known ability generally secured a respect for his wishes from his superiors. The meal having been quickly disposed of by the new arrivals, he called them to his tiny office to assign them their stations.

"Here is where we begin our web-footed existence," whispered Dick to Henry as they stood waiting their turn outside the door.

"It is a little bit of a boat, isn't it?" irrelevantly answered Henry.

"Don't say 'boat,'" cautioned Dick, "for in the Navy everything big enough to fly a commissioned officer's pennant is dignified by being called a ship."

"What is a 'commissioned officer's pennant'?" inquired Henry.

"It is a long narrow flag tapering to a point, with the wide part near the hoist, where it is attached, you know--blue with thirteen white stars in the field, and the rest is divided in half lengthwise with a red and a white stripe. Vessels commanded by a commissioned officer of the Navy only are entitled to fly it at the truck of the mainmast."

"Thanks, Dick; I reckon I am pretty green, but what's a 'truck'? It sounds like a wagon of some sort!"

"That is the name given to the very top of a mast or flagstaff. You'll soon pick up these little points," said Dick generously. "I just happen to know some of them because of being brought up in an old whaling port and having seen and known about ships all my life; but I've a lot to learn myself."

First Sergeant Douglass now called the boys in to interview them.

"Your first duty, eh?" he said after adjusting his glasses and glancing over the enlistment record which accompanies every marine in his travels. "Either of you know anything about a ship?" and he looked up at the two youngsters with an approving gaze.

Dick said nothing, but Henry spoke for him:

"Drummer Comstock does; he has been making me acquainted with some of the many things I never knew before."

"To-morrow morning I'll have Corporal Dorlan take all the new arrivals over the ship, and I want you two musics to become acquainted with every nook and corner of her. You will have to act as messengers for the Officer of the Deck and must be ready to go to any place and find any person without hesitation. If you shouldn't happen to know where the place or person or thing is located then you must be prepared to know how and where to find out about 'em in the most expeditious manner. The Officer of the Deck can't be bothered with questions, so it's up to the messenger to know."

"Is Corporal Dorlan any relation to a Sergeant Michael Dorlan who was on the *Nantucket*?" asked Richard.

"Couldn't be closer related," answered the First Sergeant; "he is one and the same person. Do you know him?"

"I should say I do," beamed Dick; "he saved the life of a boy friend of mine this past summer; but I thought he was a sergeant."

"He was a sergeant, but unfortunately an enemy of Dorlan's got the best of him, and he was reduced to the rank of corporal by sentence of a court-martial."

"My, I'm sorry to hear that," returned Dick, honestly grieved over the misfortune of his brave acquaintance.

"Yes, boys, everyone who knows Mike Dorlan is sorry, and I hope neither of you will ever have an enemy like his, nor a 'court' against your record, nor any other kind of an offense, for that matter. Your slate is clean now; keep it so, and when you've finished your enlistment you'll be wearing one of these,--and proud of it too, I'll warrant."

*　　*　　*　　*　　*　　*　　*　　*　　*

The Marine Corps Good Conduct Medal

THE MARINE CORPS GOOD CONDUCT MEDAL

Awarded to any enlisted man in the corps at the expiration of his enlistment who receives a mark of "Excellent" and who has not been tried by Court-Martial. If the man reënlists the possession of this medal entitles him to receive 83-½ cents a month additional pay. If at the end of subsequent enlistment he receives the Excellent discharge--a bronze bar is awarded to be attached to the ribbon and suitably engraved. These bars also bring additional monthly pay.

*　*　*　*　*　*　*　*　*

The old sergeant opened a little drawer of his desk and took from it a bronze medal suspended from a bar of like metal by a bright red silk ribbon through the center of which ran a narrow band of deep blue. Across the ribbon, almost covering it, were other narrow bronze bands fastened.

"This here is a Marine Corps Good Conduct Medal, and each of the smaller bands of bronze means a renewal of the medal's original significance for a whole enlistment. But to earn one of these you must 'mind your p's and q's' and be 'Johnnie on the spot' if it is your duty to be there at all."

After the boys finished their examination of the trophy, the First Sergeant continued:

"Now to return to business. Comstock, your pay number is six, your watch number is seven-twenty-one, your locker number, twenty-three, and you are in the port watch; your station at 'Abandon Ship' is in the sailing launch. Yours, Cabell, are, pay number, seven; watch number, seven-three-naught-seven; locker number, twenty-four, and you are in the steamer for 'Abandon Ship.' Report to the Police Sergeant, get your locker keys, draw your hammicks and find out where you swing. You will find plenty of work to keep you busy from now till 'taps.' Remember, I am always ready to listen to your complaints if you have any and will right them if able, but I also expect you to do your duty up to the handle. And just a word more before you go. The marines of this detachment are proud of their reputation of being the best looking, cleanest, smartest division on this ship. You are now responsible that that standard isn't lowered in the slightest degree. You will find a copy of the ship's routine on the Bulletin Board in our compartment. That's all."

The sergeant rose as he finished his talk and both boys had unconsciously straightened up to the position of attention. At their dismissal they simultaneously rendered the old veteran a military salute, but First Sergeant Stephen Douglass was too much the proper and precise marine to accept an honor to which he was not entitled.

"Wait!" he commanded as they turned to leave the office, "you salute only commissioned or warrant officers in our service, never non-commissioned or petty-officers, except at certain prescribed times during drill or ceremonies. Run along."

"I knew better than to salute him," said Henry while they were waiting for Police Sergeant Bruckner to return from some duty he was at the time engaged in, "but somehow it seemed to be the only proper thing to do, he was so fine."

"Glad to hear you talk like that, Hank, old boy! I told you that the N.C.O.'s were a pretty fine lot when you get to know them," and Dick was very well pleased that his friend was beginning to come to his own way of thinking.

Outside the office were the rest of the men who had journeyed with them, all waiting to draw hammocks. None of these men had served at sea before this, consequently their conception of a "hammock" was formed from those artistic things of net, made up in gay colors which decorated the piazzas and lawns ashore. It was quite a different article that Police Sergeant Bruckner dealt out to each of them. It consisted of a white piece of canvas, six feet long by three and one-half feet wide. Across either end eyelets were worked, through which passed the small lines called "nettles," and these in turn were fastened to a galvanized iron ring. These last two articles combined were called the hammock "clews." In addition to these, a manila rope lanyard was spliced to one of the rings to facilitate swinging the hammock between hooks fixed rigidly, in almost every conceivable corner, to the overhead beams of the ship. Each man's hammock had a small piece of canvas sewed to it about eighteen inches from the head upon which was his watch number in stencil. These watch numbers corresponded to the numbers over the hooks where their hammock berths or sleeping places were located. Every man on shipboard who swings in a hammock has two issued to him; one of them is in constant use and the other kept below in the sail-room, each division stowing their own hammocks separately in large canvas bags made for the purpose.

Mattresses made of "kapok"[#] and mattress covers were also given each man, and with these articles under their arms the new arrivals returned to the marines' compartment where, after receiving the keys to their lockers, they proceeded to "stow away their gear."

[#] Kapok is the product of a tropical American tree which was introduced into the Island of Java and there extensively cultivated. The tree has numerous uses. It puts forth a pod somewhat similar to a milkweed pod, filled with seeds to which a cottony substance is attached. This fibre is impervious to water and consequently being buoyant has been found to be better than cork for use in life-preservers. Of late years our navy has utilized great quantities of kapok in making sea mattresses, which in emergency could be used as life rafts,--also jacket life preservers. Kapok is very inflammable.

"This is like having the 'makings' for a cigarette and not being able to roll one," remarked Henry, as he gazed ruefully at the heavy canvas, the rings, strings and rope, his mattress and blankets, lying on the deck at his feet.

"The only difference being we don't smoke, while we do sleep," sagely added Dick. "Perhaps some of these other fellows will initiate us into the mysteries of this folding bed. Let's ask them."

With the help of willing hands the clews were soon tied in place, mattress and blankets rolled inside the canvas, and the lashings properly made. Then their long sausage-like beds were stowed away in the hammock nettings to remain until the proper time came for reissuing them to their owners, which was regulated by routine calls and schedule.

"I've learned another sea-going expression," said Henry as the two boys finally completed their work, "and that is, never call a 'hammock' anything but a 'hammick,' or they will know you are a rookie."

At taps the boys found it to be quite an athletic feat to get into those swinging contraptions, but having once succeeded they settled down for a well earned sleep. But who ever heard of rookies coming on board ship for the first night who escaped at least one tumble to the hard deck below, sent there by the sharp knife blade drawn across the taut foot rope, in the hand of the omnipresent practical joker? And the experience of the two music boys this first night on board the *Denver* was in no way different from hundreds of others before them.

Richard and Henry found the daily routine on board ship very pleasant. At first Henry was inclined to feel peeved because there was not a commissioned officer in command of the marine detachment which was honored by his presence. But he admired First Sergeant Douglass, and daily he was losing his snobbish ideas regarding his messmates. Shipboard life is a much closer relationship than life in the barracks, and he was beginning to find that manhood did not necessarily go hand in hand with riches, polished manners and a finely branched family tree. At the first opportunity, Richard had made himself known to Corporal Dorlan, and that worthy individual acted much in the status of guide and mentor to the two boys, nor could they have had a better, for though Michael was his own worst enemy, where others were concerned, he was constantly preaching against the "Demon Rum," as he dubbed the agent of his misfortune.

"'Twould be far better for me," said he sadly, "if the powers that be never would promote me. For whinever I git to be a sergeant, then begorra, I always have to celebrate, and it's all off with old Mike."

Having taken the necessary stores aboard for her cruise, the gunboat quietly slipped from her berth one brisk morning in November and was soon on her way down the broad reaches of the Delaware River. At the Delaware Breakwater the pilot was dropped. Many of the crew took advantage of this opportunity to send ashore last messages and letters, for the *Denver* was bound for the West Indies; her first port of entry would be Culebra Island, and her first landfall Porto Rico, a six days' voyage.

It is a peculiar fact of ocean travel that whenever a ship is about to put to sea the general topic of conversation seems to hover around one point--

seasickness. Everywhere one turned that beautiful morning the fatal word pursued one.

"Ever been seasick, Jack?"

"Well, only onct in a big typhoon coming across from Formosa," or:

"Nuh, this is the first time I've been to sea, but I've struck her some rough in the lakes, and I guess I can stand it," or:

"Son, if you get sick and want a quick cure, take a nice piece of fat pork, tie a string to it and----" but why go into further detail, when the men who never before had seen blue water were half sick before they left the wharf, so vivid their imagination, and thoroughly sick when finally the *Denver* began digging her nose in the short seas they encountered on leaving the protection of the inland waterways!

Henry Cabell had fully determined he would not be seasick, but the sight of so many in that predicament placed his resolutions in the realm of other broken vows, and he was soon *hors de combat*. Dick, on the contrary, never felt the slightest discomfort, over which good fortune he was highly elated. He did not do as many others did, namely, gloat over the misery of the less fortunate ones.

The evening of the second day out found nearly all the sick men on the upper decks, albeit many were "green in the gills" from their unpleasant experience.

"You feel as if you didn't care whether you died or not," said Henry, while he and Dick stood at the bow of the ship holding to the life-lines that encompassed the entire main deck, "but I don't reckon I'll be sick again. I feel nearly all right now, and even this sudden dipping and stomach-dropping rising hardly gives me a squirm."

Dick did not answer. He was hanging over the rail looking down at the slight lines of phosphorescence spreading out in quivering angles from the bows with each plunge of the ship. He was enjoying every moment of this new life. No longer did he regret his inability to get the appointment to Annapolis, for already the spell of the Marine Corps was clutching at every fibre of his being, claiming him body and soul for its service. In the crew's library he had found a copy of Collum's History of the Corps and for the first time he was reveling in its illustrious deeds from the day of its inception, which antedated the regular Navy and even the Declaration of Independence,--November 11, 1775, up to and including the part they took in the relief of Pekin in July, 1900. As they stood there, Corporal Dorlan, making the round of sentinels, stopped for a moment's converse.

"How goes it, me lad?" he inquired of Henry, and without waiting for a reply, he continued, "To-morrow we'll be findin' of ourselves in the waters of the

Gulf Stream, and ye will believe that ye never saw such blue water in yer livin' born days. And ye will keep on believin' that till ye see the waters of the Caribbean and then ye will be changin' the moind of ye, like as not."

"I'd rather see some good brown earth and a little green grass at this present moment," said Henry, wistfully.

"And there'll be a-plenty of both on this cruise, I'm thinkin'," said Mike cheerfully. "But do you know where we're goin'? If ye don't then I'll tell ye. We're bound for Treasure Island, and a foine place it is to roam around in for a bit. Ye can't git lost and ye can't git into trubble unless ye look for it, and that's more'n ye can say for most places. Its right name is Culebra, which is the Spanish for 'shnake,' but some feller wrote a wonderful story about it under the name I've just mentioned to ye, so like as not if ye look in the right spot ye may yet find some of the old pirates' buried gold. Heigho!--I'd better be on me way, for it's about time to make me report of lights to the bridge. Good-night, me lads," and off he tramped.

"And as a better man than I just said," remarked Dick a few moments later, "'Heigho! I'd better be on me way'; let us get to bed."

"I second the motion," said Henry, "for I'm getting sick of this motion, and the 'hammick' sounds good to me. Maybe by to-morrow I won't be bluer than the Gulf Stream, after a good night's rest."

CHAPTER VIII

AN ADVENTURE ASHORE

Saturday afternoon! Under the azure dome of the tropic sky the verdured hills of "Treasure Island" sparkled with emerald brilliancy. Stretches of glittering-white, sandy beaches connected abrupt, green-clad headlands in the semblance of Nature's own rosary. Coral reefs everywhere, with varying depths of water over their treacherous beauty, afforded so many wonderful shades of blue and green that the cleverest artist would despair of reproducing their tantalizing colors on his canvas.

In the deep but sheltered waters of Target Bay, close anchored to the beach, swung the *Denver*, her graceful outlines reflected with startling perfection in the mirror-like depths. Under her white spread awnings, members of the crew dozed, conversed or played games as their fancy dictated. On the bridge, the ever alert Quartermaster attended the duties of his watch; while pacing the quarter-deck, the Commanding Officer of the ship, Commander Bentley, and his Executive Officer, Lieutenant-Commander Ogden, were earnestly conversing. Near by, the Officer of the Deck, with a telescope, the insignia of his office, tucked beneath his arm, was trying to catch the drift of his superiors' conversation without appearing to be too inquisitive.

"It is apparent, Mr. Ogden, that someone ashore is furnishing liquor to our men. The reports at the mast[#] for the last few days show it clearly. In spite of all the 'Alcalde' at Dewey may say, the men are getting the stuff somewhere."

[#] The "mast"--A fixed place on deck, often not near a real mast, where complaints against the conduct of enlisted men are heard by an officer, and judgment passed on them.

"I agree with you, Captain, and I wish we could get a clue sufficient to convict the guilty party. By your order the men are not allowed in the towns of Dewey or Roosevelt, and every day that liberty parties are ashore I have had patrols along the trails to stop men going in that direction. Furthermore, we maintain a patrol in town, each ship taking a turn at it, to arrest any of the men seen inside the restricted district. The revenue officer on the island has assured me that not a store or shack this end of the place has a license to sell alcohol."

"It beats the Dutch," remarked Captain Bentley, after a short silence, "how enlisted men will go out of their way to get into trouble. A lot of youngsters think it smart to be tough and rough, imagining they are then real sailors. They haven't the brains to see that the navy man is revolutionizing his habits and trying to live down the idea of him which years ago was so prevalent.

The desire to 'spend their money like a drunken sailor' still holds an attraction for some of these brainless idiots. Our older men have been through the mill, and the worst element among them is weeded out. They have sense enough to keep out of harm's way, but---- Oh, well, the fact still remains, they are getting liquor, and bringing it on board too."

"I have had a talk with the officers and they in turn with their C.P.O.'s, and also I have put Sergeant Douglass on the trail, so I hope of getting some results soon."

"Keep at it, Mr. Ogden, and for the sake of all hands I hope we can run the parties to earth; nothing is worse for the discipline of a ship," and with that parting remark Commander Bentley turned and descended to his cabin.

For over a month the cruiser had been in and around the waters of Culebra Island, generally anchoring for the night in Target Bay, but during the day, excepting Saturdays and Sundays, joining with three other ships of her class in division drills and maneuvers while at the same time preparing for target practise.

The *Denver's* marines, having only two six-pounders in their charge, did not take as great an interest in the gunnery work as marines generally do on board the battleships and dreadnaughts, where they have guns assigned them of larger calibre. During this time they were mostly occupied with work pertaining to their profession on board, or with boat drills, and hikes on shore. For this latter drill they were landed twice a week and worked in coöperation with the detachments from the other vessels. Later on when the Fleet arrived combined maneuvers ashore on a grand scale would be carried on.

Liberty was granted, to those whose duties did not intrude, on Saturday and Sunday afternoons. On this particular Saturday, Drummer Comstock and Trumpeter Cabell went ashore in the first liberty boat to leave the ship. Dick, already having made a name for himself as an oarsman, was a member of the marines' dinghy racing crew, and this afternoon he and Henry helped pull the big cutter ashore and well up on the coral beach in Firewood Bay.

From this spot it was about a two-mile walk over the hills, down into the valley past Laguna de Flamingo to the perfect, crescent-shaped, smooth, level sands of Flamingo Bay, where the mighty rollers swept in with unrestricted grandeur from the blue Atlantic, stretching northward farther than the eye could reach. Here, in spite of the wonderfully high surf there was little or no undertow and the bathing was considered safe, and free from venturesome sharks.

According to their habit, the two boys undressed at Firewood Bay and leaving their clothes in the cutter, wearing only rubber-soled sneakers and bathing trunks, they were soon dog-trotting over the narrow trail leading to a group of shacks on the saddle of the ridge they had to cross. With their swifter pace they soon passed the others of the party. After breasting the summit of the ridge they followed the torturous downward trail to the Lake of the Flamingos. The trail led past an unused hut half-way down the hillside, at one end of which it abruptly turned to the left.

Dick, well in the lead, having turned the corner of the hut, saw a man dashing towards him, mounted on a fiery little West Indian pony. There was plenty of room for the rider to turn aside so as to avoid the boy, while ordinary politeness would have led him to do so, therefore Dick continued at his slow trot in the center of the path. Nearer came the rider, and the boy now saw he was reeling in his saddle and lashing his horse viciously as he came tearing up the hill. Still the boy did not change his course. The next moment the pony had of its own volition jumped out of the trail to avoid collision.

At the moment he passed the native rider cut Dick a fearful lash across the shoulders with his leather quirt, yelling loudly some vile expletive in Spanish. For the fraction of a second Dick did not comprehend what had happened. The blow across his bare back nearly brought him to his knees and, missing his footing, he fell headlong. In an instant he was up again holding a rough, jagged piece of rotten-rock in either hand and running back after the reckless horseman.

Never before in his life had Dick been thoroughly angry--never before had he felt that insane rage within him that knew no other impulse than the desire to inflict bodily harm on another human being.

The horseman must have disappeared behind the deserted shack, for he was nowhere in sight. By this time Henry came swinging along the trail, and he was surprised to see his chum coming towards him like a raving maniac.

"Did you see him?" yelled Dick furiously.

"See whom?" questioned Henry.

"That black drunken scoundrel on horseback."

"What are you talking about, Dick? I've seen no horseman."

"Didn't a native just pass you on the trail, riding a pony like mad and lashing the poor brute with a rawhide quirt?"

"Nope,--I reckon you must have been seeing things, Dick," and Henry started to laugh.

"'Seeing things,' nothing! Look at that red welt across my back, if you think I've been 'seeing things'!" shouted Dick, and he turned while Henry examined with amazement the angry looking ridge across the broad, sun-browned shoulders.

"I see it, right enough, Dick, but--you say a man on horseback did it?"

"Yes, and if he didn't pass you on the trail then he turned by this hut and went off into the bush, and I'm going to get him and thrash him before this day is over," said Dick, and having delivered his outburst he rushed off towards the clump of bushes, tall grass and cabbage palms, clustering close to the far corner of the hut.

"Hold on, Dick," called Henry, "we can't get through that jungle without our clothes. You stay here on watch while I go back and fetch them. The rest of the liberty party will be along any time now and they will lend us a hand."

"I don't need any help to thrash that cowardly Spig,"[#] muttered Dick, but seeing the wisdom of Henry's suggestion he consented to wait.

[#] "Spig" or "Spiggoty"--A generic term for all inhabitants of Latin-American countries and of the Philippines and Guam, given by sailors, soldiers and marines only since the Spanish War of 1898.

Left to his own devices, he began a systematic scouting of the ground in the vicinity. The trail, baked hard by the sun, showed no signs, but across the ground in front of the palm-thatched hut he found distinct traces of recent hoof prints. Following them he came to a newly broken trail through the long grass leading to the thicker undergrowth beyond. Returning to the hut he pushed open the dilapidated door and entered the musty interior. The place was bare of furniture or utensils, a few bits of rubbish littered the floor and in one corner were several bottles and flasks, all empty. Picking up one and extracting the cork he found a strong smell of whisky. Evidently this was the rendezvous of those men from the ships recently found under the influence of liquor while on shore. Presently he heard the sound of footsteps coming down the trail. Probably members of the liberty party with whom he came ashore, thought Dick.

"Say, Joe," he heard a voice question, "where do you suppose that marine was hot-footing it to?"

"I dunno," answered the one addressed, "when he ducked past me he yelled something, but I didn't get it, did you?"

"Nuh! Glad he's out of the way, 'cause him and the kid he runs with think they are some class. They'd put a crimp in our game if they got next to it."

"Any of the others in sight?" Joe now asked as the two stopped beside the corner of the shack.

"No; get a hustle on," and with that Dick heard the two speakers run past the front of his refuge and dash into the woods near the spot he had just been investigating.

"The plot thickens!" mused Dick, looking at the empty bottle he still held.

Again the sound of footsteps, but this time the men passed the shack without stopping. These men were bound for the beach at Flamingo Bay.

At first the boy thought of calling them back, but on second consideration he decided not to. He preferred working out this affair with only Henry's assistance.

That very morning First Sergeant Douglass had given the marines a talk about the liquor traffic and asked them to try and trace it. He had said it would be a feather in their caps could they succeed in finding the guilty parties. For that reason, all the more honor if he and Henry carried it through by themselves.

It seemed an interminable while before the soft patter apprised him of his companion's return. As Henry reached the corner of the hut, Dick's warning hiss attracted his attention to the open door.

"Come in here, Hank," he called, and Henry entered, breathing hard from the grind of his strenuous race up-hill.

While he dressed, Dick explained more fully about the drunken native and of what had transpired during Henry's absence. The young trumpeter was equally enthusiastic over the prospect of an exciting adventure ahead of them and thoroughly agreed they alone could manage the business.

"I reckon we are on the right track for sure," said Henry, struggling into his O.D. shirt. "That fellow Joe Choiniski is one of the tough nuts who joined us from San Juan in the last draft right after we came here. He's been on some 'spit-kit'[#] stationed down in these waters for a long time and speaks the native lingo. The man with him is a bad egg too, though he has never been caught so far."

[#] "Spit-kit"--Really "spit-kid," a small wooden cask set about the deck for spit-boxes. Spitting upon decks is an unpardonable sin. The name is slangily applied to the smaller vessels of the Navy.

"What is his name?" asked Richard, preparing to open the door.

"Never did hear his right name; the men on board call him 'Slugger.'"

"I know now," said Dick, "they say he used to be a prize-fighter and he's all the time bragging how he can mix it up with the gloves, but no one ever saw him put them on since he came on board. He's husky enough, but all out of training."

"That's the fellow,--a tough customer, I reckon."

The boys, finding the coast clear, emerged from the hut and were soon following the trail which the two men and horseman before them had presumably travelled. For a while the way led through a veritable tangle of briers, weeds, bamboo and underbrush, but after a quarter of a mile with no break on either side the path joined into a wider and well worn trail through a piece of timberland leading almost due north and south. In the shade of the tall hardwood trees the ground was softer and the spoor of the horse was distinctly shown turning to the right. This fortunate discovery saved the boys any possibility of going wrong.

The island at this point was sparsely settled, as in 1906 the Navy Department had required all squatters to move off the government reservations. The trail was now nearing the boundaries of the northern tract. For another quarter of a mile they went on, each moment hoping to discover some evidence to substantiate their deductions, but the silence of the wilderness was about them, only broken occasionally by the cooing of the blue doves high up in the tree-tops.

Here and there the woods gave place to clearings covered with waving grass or untended banana patches, affording long vistas of land and water but not a house nor animal nor human being rewarded their sharp searching. To their left was South West Cay, separated from the larger island they were on by a narrow dangerous channel. To their right they caught occasional glimpses of Flamingo Bay or the distant top of Mount Resaca.

During one of their halts before emerging into plain view on the hog-back trail, Henry caught Dick by the shoulder and pulled him down in the shelter of the long grass which carpeted a steep slope on their left, down to the very edge of the water.

"Look, there is your horseman!" he whispered excitedly, forgetting his voice would not reach half the distance to the object at which he was pointing.

"LOOK, THERE IS YOUR HORSEMAN!"

LOOK, THERE IS YOUR HORSEMAN!

"I see him," said Dick grimly, "coming up from that shack at the foot of the hill."

"Yes, and see those two sailors going down to the beach; they're toting sacks or something over their shoulders. They can go around to Firewood Bay that way. We've got 'em, all right," exclaimed Henry joyfully. "What do you reckon we'd better do now?"

"I 'reckon' there's going to be one native of this 'Treasure Island' who's going to get the beating of his life in just about five minutes," answered Dick, taking an extra tug to his belt. "That fellow is coming right up the hill to this trail, and I'm going to be right at the top to welcome him. Come along, Hank, but lie low and leave him to me."

Stooping low, both lads ran across the open space till they came to the edge of the farther wood, where they found an entrance to the trail up which the lone horseman could be seen spurring and lashing his worn-out steed. The animal was too far gone to respond to the cruel treatment, and plodded slowly and wearily upward.

"Hank, you go to the other side in case he should happen to turn that way," directed Dick. "That brute won't escape us; and let me tell you something, I'm not going to beat him up for lashing me, alone, I'm going to try and even up some of the debt for that poor dumb animal he's torturing."

Henry scuttled to the north side of the trail, while Dick waited impatiently where he first had hidden.

The labored breathing of the horse came to his ears, and then, preceded by a volley of oaths, rider and horse reached the ridge trail. The native, a dark, swarthy, pock-marked man, about thirty-five years of age, with black, bloodshot eyes and long, yellow teeth, was broad shouldered, and though slender, was well knit. On reaching the crest of the hill the horse's head was turned southward and again the rider raised the heavy quirt to bring it down on the bleeding, swollen flanks. That blow never fell, for with the quick spring of a tiger Dick grabbed the rider around the waist and tore him from the saddle, throwing him to the ground. At the same time he snatched the quirt from the surprised man's hand and began belaboring him as he groveled at the boy's feet. The startled horse meanwhile had turned down the slope and was stumbling towards the foot of the hill.

"How do you like that, you yellow cur?" questioned Dick coolly, giving the coward a final blow across the legs. "Do you think you want to try any more tricks on me?"

"No! No! Señor! Pardon, Señor! Por Dios, no mas!" cried the man as he saw Dick's arm rise again and the lash snap ominously.

"Get up and vamoose," ordered Dick, pointing along the trail they had followed. "Never mind your horse; you can get him when I get through with you."

Never taking his eyes from the man, Dick made him march in front of them. The native limped along protestingly, but every time he stopped to argue Dick applied the lash with good effect.

On reaching the trail leading down to Firewood Bay, Dick pointed towards the town of Dewey.

"You savvy Dewey?" he inquired.

"Si, Señor," came the surly response, and the shifty black eyes glared for a moment at the boy.

"Well, beat it--pronto," ordered Dick, and with the words he gave the man a push in the right direction, while both boys, as if performing a military drill, simultaneously aided him with a persuading kick.

"Just to help you along a bit," called Henry and then he turned to Dick. "Shake, Dick; that was a job well and nobly done."

As he spoke five bullets whistled past them, one dusting the ground at their feet and ricochetting with a shrill "Z-z-z-i-i-n-n-g."

Instantly the startled boys dropped to the grass beside the trail and, keeping under cover until a fold in the ground effectually protected them, they ran for the boat landing.

"Wonder why he didn't use that shooting iron before?" questioned Dick, looking back over the trail.

"Reckon he was too plumb scared to remember he owned a gun," said Henry, still beaming with joy over the adventure. "Do you believe he'll take any more pot shots at us?"

"No, we are out of pistol range down here, and he can't come down the hill without being seen. Those shots were too close for comfort to suit me, and yet I hated to have to run away as we did. Still it would have been worse than foolhardy to tempt Fortune by hanging around up there with that rascal in hiding. How do you like being under fire?"

"Can't say I've any hankering for it, but it didn't scare me as I thought it would," said Henry.

The men from Flamingo Bay were now coming over the brow of the hill and soon reached the boat. They had not seen the native on the other side of the hill, but all had heard the five shots. The boys did not enlighten them as to the cause, having decided to report the whole matter to First Sergeant Douglass on their return to the *Denver*.

While they were shoving the heavy cutter into the water the two men, Joe Choiniski and "Slugger" Williams, came from around the point and joined the group. Both men wore rubber boots, and Dick remembered that they had taken them ashore that afternoon under their arms, whereas now they carried their shoes, from the tops of which were sticking some finely branched pieces of unbleached coral. Dick also noticed how carefully they got into the boat when all was ready to shove off for the ship.

"Wonder where they hid their booze," said Henry, "for I'd bet a month's pay they have it somewhere."

"I guess I know, and you watch Corporal Dorlan frisk them when they go up on deck," answered Dick with a knowing wink.

Arriving at the port gangway, the liberty party went aboard and fell in on the quarter-deck for inspection before being dismissed. Corporal Dorlan, standing at the top of the gangway, was surprised to hear Dick whisper as he passed, "Search the rubber boots, Corporal," but he was not slow of comprehension, and as soon as the men were all in line he went directly up to Joe and "Slugger" and feeling down their boot legs brought forth several flat flasks carefully wrapped in dry seaweed.

"What is this?" said Mr. Thorp, the Officer of the Deck.

And Corporal Dorlan merely answered:

"'Wilson--that's all,' sir."

"That is fine work, Corporal. I congratulate you," said a hearty voice behind the line of men who had witnessed this little scene, and turning Dorlan found Commander Bentley standing near him.

"It's not me what discovered it, sir. All the credit belongs to Drummer Comstock. He's the lad what put me wise, sir."

"We will hold 'mast' and investigate this matter at once, Mr. Thorp; have Comstock report here immediately."

Dick, having heard his name called, approached.

"Now, young man, tell me all you know of this business," ordered the Captain, and having heard the entire story of the exciting afternoon ashore he ordered Dick to go to the Executive Officer's office and dictate a full report to the Yeoman.

"A man like the one you describe has no business to be at large," he said. "I will communicate with the authorities ashore and have him locked up. In the meantime, Mr. Thorp, send a detail of marines ashore under arms to search and destroy the shack these two boys discovered. It's on the government reservation and has no business there. Trumpeter Cabell will go ashore and act as guide."

Then turning to the two culprits, Commander Bentley said:

"I'll keep you men in close confinement until a court-martial can dispose of your case. Have these two men taken to the brig[#] at once, Mr. Thorp."

[#] Brig--Cell for confinement of men under punishment.

"Aye, aye, sir!" and Ensign Thorp gave the Master-at-Arms the necessary orders.

CHAPTER IX

HISTORIC BATTLEFIELDS

"Speaking of that report against our horse beater," remarked Henry a few days later, "reminds me, Dick, that I never thought to inquire if you ever heard from the report you wrote out in Washington against those plotters."

"No," answered Dick, looking up from the signal card he was studying, "I wrote it the following Monday and sent it to Dad, but never heard anything from it."

"We heard from your last report," said Henry. "That Spig was a wise hombre, right enough. The revenue officer found out all about him, but 'Mexican Pete' was too quick. He left for parts unknown that same day, and all the authorities in Porto Rico are on the lookout for him. He's a famous smuggler down in these regions and a regular bad man in the bargain. It's said he has served jail sentences in nearly every town from here to Vera Cruz. He's a Mexican by birth, a bad man by nature and a wanderer most of the time by necessity."

"That is all true, Hank, but it is not getting down this Morse code," replied Dick. "We've learned the semaphore, wigwag and Ardois, and I think we can give the signal boys on the bridge a run for their money; but I can't seem to get these sound signals. Guess my ear isn't attuned properly!"

"I don't see why you want to bother with it, anyway. You don't have to learn it."

"Never can tell when such knowledge will come in handy; besides, Hank, it helps pass the time when we've nothing else to do. It proved pretty useful last week when we were having that scouting drill ashore and by knocking two rocks together I was able to tell you to go to the left of that clump of bamboo. If you'd gone the other way the enemy would have captured you and your message, which would have meant the capture of our whole detachment."

"Yes, I'd forgotten that, Dick, and seeing that we both hope to be made privates some day the extra pay we will pull down as first class signalmen is not to be sneezed at. Well, here goes; see if you can get this!"

Thereupon Henry began a quick tap-tap with a pencil against the rim of the brass bugle he held on his knees.

For an hour the two boys practised at their self-appointed task, never using a spoken word in the meantime, but often smiling at each other over the messages they sent back and forth.

Richard Comstock was not wasting his time in the service. He had enlisted with one stated purpose in view, and all his work was to him a means to an end. Every new bit of knowledge acquired connected with his profession was just one more step in the ladder he meant to climb, until his hopes and ambitions were realized.

The friendship existing between Henry Cabell and himself was of great help to both boys. They often had their differences of opinion, but petty quarrels and bickerings never entered in their discussions. Both lads were high spirited, quick to take offense but as quick to acknowledge their errors in the light of reasoning. Day by day, Henry was losing his attitude of snobbishness. His association with Richard, who tried to find something worthy in every person with whom he came in contact and to see the bright side to every cloud, was the best thing which could have happened for the hot-headed Southerner.

Their duties on board ship were not particularly arduous. They stood four-hour watches as messengers for the Officer of the Deck, dividing this duty with the ship's sailor-buglers; assisted in the work of keeping their part of the ship clean, accompanied the marines on their drills ashore and participated in the routine drills of shipboard life. Sometimes the musics on the larger vessels are members of the secondary battery gun's crews or have other battle stations at "general quarters,"[#] but not so on the *Denver*, which was only a third-class cruiser of a little over three thousand tons. Also on shipboard the marine drummer has but little use for his drum and sticks, which are generally put away in the storeroom and a bugle issued in lieu thereof, as all calls are given by means of the trumpet or the piping of the boatswain's whistles. Therefore, in so far as their duties were concerned, the boys did identically the same work on the *Denver*, and except when their watches interfered they were generally to be found together.

[#] When the ship is ready to go into action. The drill for this preparation is called General Quarters.

One day they were conversing about the former achievements of the marines, and Dick, who by now had read Collum's history from beginning to end, said:

"I wonder if when they put those new dreadnaughts in commission they will reverse the time-honored custom and move the marine detachments up forward!"

"I don't reckon I know what you mean, Dick; why shouldn't they put the marines wherever they want to on the ships?"

"These days there is no real reason why they shouldn't," said Dick. "But you know what the relation of the marines was originally as regards the ship's crew, don't you?"

"Y-e-e-s; at least I think I do. They were the policemen on the ship, weren't they?"

"Oh, Hank, you simply must read the history of this organization before you go any further. It will be the best thing to make you get the right kind of ginger into your work. It will make you proud of your job and proud to be a U.S. Marine; it is one of the chief things you need:--*esprit de corps*--it's what has kept this outfit up to snuff, and without it no organized body of men could make a name for themselves any more than you can 'make a silk purse of a sow's ear.'"

"All right, if you say it takes *esprit* to make that purse, Dick, I'll take your word for it, but don't get started preaching. Now tell me why should or should not the marines be moved, and if not, why not, or whatever it was you began on when you lost yourself on Pulpit Street. Go ahead, I'm listening!"

"To begin with, the sailors in the early days were a mighty tough lot of customers, picked up from nearly every nation under the sun. They were employed to work the ship; whereas the marines were organized to do the fighting and were picked men. Because of the mixed and unruly element in the crew the sailors often became mutinous. In those days all weapons, and firearms particularly, were stored in the after part of the ship where the officers had their quarters and having this advantage, they were able to keep the crews under subjection. But there were only a few officers as compared to the crew, consequently the trustworthy marines were given that part of the ship to berth in between the officers and the sailors, who generally were berthed in the forecastle. I don't know just when this was made the fashion, but I do know that it has been handed down to the present day and you will always find marines in a compartment next the ward-room. Now do you see what I mean?"

"I understand what you have said, Dick, but what has it to do with the new battleships?"

"Why, I was wondering if another old Navy custom is going out of vogue, that's all. For in these new ships the officers are going to change places with the crew--their living space is going to be the forecastle instead of the stern. Question: What will they do with the marines?"

"When did you say that custom started, Dick?"

"Oh, I don't know, Hank; way back in the days of bi-remes and tri-remes, I guess."

"Then all I have to say is that it's high time a change was made; allow the officers a chance to take care of themselves--we marines have nursed them altogether too long," said Henry, and they were yet laughing at the remark when Police Sergeant Bruckner came along the deck seeking them.

"The 'Top'[#] says you boys should go with me to the storeroom and draw rifles, so come right along and get 'em."

[#] "Top"--Top sergeant--first sergeant, or also applied to the highest ranking sergeant at a post.

"Get rifles?" questioned Dick. "What are we going to do with rifles, I'd like to know?"

"Ask the Top; don't bother me with your questions;" and Bruckner led the way below.

"They're brand new shooting irons, and you will have some job getting off the cosmoline, so I adwise you to get busy before you report to the First Sergeant," cautioned Bruckner, whose German origin accounted for the manner in which he pronounced his letter "V" on occasions. He had come to the United States as a lad of fifteen years and after ten years spoke, with this exception, almost like a native-born citizen. Six of these ten years he had spent in the Marines.

After noting the number of each rifle in order to enter them on the public property card of the musics, they all repaired to the upper deck and the work of cleaning the new rifles was soon under way.

"You musics will fall in for aiming and sighting drill each morning," called out Sergeant Douglass, who saw them at their labors. "Although you aren't required to handle a gun you are required to know how to shoot straight. Come to my office when you get through with that work, and I'll give you each a score book which one of our Marine Officers got up and it will give you all the best dope on rifle shooting."

It was not long before the boys were applying for the promised books.

"When shall we have a chance to fire on the range?" asked Dick.

"From the 'galley yarns'[#] flying about the ship, it would not surprise me if we were on our way to Guantanamo in a day or two, and when we get there I'm going to try my best to have the guard put through the regular Marine Corps practice as well as the Navy course, and I want to keep our high showing up to standard."

[#] In some mysterious way stories get started on shipboard, generally founded on guess or rumor and turn out to be true; all are supposed to start in the "galley," hence the name.

"Do we get a medal or anything like that out of it?" asked Henry.

"Yes, you have an opportunity to get a number of things out of it. The marines shoot the same course for qualification as that prescribed for the army. There are three grades which pay you well for trying to do your best. The highest is that of expert rifleman. If you qualify, you get five dollars more pay per month from the date of qualification to the end of your enlistment and also a silver badge,--crossed rifles with a wreath around them. Sharpshooter pays you three dollars per month till you next shoot for record the following year and a badge consisting of a silver Maltese cross, while a marksman's qualification pays two dollars and you get only a silver bar with 'Marksman' on it. But you will find out all about it in those books. Run along now and don't bother me any more with your questions. By the way, Cabell, to-morrow morning you will report to Ensign Gardiner as orderly for the summary court-martial at ten-o'clock, in the ward-room. Mr. Gardiner is the recorder of the court."

"What is the recorder of a court?" asked Henry, who was as full of questions at times as a hive is of bees.

"He is to a summary court what the judge advocate is to a general court, and the prosecuting attorney to a civil court," answered the First Sergeant patiently, "and I hope your acquaintance with all of these gentlemen may be that of an orderly or a witness only. And, Comstock, speaking of witnesses, reminds me you had better stand by for a call, as both Williams and Choiniski are to be tried to-morrow for smuggling liquor on board ship."

Promptly at ten o'clock the next morning the "musics" were in attendance at the meeting of the court-martial, but no testimony was required, as the accused sailors both pleaded "guilty" to the specifications[#] preferred against them, and merely put in a plea for clemency.

[#] The written statement of specific acts for which the accused person is being tried.

Richard was standing outside the ward-room door when Chief Master-at-Arms Fitch brought the two prisoners aft for their trial.

"I'll get you for this, you fresh Leatherneck, and I give you fair warning to keep out of my way when I get out of the brig," muttered Choiniski, glaring malignantly at the drummer.

"Shut up and don't talk so much or I'll see that you get hung," snapped Fitch on hearing the remark. "After you two birds get out of your cage you'd better be looking round for friends, not enemies, I'm thinking."

And two days after the trial with the entire crew of the *Denver* mustered aft on the quarter-deck, the sentences were published to the two offenders.

"Whew! You'll never catch me smuggling any liquor on a man-o'-war," said Dick to his friend, Corporal Dorlan, as they sat talking in the marines' compartment soon after the crew had been dismissed.

"No, it's bad business no matter how ye bring it on board, inside or outside," said Mike, dolefully, "and it's meself who should know, bad 'cess to the stuff."

"Have those two men got to stay in those hot little cells up forward with nothing but bread and water to eat for thirty days, and lose three months' pay, and in addition, do three months' extra police duties with no liberty meanwhile?"

"Not quite that bad, me lad; they'll be after gittin' a full ration on every fifth day, so as to show them what they're missin' in the way of good chow,[#] and accordin' to my way of thinkin' it will do them both a world of good. Until they came to this packet 'twas the happy ship; but the likes of them are always makin' trouble."

[#] A Chinese term generally used by men in the service for food.

"Did you hear that we are going to Guantanamo Bay before the fleet arrives here, Mike?" questioned Richard.

"Well, it won't be the first time Michael Dorlan has been in that place, and well I remember the time we showed the Spaniards they couldn't fool with Uncle Sam's Marines and git away with it."

"Were you in a fight there during the Spanish War, Corporal?"

*　*　*　*　*　*　*　*　*

The Sampson Medal

THE SAMPSON MEDAL

The medal commemorating the U.S. Naval Campaign in the West Indies, during the war of 1898. The ribbon has a blue center with red on either side. Commonly called The Sampson Medal after the Commander-in-Chief-- William Sampson, U.S.N.

A similar medal for Admiral Dewey's victory in Manila Bay was awarded, suspended from a ribbon with broader band of blue in center and yellow on either side.

*   *   *   *   *   *   *   *   *

"Right ye are, me lad, and 'twas no slouch of a scrimmage, at all, at all. The Navy wanted a good sheltered harbor as a base for their ships close to Santiago, where that foine old Spanish Admiral, Cervera, was bottled up. So Guantanamo Bay, being the foinest kind of a place, they decided to go in there, dhrive away the enemy and hold it. Well, the ships shelled the beach before we landed and then us marines was sent ashore under Colonel Harrington; and a hot reception we got, I'd like ye to know."

"How many marines were there in the fight?"

"About four hundred altogether, and out in the bosky[#] there were over three thousand Spaniards pouring the lead into us at every opportunity. We took the beach with a rush and charged up the hill back of our landin' place, and then havin' got a toe-hold we dug in and we stayed dug in, with the Dagoes a-takin' pot shots at us every time we showed a hat."

[#] Really the word "Bosque"--Spanish word meaning wood, and pronounced--boskay.

Henry, having joined the little group surrounding Dorlan and Richard, as usual asked a question at this point in the recital:

"Did the army come to help you, Corporal?"

"Army nothin'. They was busy gettin' ready to take Santiago, and didn't bother about us. We marines was the first to land and the first to fight, but unless we drove those Dagoes out of the woods it wasn't goin' to be a very healthy place to stay put."

"And did you drive them away?" inquired Dick. He had read all about the fight, but to get first hand news from one who had participated in the actual fighting was much better than reading it from a book.

"Of course we did. You see, the Colonel learned from friendly Cubans that the Spaniards in that region depended for all their water on a well a few miles away over the hills--Cusco Well, it was called. So if we took that well then they'd have to git out of the country. It was up to us to destroy the well. We made all the arrangements, and one of the ships was told to shell the locality where the well was located. Finally we started off dhriving the Dagoes ahead of us, when suddenly the shells from the ship began droppin' all about us instead of into the ranks of the enemy. Every minute they kept comin' hotter and faster and there was little chanct of us bein' successful as things were goin'. Then I saw one of the nerviest jobs pulled off that mornin'--one of the things ye often read about and believe is fiction. Right behind us in plain view was a high bare hill and on the top of that there hill, his back to the Spaniards and facin' the flashin' guns of the ship, was a marine sendin' wigwag messages to the ship and tellin' them where to shoot. Begorra, the bullets was a-flyin' around him like hail. Kickin' up little spats of dust at his feet, cuttin' down the cactus on either side of him, singin' through the little flag he was a-wavin', but did he stop? Not onct--and before long the shell fire lifted and began fallin' among them Dagoes and off they went with us marines after them, chargin' and yellin', sweatin' and swearin'. Yes, we found the well and destroyed it and went back to our own lines carryin' our dead and wounded with us. And onct again the good old Corps had scored, for Sergeant Major John Quick, the feller what did the signalin', won the first medal of honor in the War of 1898."

"Tell us some more, Dorlan," one of the bystanders pleaded.

"Ah, g'wan with ye. Sure I'm so dhry now from so much blabbin' I can drink the scuttle-butt[#] dhry, and that without half tryin'."

[#] A tank holding drinking water.

"Let us see the campaign medal the government gave you, will you, Mike?" asked Dick. One of his chief ambitions was to be able some day to wear some of those little bronze medals suspended from the bright colored silk ribbons on his own coat. Their intrinsic value was small but what an honor it would be to have the right to wear them.

Mike Dorlan opened his ditty-box, upon which he was sitting, and fumbling around in its interior brought forth two bronze medals; one considerably larger than the other.

"This one," said he, holding up the larger medal, "is the Sampson Medal, given for bein' on board of a ship of the U.S. Navy in some of the actions against the coastwise towns or with the Spanish Fleet. You all know that Admiral Sampson was in command of our naval forces that bottled up Cervera in the harbor of Santiago. That feller Cervera was a brave man indeed, and he fought like the gentleman he was, with no more chance of escapin' than I have o' bein' made the Commandant of the Corps, and you know how likely that is, bedad. This other little piece of bronze is the regular medal everyone got who was in Cuban waters or on Cuban soil durin' the war. It's the Spanish or West Indian Campaign Medal."

"Why don't you ever wear your ribbons and medal, Mike?" asked Dick. "Believe me, if I had 'em I'd be so proud I'd want to show 'em to everybody I met. I would like to see you with them all on some day at inspection."

"I'll tell ye why, me lad, and ye can belave it or not, as you please; there's one medal I want mor'n all of these combined and until I can wear that one, I'll not be wearin' of any."

* * * * * * * * *

Medal for Campaign in the West Indies and for Spanish War

MEDAL FOR CAMPAIGN IN THE WEST INDIES AND FOR SPANISH WAR

Issued to those of the Army, Navy and Marines who served on the high seas en route to or in immediate vicinity of Cuba, Porto Rico or Philippines between certain dates. In case if the army or navy service was not in the West Indies the inscription read "Spanish Campaign."

     *   *   *   *   *   *   *   *   *

"Which one is that, Dorlan?"

"It's one of them good-conduct medals the Top Sergeant was showin' of ye that first day ye come on this ship, and I'll git one yet! In three days more me present enlistment expires. I'm going to ship over right off, and I'll be makin' a bargain with ye right now!"

"What's the bargain?" asked Dick.

"Well, if I don't git one of them little bronzes at the end of my next enlistment, I'll be givin' all the rest o' me medals to ye, and ye can melt 'em up into copper pennies; but if I do git it, I'll string the hull lot of them across me chest at the first inspection what comes along."

And midst much laughter from the group surrounding them, Dorlan and Richard shook hands on the "bargain."

Ten days later the "galley yarns" came true, as they sometimes do, and the *Denver* steamed through the narrow entrance and into the wonderful, green bordered, blue waters of Guantanamo Bay, where she anchored for an indefinite stay.

Upon the first opportunity, Sergeant Douglass took the entire guard ashore for a view of the historic battlefields. Landing at Fisherman's Point, they climbed the steep slopes of McCalla Hill, where stands the monument erected in memory of the heroes who lost their lives in the memorable engagement. But it was Corporal Michael Dorlan who explained to the interested men every phase of the landing and the attack; who showed them the hill from which the intrepid Quick had signalled so calmly oblivious of personal danger, and finally he took them through the dusty cactus and chaparral to the old well, the destruction of which forced the Spanish troops to evacuate and leave the field to the sturdy soldiers of the sea.

At a later date, the boys in company with Dorlan and others made a week-end "liberty" to Santiago, where the winning battles of the war were fought on land and water. They saw the exact spot where Hobson and his brave crew blew up the *Merrimac* in the harbor entrance; they scaled the walls of Morro Castle, which withstood with hardly a scar the fierce bombardment of our fleet; and they rode out to San Juan Hill, where the gallant soldiers of Shafter's army fought so valiantly and successfully.

These little trips to old battlefields resulted in a great demand for books dealing with the wars of that period, and the crew's library of the *Denver* was more popular than it had been for months.

CHAPTER X

WINNING HIS FIRST MEDAL

Overhead the sun shone mercilessly from a cloudless sky. Hardly a breath of air stirred the stubby grass and scrubby bushes which covered abrupt little hillocks of piled-up coral lightly spread with clinging bits of sandy soil. From the floor-like level of the baked sand flats, covered with white streaks where the sun's rays had gathered up the water and left small deposits of salt, the heat-waves rose, bubbling and boiling, a snare to the unwary or unknowing riflemen, who, from various ranges and positions, were sending little pellets of lead encased in steel jackets at rows of paper targets surmounting the earth and concrete parapets, known as the "butts."

It was a busy and interesting scene of action. Marines in khaki and sailors in white were sprinkled over the vast plain, all intent on watching the bobbing rectangles of brownish paper with black, round, bull's eyes whereon was marked each shot-hole caused by the bullets in their flight.

For days the preliminary drill had been under way. To the men who never before had fired there seemed to be much useless labor and time wasted. Position and aiming drills are monotonous at best, and to stand at long intervals raising the rifle from the hip-position of "load" to a certain height, then bringing it to rest against the right shoulder, bending the head and squinting over the sights at small round black pasters an inch in diameter stuck to a bulkhead or wall and finally snapping the trigger, seemed the height of folly. When, however, the sighting drills progressed to their making tiny triangles by getting points on a piece of white paper twenty feet distant from the rifle sights and connecting these with straight lines, followed by explanations why certain triangles were good and if a bullet had actually travelled along the indicated path, excellent or poor scores would have resulted, then the drills held more interest for Richard and Henry.

Each day Sergeant Battiste, one of the famous shots of the Corps and attached to the *Denver*, gave lectures on rifle shooting. A celebrated coach, member of many winning teams in the National Rifle meets, holder of the coveted Distinguished Marksman Medal, and Military Rifle Champion of America for two consecutive years, he was well fitted for his task.

Marines are entitled to fire the regular record practise for qualification under the Small Arms Firing Manual of the United States Army once during each target year; but those men who made the grade of Expert Rifleman were not required to fire again during their current enlistment and for that time received each month the extra pay which is a reward for their merit. Naturally all hands were anxious to make the score necessary to acquire these benefits and Sergeant Battiste left no stone unturned to help them in their desires. Each step had been carefully rehearsed, instruction practise completed and to-day the record firing would decide their final merit.

"I've already told you," said Battiste, the men being gathered around him on arrival at the 200-yard firing point, "not to get excited and to take your time. Get your rear sight in perfect alignment with the front sight and the 'bull' sitting oh top; fill your lungs--then, the moment you are ready to fire hold your breath for that instant and squeeze the trigger--don't pull or jerk it, first take up the 'creep,' and by now every one of you should know just when that little additional pressure will be sufficient to release the firing-pin. We've a perfect day for shooting, and if you don't make good scores it's your own fault. As we go back to the longer ranges the wind will come up, but it will blow steadily from the left or nine o'clock,[#] if I know anything about this range and the action of the wind here, and I claim I do. We shall have to watch out for mirage. Your targets have been assigned. Each man knows the number he will fire at and there is no excuse for shooting on the wrong target. To do so would possibly spoil another fellow's score, and it means you will receive a 'goose egg'[#] for your own shot, and goose eggs mean low qualifications."

[#] When facing the target the range is supposed to represent the face of a clock. Twelve o'clock is at the target; six, at the firing point; three, to the right, and nine, to the left. The direction of the wind is easily designated by reference to any hour of the clock dial. A clock-face is also imagined on the target-face; twelve at the top and six at the bottom, facing the firer.

[#] A Zero on the score.

"Are we permitted to blacken our sights on record practise, Sergeant?" inquired Dick, as Battiste paused for a moment.

"Yes, you may blacken both front and rear sights. I'd suggest the use of camphor, and I should also smoke the barrel well, as this sun makes the blued metal glare badly. The red flag is up in the pits, so the 'sand rats'[#] are ready for us to begin. Get on the line, men, and begin firing when your target comes up. Each shot will be marked. If you fail to hit the target a red flag will be waved across its face, indicating a miss; the white disk placed over the shot hole means a bull's-eye, or five; the red disk, four; the black and white disk a three and the black a two. If any of you wish to challenge the marking, Mr. Gardiner, who is the Range Officer, will call up Mr. Thorp in the butts and have the target gone over carefully. Remember to keep your own score in your book and see that it corresponds with the marking and with the scorekeepers' records."

[#] Men who operate the targets and signal the hits from the butts.

"How many shots do we fire?" called out Private Jones, the most inattentive man of the guard, but also the one always spotlessly clean, which reputation had gained for him the position of one of Commander Bentley's cabin orderlies.

"This is slow fire at 200 yards," answered the coach, who seldom lost his temper and had the patience of Job. "Each man will fire two strings of five shots each from the standing position, then we shall move back to 300 yards, and fire the same number of shots from either the sitting or kneeling position. No sighting shots allowed at either of these ranges. The targets are up, men! Commence firing!"

Immediately following the command came the crack of rifles all along the line--the record practise was under way.

Neither Richard nor Henry, before this week on the range at Guantanamo Bay, knew anything of rifle shooting, though both, one in the New England woods, the other along the bayous of the Mississippi, had spent many happy hours with dog and shotgun. Practise with the high-powered military rifle was a decidedly different proposition, but they took to it as a duck does to water, and during instruction practise they agreeably surprised Sergeant Battiste with work that was excellent for beginners.

Dick, having more patience and being more cool-headed, strong and nerveless, was without doubt the better of the two. Henry's one failing was his impatience to "get the shot off." In case he failed to bring his sights in perfect alignment on the bull's eye with a steady hand, he would fall back on the quick "fly shot" so necessary to the hunter armed with a fowling piece, but disastrous to one who aspires to perfection with the military weapon.

"Five o'clock three for you, Cabell," sang out the coach; "must have pulled down on your gun at the last moment. Remember my caution--take your time and squeeze the trigger. Good work, Drummer Comstock; you've found the bull first shot. It's nipping in at twelve o'clock.[#] It pays to be calm and deliberate."

"I'm way off to the right, Sergeant," called out Jones irritably; "all three of my shots have gone in the same place--twos at three o'clock, and you said there wasn't any wind blowing."

[#] "Nipping in at twelve o'clock"--A rifleman's term for a bull's-eye just barely cutting the black at the top.

"Not a bit of wind, Jones, and if you would only remember to set your wind gauge properly those twos would have been bulls, every one. You have almost three points of right wind on, and you shouldn't have any. Apply your quarter-point rule. Each quarter-point on your wind gauge at 200 yards moves your shot how many inches on the target?"

"It moves it two inches, and three times two is six inches," said Jones smugly. "My shots are about two feet from the center of the bull, so there must be wind blowing from the left."

"Your arithmetic needs a little oiling, Jones. There are four quarters in every full point and that makes twelve quarters altogether for your three points. Each quarter point moves you two inches, making twenty-four inches in all. You see, that is the two feet that your shots are out, which is what I said in the beginning."

Jones sheepishly corrected his sight, and the next shot on his target was marked a "pinwheel."

Thus it was the coach went up and down the firing line, offering the advice of long and successful experience.

At the completion of the firing at 200 yards the line of riflemen moved back to the 300-yard point, and taking the sitting or kneeling position, began the next stage of the course. A "possible" or perfect score of ten shots would mean fifty points towards the three hundred points necessary to qualify the men as marksmen, and this they would have to get in order to be permitted to shoot the sharpshooter's course. The firing at 200 yards was the hardest in Dick's estimation, and though he had started off with a bull's-eye, or five, as already stated, he did not continue to see the little white marker or spotter in the black space as he hoped would be the case. His first and last shots were fives and the rest fours, making his total score forty-two. Henry was six points below centers, or thirty-four.

Three hundred yards was an easy range for Dick and he surprised himself with the high score at that stage--forty-seven points, all bulls but three, which fell close outside in the four-ring. Henry had made one over centers, or a score of forty-one.

"Now we will go back to five and six hundred yards," said Battiste. "Each man must fire two sighting shots at both those ranges before he can count his shots for record. The firing will be the same as it was in instruction--from the prone position. I expect every man to average up his score at the 500-yard range, for the bull looks as big as a barn-door, and you can't miss it. You know we change the size of the targets now and use the mid-range or B-target, and the bull's-eye is twenty inches in diameter. In the short-range or A-target it is but eight inches, and in the long-range or C-target it is thirty-six inches. For this reason B-target at 500 yards and C-target at 800 yards are what we call 'easy marks.'"

"Supposing we fire the twelve shots and the first ten are bulls but the last two goose eggs, would the latter count against you?" asked Henry, as he rearranged the leather sling on his rifle around his left arm before lying down.

"It's your last ten shots which count," replied the coach. "Firing regulations require you to take the two sighting shots, and you can't juggle them around to suit yourself; they've got to be the first two fired. The mirage is no longer boiling straight up,[#] but it's moving off to the right a bit, so I'd advise you all to take your sighting shots, make your own deductions and then wait for me to see how nearly correct you are."

[#] Mirage--Heat waves near the earth, visible on some days to the naked eye, but more clearly seen through a telescope. It is really the air travelling on the range, and the best guide for windage, as it is the actual air through which the bullet travels. When there is no movement to left or right the wind is either still for a moment or carrying the mirage directly towards or from the target. It appears to rise and is said to be "boiling."

The moment Dick's target appeared he lay flat on his stomach with his body at an angle of about forty-five degrees to the firing line, feet spread apart with the heels turned inwards. His leather sling was fastened tightly about the upper part of his left arm, and the left hand was well under the rifle, bearing against the lower swivel, which held one end of the sling. The butt of the rifle was placed, with the aid of his right hand, against the right shoulder, both elbows on the ground, the right hand grasping the small of the stock with the forefinger curling around the trigger. His cheek was against the left side of the stock and his right eye so near the rear of the cocking-piece that to one uninitiated it would appear dangerous. But it was the safest position he could assume, and the rifle in his grasp was steady as a rock.

Crack! Crack! The first shots sped on their way to the butts, as Dick and the man on his right fired almost simultaneously.

Nothing followed! Dick's target screen did not move. He was certain his position, his aim, his pull, were all perfect. The shot must have gone through the black paper in the center or one of the black annular rings and was not seen by the "sand rat" in charge.

"Mark number three target," shouted the sailor who was keeping Dick's score, and the man at the field-telephone relayed the message to the butts. A second or two later "number three" was "sashed," or pulled down; then up it popped with the fatal red flag waving back and forth across it as if in derision.

Dick was surprised at this, for he was positive his first shot must have been a bull's-eye. He looked at his sight critically. What was wrong? Perhaps the wind was blowing enough to throw him off the "bull," but never could that light breeze throw him off the target altogether. He had one more sighting shot, and unless he found the target with that one he would have no "dope" for his ten record shots that were to follow. Already he had a quarter-point of left wind on his gauge, which meant, at this range, if he took one-half a point windage that would move the shot one-half the width of the "bull"-- enough to put him in the four-ring if his aim deviated the slightest and his "dope" happened to be wrong.

He was about to make the change, even though against his better judgment, when the man at the end of the telephone called out:

"Two shot holes in the bull on Number Four target!"

Dick drew a long breath of relief. He had fired his first shot not at his own but at his right-hand neighbor's target.

"Thank your lucky star, young man, for the sighting spots, or else your score would have been spoiled in the making," quietly remarked Sergeant Battiste, who was standing back, enjoying the lad's perplexity. "Let it be a lesson to you--always take a squint through your peep sight at the number below your target before you fire. One of those fives in Four Target was right in the center--a pin wheel! How much windage did you have?"

"A quarter-point of left wind," answered Dick.

"Just right--now, go ahead and make a possible."

And that is exactly what Drummer Comstock did--every one of his following shots hitting the bull's-eye for a perfect score, and to the present day he shows that page from his score book with great pride.

Dick's luck continued with him at 600 yards, which to many old and tried riflemen is one of the most interesting ranges. With forty-three points here and the fifty at 500 yards, Dick now had a total score of one hundred and eighty-two points.

"What's your total, Hank?" asked Dick while they rested during the noon hour.

"One hundred and sixty-three, so far; but do you know who has the highest total for the day?"

"No, I didn't get through at six hundred in time to look over the score-boards; why, who is it?"

"Oh, a fellow named Richard Comstock! Great Scott! If you keep this up they will be hailing you as the Military Champeen of the World, Dick. That was great shooting you did at 500 yards, old man."

*　　*　　*　　*　　*　　*　　*　　*　　*

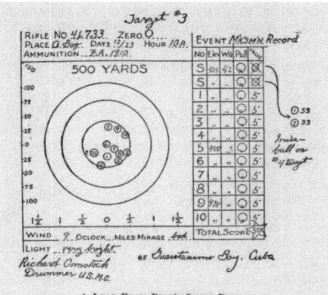

A LEAF FROM DICK'S SCORE BOOK

1. This leaf is from Dick's Score Book, which he inked in after he left the range.

2. It will be noticed the mirage was bad and Dick's 2nd sighting shot and first four record shots were low, therefore he raised his sight 25 yards. The bull's eye of this target (B) is 20 inches in diameter. 25 yards up on sight gauge would be about 6¼ inches.

3. "The square rule" is, changing the elevation 100 yards at any range gives change on the target equal to the number of inches in the square of the range. Example: at 500 yards equals 25 inches.

4. On the 9th and 10th shots, Dick raised his sight again and kept in the bull. The mirage had increased, tending to "throw" his shots low.

A Leaf From Dick's Score Book

A LEAF FROM DICK'S SCORE BOOK

1. This leaf is from Dick's Score Book, which he inked in after he left the range.

2. It will be noticed the mirage was bad and Dick's 2nd sighting shot and first four record shots were low, therefore he raised his sight 25 yards. The bull's eye of this target (B) is 20 inches in diameter. 25 yards up on sight gauge would be about 6-¼ inches.

3. "The square rule" is, changing the elevation 100 yards at any range gives change on the target equal to the number of inches in the square of the range. Example: at 500 yards equals 25 inches.

4. On the 9th and 10th shots, Dick raised his sight again and kept in the bull. The mirage had increased, tending to "throw" his shots low.

*   *   *   *   *   *   *   *   *

"I am proud of it, of course, but when you read how some of these crack shots make a string of bulls as long as your arm at that range then it loses some of its lustre as a star score."

"They didn't get those wonderful records, though, on the first real practise, as you have done, Dick; and Battiste says you have a natural gift for shooting which further practise will surely develop."

"Yes, I got along pretty well with the slow fire, Henry, but I'm rotten in rapid fire, especially at 200 yards. Somehow I can't get the knack of it."

"That is funny, for I am perfectly at home in rapid fire," said Henry.

"If I can get on my tummy and shoot 'em I am safe, therefore I don't fear the skirmish runs. How many more points can be made from now on? Let's figure it out!"

"We could make three hundred more. Each of the two skirmish runs counts one hundred, and the scores at rapid fire at 200 and 300 yards are fifty each, but I don't reckon we will get anything like that. Besides, you shouldn't worry, and I need but one-thirty-seven to qualify as marksman, and you a hundred and eighteen."

"You are wrong, Hank. It's true you require but three hundred points to make you a marksman, but you need as many points as you can get. I'm not satisfied just to scrape through in a matter of this kind, and because the thing appears easy is all the more reason we should try for the highest score we possibly can get. Then there is another reason; your marksman's score is added to what you make in the sharpshooter's course, and you've got to make a total of four hundred and fifteen points to get the qualification, which then gives you the right to shoot the expert test."

"You are right again, Dick, and thank you for the tip, or I might have missed my badge and the extra pay."

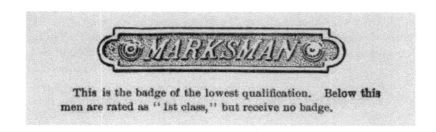

This is the badge of the lowest qualification. Below this men are rated as "1st class," but receive no badge.

Marksman badge. This is the badge of the lowest qualification. Below this men are rated as "1st class," but receive no badge.

That night when the different divisions of the *Denver's* complement returned, tired and hungry, to their ship, Sergeant Battiste worked till late arranging the scores of those who had fired, and out of twenty aspirants for the honor all had qualified as marksmen and would shoot the following day. Of the twenty, the top notch shot was none other than Dick, and fighting for last place were Trumpeter Cabell and Private Jones, both with 323 points to their credit. Dick had made the excellent score of 449 out of a possible 500 points.

THE BADGE AWARDED TO
HENRY CABELL

The Badge Awarded to Henry Cabell

The following evening when the shooting cohorts returned on board having finished the Sharpshooter's[#] Course, he was still leading the detachment with a total score of 586 points.

[#] This course consisted of ten shots slow fire at 800 yards, same at 1,000 yards, and ten shots rapid fire at 500 yards; a possible score being 150 points.

"The 1,000-yard range was my Waterloo to-day," he explained to First Sergeant Douglass, who did not have to fire, being already an expert rifleman; "a fellow needs a lot more practise than I've had to be able to find and hold the bull at that distance, especially if there is a 'fish tail'[#] wind blowing, as happened to-day. Anyway, I'm sure of my Maltese Cross; but I want to pull down that expert's badge to-morrow, for it's the finest of the lot."

[#] A wind coming from a direction nearly parallel with the flight of the bullet:--the course the bullet travels through the air is called its trajectory.

The expert rifleman's test consisted in first firing ten shots slow fire from 600 yards over an embankment at the silhouette of a kneeling figure of a man with his arm raised as in shooting. Then came five shots at 500 yards and five at 400 yards at the same figure, only in this shooting it bobbed up above the butts for five seconds and might show up at any point, with five-second intervals between appearances. Next, two strings of five shots each at the "ducks," or Target F, the silhouette of a man lying, are fired at 500 yards. These "ducks" are supposed to fall over when hit, and at 300 and 200 yards the target first fired at, Target E, is pulled across the range on a track fifty yards long, in thirty seconds, while ten shots are being fired. Every hit counts one point, and the firer must make twenty-five hits out of fifty shots to qualify.

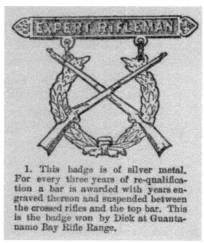

1. This badge is of silver metal. For every three years of re-qualification a bar is awarded with years engraved thereon and suspended between the crossed rifles and the top bar. This is the badge won by Dick at Guantanamo Bay Rifle Range.

Expert Rifleman badge.

1.   This badge is of silver metal. For every three years of re-qualification a bar is awarded with years engraved thereon and suspended between the crossed rifles and the top bar. This is the badge won by Dick at Guantanamo Bay Rifle Range.

It is a true test of the individual's ability, where steady hand, quick eye and excellent judgment are prime qualities for its successful accomplishment, yet, in spite of his fine showing on the two previous days, Dick barely scraped through with the exact number of hits to win out. But he had won, and two months later when the little silver emblems were received from Headquarters, it was with mingled pride and thankfulness he saw his own name neatly engraved on the reverse of the pin which Sergeant Douglass handed over to his keeping.

Five new experts, eleven sharpshooters and four marksmen was the final result of Sergeant Battiste's course of training.

"Well, I don't believe," Dick remarked as he strained his eyes to see the bright new badge he had pinned to his khaki coat preparatory to Saturday morning inspection, "that I'll ever have as much pleasure in winning anything as I had in winning this, my first real medal."

"You may be right, Dick," said Henry, looking a little regretfully at the new sharpshooter's badge he held in his hand, "but what appeals more to me is that extra pay these little silver gadgets bring in each month."

CHAPTER XI

A REPUBLIC IN DISTRESS

Christmas and the New Year's holidays passed by uneventfully, and the *Denver* still remained at anchor in Guantanamo Bay. Other vessels arrived and departed, but no orders came for the cruiser, much to the disappointment of all hands.

Rumors of trouble at various points often reached their ears, but the crew finally began to lose hope of moving. The Department must have forgotten them! The Secretary of the Navy was going to make her a station ship! The Admiral of the Fleet had it in for the Captain, and wouldn't let him move! All sorts and kinds of excuses and reasons were forthcoming, but they were as unsatisfactory as they were improbable.

Over six months of outdoor life, swimming, boating, fishing, riding horseback, taking a leading part in athletics, for which his days at Bankley High School and the healthy life in the New England seaport formed a splendid foundation, had developed Richard Comstock into a tall, broad-shouldered, small-waisted, powerful young man, one able to give an excellent account of himself, no matter what the situation. As bow oar of the winning marines' dinghy race-boat crew he had already given evidence of the strength and endurance of his well-knit muscles. He was nearly as brown as the Cubans who plied their bum-boat[#] trade at the port gangway during meal hours, and with his straight black hair and dark eyes he might easily have disguised himself as one of them.

[#] A shore boat which sells fruit, post-cards, curios, etc., to ships visiting the port.

The months had likewise worked a change in Henry Cabell, but his figure was much slighter and less robust than that of his boon companion. The boys were trying to master the Spanish language, and when ashore on visits to Caimanera and Guantanamo City, as frequently they were, it became a practise to carry on all their conversation in that tongue, much to the amusement of themselves and particularly the natives with whom they came in contact. However, the practise was good for them, and they were able to converse quite fluently, and to chatter glibly with the Phillipino cooks and mess attendants, of whom a number were attached to the ship.

Usually their evenings were spent ashore at the Marine Barracks on Fisherman's Point, where a nightly programme, consisting of the best moving-picture plays, were shown on the screen or boxing and wrestling matches, in both of which Dick occasionally took part, helped pass the hours.

In the meantime Joe Choiniski and "Slugger" Williams, having completed their term of punishment in solitary confinement, were released and restored to duty. The long enforced diet seemingly wrought a change in Williams' attitude towards the world in general; and the ship's athletic officer, Lieutenant Robling, hearing of the "Slugger's" reported prowess with the gloves, had interested him anew in boxing, and he had gone into training with a view of winning laurels when the Fleet should finally put in its appearance during the winter maneuvers and target practice. Choiniski belonged to the "black gang,"[#] and his living space was far removed from the marines' compartment, consequently the boys rarely came in contact with him, but if black looks could speak for anything it was certain that Joe's feeling for them was still full of animosity.

[#] A nickname for the Engineer Division on shipboard.

Altogether Captain Bentley's ship was having a peaceful, rather than a wildly exciting time.

Then like a bolt from the blue came a cable message--received at the little station near the lighthouse.

"Revolution in San Domingo. Proceed immediately to Monte Cristi and report to Senior Officer Present for further assignment on arrival."

Thus ran the order.

It was Saturday afternoon, and most of the crew were ashore. Immediately the "Cornet"[#] was hoisted at the foremast, which was a peremptory order for everybody to return on board at once regardless of length of leave. It told those on shore that the ship was under sailing orders and about to get under way.

[#] A signal flag used to recall all boats and liberty parties.

Conjectures were rife in the boats hurriedly returning from all the various places to which they had gone for the afternoon's outing. Swimming parties hardly waited to get into their clothes before shoving off for the cruiser; officers playing golf did not stop to look for the balls they had sent flying along the "fairway" or bouncing into the "rough"; the baseball game in progress halted as a batsman in the act of making a "home run" cut swiftly across the diamond from second base and, grabbing his sweater, made his final spurt for the boat landing.

"Back to the good old U.S.A. for us, boys!"

"Hooray! Broadway and the white lights, fellers!"

"Philly's good enough for me!" called out one enthusiast from the stern sheets of the loaded sailing launch.

These and many other such remarks filled the air.

"Whoop her up, boys, for ten days' leave in the old home town, no matter where it may be!" yelled one joyful youngster, and all who could lent a willing hand on the heavy oars.

Then came the disappointment!

Within an hour the gangways and boat booms were rigged in, awnings furled, cutters and steamers hoisted aboard, life-boats secured for sea, all the hundred and one things necessary to the departure of a man-of-war attended to.

Last of all the mail was sent ashore, for this might be the only opportunity for days,--possibly weeks; who could tell?

Now came the peeping of the boatswains' whistles and raucous voices bellowing throughout the ship.

"All hands, Up anchor!"

Silently the divisions fell in at their proper stations. Slowly the propellers began their revolutions, which would not cease until the arrival at that island of trouble, San Domingo--the Hispaniola of the Spanish Main.

Ashore the little garrison of marines lined the beach at Fisherman's Point. They had heard the news and when the *Denver* passed, clouds of smoke issuing from her funnels, her ensign snapping in the breeze, and her crew drawn up on deck, the envious men ashore gave her three rousing cheers to speed the parting guest. On past the lighthouse, out through the narrow entrance of the harbor into the deep indigo waters of the Caribbean, where, once the coral shoals were well astern, the course was changed to due east, and one by one, buildings, bay, and lighthouse were swallowed in the distance and the bluish haze which hovered over the terraced hills and shore of Cuba's southern slopes.

Captain Bentley, unlike most naval officers of his day, believed in informing his officers of all the reasons underlying his official actions and the movements of the vessel he commanded. The idea which so many officers held,--divulge nothing, keep officers and crew in ignorance of situations, destinations and intentions until the last possible moment, was not in accord with his conception of good management, executive ability and coördination, therefore, unless absolutely forbidden by his instructions, he made it a point to explain fully all orders which would sooner or later affect them, so that they might familiarize themselves with all the ramifications of the probable events.

Following out this policy he summoned the heads of all departments to his cabin after supper, and there being no officer in charge of the marines, he included First Sergeant Douglass among those present, and furnished them with a short résumé of all the messages he had received since the first one ordering him to sea so unexpectedly.

"Gentlemen, for some months the political situation in the Dominican Republic has been hovering on the brink of another revolution, and from these despatches received to-day, armed conflict has at last become a fact. Our government anticipated this state of affairs, but owing to various causes we have not sufficient ships in San Domingan waters adequately to guard the interests of American citizens nor protect the customs, which as you are aware, are under the supervision of the United States. The situation is so acute, in the belief of the Department, that already marines are embarking on board the *Dixie* at Philadelphia, and by morning will be on their way to Monte Cristi, where the greatest activity against the organized government seems centered. It will be five days at best before the marines will reach here. I have been ordered to proceed there also and report to the S.O.P. for assignment. Barring unforeseen accidents we should arrive at our destination on Monday morning. It is advisable for us under the circumstances to make ourselves acquainted with such facts as are available regarding the political, economical and geographical features of the unfortunate republic. Our duties may take us to any one of its ports; therefore a study of the charts and a glimpse at the island's history will be beneficial to all. I believe the day is not far distant when San Domingo will become a territory of ours, or at least a protectorate under us."

"If you have time and inclination, sir, I believe all present would appreciate a short talk along the lines you indicate," said Lieutenant Commander Ogden.

"Very gladly, and I will not waste time on preliminaries," said Captain Bentley. "Of course, you all know Christopher Columbus discovered Santo Domingo on his first voyage, and by his direction his brother Bartholomew founded the first European settlement in the New World on August 4, 1494, naming it New Isabella. From this time to the present the island has been the scene of more continual fighting, and strife, and dissension, than any other portion of the globe of equal size. The Spaniards were the first people to believe in the policy that 'a good Indian is a dead one,' and they proceeded to make them 'good.' English, French, and Spanish armies and navies have fought along and on its shores. Revolution has succeeded revolution. The French end of the island was declared a republic in 1801 after an uprising of the blacks under Toussant L'Ouverture, who incidentally was the son of a Royal African King. The French and Spanish long disputed certain portions of the island, and a treaty establishing the boundary was made January 3, 1777, but with the independence of Haiti the whole island came under the rule of the negroes. Soon the Spanish element revolted against the blacks and formed an independent republic, and the old boundary lines were reëstablished in 1844. In 1849 President Baez endeavored to lease Samana Bay to the United States, but our President, Mr. Pierce, did not succeed in putting the measure through. The countries of Europe were fearful of our securing a base in the West Indies of such prime importance, and a revolution against Baez, incited so it is claimed by the English, overthrew the government.

"Strife was again rampant, and finally Spain was invited to take over her former colony by the people in 1861.

"This lasted till 1865, when the Spanish yoke was again thrown off and another futile attempt made to interest us in Samana Bay. Hardly a year has passed since without dissension and bloodshed. In the interests of our own and foreign citizens, and to carry out the policy of the Monroe Doctrine, the United States has at all times endeavored to settle these sanguinary conflicts, and with some success; but never has a permanent peace resulted.

"About 1905 we agreed to manage their customs for San Domingo, and to assist them to liquidate many of the enormous financial claims against their government by various foreign and domestic concerns. Germany, ever on the alert to expand her power, was only too anxious to establish herself in the Western Hemisphere, and in order to continue our stated policy of protection against such invasion, some such act on our part was absolutely necessary. Deprived of the rich benefits of custom dues, revolutions did not prove profitable, and a period of comparative quiet ensued. But it seems that a Latin-American people cannot long remain stable, and now they are again on the rampage. European influence is undoubtedly behind it, but I do not feel free to divulge that phase of the matter. I hope I have not bored you."

"Are you able to give us the present situation regarding the contending forces?" asked Lieutenant Robling, the engineer officer.

"Only in a general way. The rebels seem to hold the interior towns and country, and with the exception of Monte Cristi the seaports are all in the hands of the government troops. A great amount of smuggling is being carried on between the rebels and Haitians, and the officials are powerless to prevent it."

"Do you believe we shall land?" inquired the Executive Officer.

"That I cannot say; however, we must be prepared for any emergency."

"I will make all arrangements for the landing force to be ready for instant service. To-morrow is Sunday, but with your permission I will 'turn to' in the morning, go over the details, and break out and stow on deck our equipment."

"Go ahead with the work as you see fit, Mr. Ogden, and be sure that the gunner gets his small-arms ammunition ready for issue. Turn over to First Sergeant Douglass enough rifle and pistol ammunition to equip the guard. The marines may be needed immediately on arrival for service ashore. If that is all, gentlemen, I will bid you good-evening."

No feeling of disappointment prevailed among the *Denver's* crew upon receipt of the news that they were en route to aid in putting down a full-fledged rebellion, and everybody was once again full of cheerfulness and smiles. This elation was particularly noticeable among the marines, for if there was "anything doing" ashore their participation was a foregone conclusion. The mere fact that a thousand of their fellows were already sailing from Philadelphia was indication enough that the situation was critical.

Time and again the marines had been rushed here and there and everywhere to police up this or that fractious republic; it was an old yet ever new story with them, and though the activities and general status of this fighting branch of Uncle Sam's armed forces were obscure to the majority of people at home, they were well known and greatly respected in those lands where they labored, fought and often died in their country's service.

Richard and Henry were greatly excited over the prospect and worked with a will the following day in getting out stores, munitions, clothing and otherwise preparing for the hoped-for duty ashore.

"It's lucky we went to Guantanamo, Dick, else we might not have had any experience with these big Colt's forty-fives we pack around on our hips," Henry remarked.

The two lads were at the time carefully oiling and cleaning their heavy revolvers, the weapons the "musics" of the Corps carried into conflict. Splendid shooting arms they were, too, and during the stay in Cuba they had received a certain amount of practise with them in connection with the Navy Small Arms Course, wherein scores with both rifle and revolver were required.

As he spoke, Henry whirled the open cylinder about, and with a clever twist of the wrist snapped it shut, then pointing the empty revolver at a passing man he snapped the hammer rapidly.

"Stop that!" came a curt command, and looking up Henry found Corporal Dorlan standing over him. The look in Dorlan's eye was not pleasant to see, and the usual good-natured smile was missing from the older man's face.

"Stop what?" asked Henry, flushing because of the harshness in Dorlan's voice and glance.

"Stop that foolishness! Ye ought to be gettin' sense in the noodle of ye after bein' these months in the marines."

"I reckon I've as much sense and maybe a little more than some marines around here, who've been in as many hitches[#] as I have months, and I don't need a trial by Summary Court to teach me lessons," and Henry glared hotly at the veteran soldier.

[#] "Hitches"--Enlisted man's term for enlistments.

"If that's the case, me lad, let's see ye use it, both in yer actions and yer manners," said Dorlan, and the twinkle was now returning to the gray-blue eyes; "but I'll tell ye one thing sure;--it won't be a 'summary' but a 'general' ye will be after gettin' if ye go around so careless like aimin' and shootin' yer gun at human bein's, and ye can put that in your pipe and shmoke it for the rest of yer life, and 'twill do ye a wurrld of good."

By this time Henry's better nature asserted itself and rising he put out his hand frankly and asked the elder man to excuse his unwisely chosen words.

Richard, witnessing the incident, was happy to see these two good friends of his settle so amicably what might have developed into a bitter animosity on the part of the young Southerner.

"Now that 'the battle is over, Mother Dear,'" quoted Dick, "suppose you sit down, Corporal Michael Dorlan, and tell us the causes of the Revolutionary War."

"And I could do that too, me lad," said Dorlan, smiling at Richard, whom he claimed as his own particular protégé, "but I'll sit me down and tell ye somethin' that may be of interest and profit to the two of yez."

Seating himself on a near-by sea-chest, Dorlan continued:

"Just a bit ago, young man, I saw ye pointin' a gun at one of yer shipmates and not only that, but pullin' of the trigger," and he looked severely at Henry.

"What of that? The revolver wasn't loaded--it couldn't harm anyone," stated Henry.

"That's where ye are wrong, lad, for it's the gun what ain't loaded which generally goes off and kills yer best friend. It's the kind of accident ye read about in almost any paper ye pick up in any part of the world, and I'd make a bet with ye that the weapon the other fellow 'didn't know was loaded' since the invention of gun-powder has caused more deaths and serious accidents than have the aimed shots in actual warfare."

"But, Corporal, I knew my pistol was empty," protested Henry; "I looked through the cylinder before I closed it. Besides, we've had no ammunition given us."

"Nevertheless, what I say is true, Henry, and here is a safe rule for ye to follow for the rest of your life: never point a gun, loaded or unloaded, at any human bein' unless ye mean to kill or wound him."

At the instant Dorlan finished speaking a half dozen laughing bluejackets came running around a corner into the marines' compartment. Following in close pursuit was a companion flourishing a noosed rope in one hand and a revolver in the other. As he appeared he called out:

"Catch the bandits!"

It was innocent horse play and the men in the vicinity turned to watch the chase. The "bandits" disappeared through a door on the port side of the deck, the pursuer aimed his revolver at them and pulled on the double-action trigger. There was a loud report and a leaden bullet flattened itself harmlessly against the iron bulkhead.

The young apprentice seaman who had fired the shot stopped short and, with a white face, looked in horror at the smoking weapon as it fell from his nerveless grasp to the deck.

"I never knew it was loaded!" he cried hoarsely.

Reaching for the heavy Colt's, Corporal Dorlan picked it up and broke open the cylinder,--every chamber but the one just discharged was filled with death.

"Come up to the Officer of the Deck, young feller," ordered Dorlan grimly, taking the trembling sailor by the arm, and as they turned to leave, he looked towards Dick and Henry, saying:

"As I said before--never point a gun unless ye mean to kill."

No more salutary lesson could have been given than old Mike's talk and its startling sequel.

Out into the windward passage; northward then eastward into the trade-wind-tossed, white-capped waters of the Atlantic; past the mountainous shores of Haiti and the famous or infamous island of Tortuga, whence came the buccaneers and their notorious chief, Sir Henry Morgan.

Then the character of the land changed from rugged mountains rising at the shore line to low, gray, misty ranges rearing their serrated ridges far inland. Finally from out the sea a lone peak reared its crest; growing ever higher and higher--the well-known Monte Granero, so called by the great discoverer when he first saw it, and from the summit of which can be seen the site where now are the ruins of New Isabella on the northern shore of San Domingo. On the low-lying plain a few miles southwestward from the base of the mountain was the straggling town of Monte Cristi, sweltering in the morning sunshine.

Since before dawn the spluttering snap of the wireless filled the air on board the *Denver* as the message sped through the intervening miles of space to the flagship lying in the open bay off Cabras Island.

Captain Bentley on the bridge read the aerograms with interest, and particularly the last one.

"Large force rebels reported operating vicinity Samana Bay. Proceed to Sanchez, investigate conditions, protect American and foreign lives and property. Guard customs. Report conditions."

"We will continue on our present bearing, Mr. Ogden," said the Captain; "read this, and send word to the Navigating Officer to report to me at once in my cabin."

Captain Bentley then went below, and soon was poring over the chart of Samana Bay, one of the finest harbors and most desirable bases in the whole of the West Indies.

CHAPTER XII

SEÑOR PEREZ ASKS FOR AID

Before the mud caused by the dropping anchor rose to the surface of the water, a shore boat containing two oarsmen and one passenger put out from the wharf and pulled for the *Denver*. That the passenger was in a hurry was evidenced by his gesticulating hands, and by the black cotton umbrella held by its bulging center which he waved in an attempt to make the clumsy boatmen pull together. From under the white cork helmet his dark face worked spasmodically as with a mixture of Spanish, English and German words he urged on his laggard crew.

Interested sailors and marines lined the ship's rail, watching the approach of the stout, excited little foreigner. His rapid speech was now quite audible though not intelligible.

"He is giving those peons what my mother would call 'gowdy,'" said Dick to Henry, "and that is her worst swear word."

"Meaning our excitable friend is rather strong in his choice of expletives?" inquired Henry.

"You've got it, Hank! His language is hot enough to make a bottle of Tobasco sauce weep tears of envy."

By this time the boat was within a few yards of the ship.

"Boat ahoy! What do you want?" hailed the Officer of the Deck.

"I want to see the Captain. I am the consul. I am Señor Perez. There is much trouble."

"Come alongside," ordered the Officer of the Deck, and walked to the gangway to meet the consul who, with surprising agility, sprang from his boat and waddled hurriedly on deck.

"Excuse the absence of honors, Señor, but we did not expect you. The Captain will see you at once, sir."

"I do not want the honors, I want the protection. I want----"

"Orderly, conduct Señor Perez to the Captain's cabin," said the officer, and still talking volubly the little man disappeared below, the marine orderly leading the way.

"It was a regular vaudeville show," said Private Jones later, hardly able to control his laughter while he related the interview to a group of friends accosting him for news after he came off watch. "The little Spig is our consul, all right enough, and after the Old Man had quieted him down a bit he appeared to be a pretty agreeable sort. But, say! He was going strong when he first opened up, and that's no idle jest."

"All right, Jonesie, cut that part and tell us what all the excitement's about."

"From what I gathered seeing the door to the cabin was open all the time," continued Jones, "he's all wrought up over the arrival of a bunch of rebels in the hills back of the town. He has just returned from a trip to the States; came on a Clyde Liner Saturday. His daughter was struck in the leg by a stray bullet during the revolution two years ago and has been in New York for treatment. He brought her back, also a new German governess for his four children, the oldest being this little girl--her name is Sol-la-de-da or something like that----"

"Guess you mean Soledad," volunteered Dick.

"That's it,--Soledad! Well, last night the rebs shot up the town, but no one was hurt. The little girl--he sort of worships her--was scared stiff, and so was everyone else. The government troops were afraid to leave the fort, but added their shots and shouts to the general uproar.

"Some of the bullets hit the consulate, and Perez believes, because he is the American Consul and Americans are unpopular with the rebs--also because he was active in electing the present president--that they are after him. He's a native of San Domingo, and I expect he ought to know what he's talking about."

"What did the Old Man tell him?" asked one of the men.

"The Captain told him he'd received orders not to send any forces ashore unless absolutely necessary; in other words, that we are not to get mixed up with any of the fighting at all if we can help it. He offered to take him and all his family on board for a while."

"What did the Spig say to that?"

"Oh, he went up in the air at first, but it was finally settled to arrange signals from his house to the ship, and if he was actually attacked he could send up a rocket or two and we'd land in a jiffy. You see, there are only about fifty insurrectos in the hills, so it's estimated, and there are two hundred government troops in the town, and the rebs are afraid to come in to attack, even though the federals are afraid of them. We are going to keep our search-lights on all night, and though we can't see the Spigs in the bosky they'll think we can, and that'll be enough to scare 'em. After that Mr. Consul went ashore with a bundle of rockets under one arm and his old bumbershoot under the other, mollified but not satisfied."

"Is that all you know?" inquired another inquisitive man.

"You can't expect me to remember everything; besides, I'm no evening paper," answered Jones.

"You ain't no yeller journal, that's sure," said Joe Choiniski, sneeringly, from the edge of Jones' audience. "I, for one, wouldn't give two cents to read all you've chawed about so far."

"Nobody asked you to butt in and listen," promptly answered Jones, looking at the speaker, who was none too popular, especially with the marines, "but I've got a dime thriller up my sleeve for the Sunday edition."

"Loosen up, Jonesie," said a big marine, tossing into the circle a quarter, which Jones deftly caught, "here's two bits; you can keep the change. What's the scandal?"

Rather proud at being the center of so much attraction, an honor not ordinarily accorded him, Jones continued:

"Well, the chief thing old Perez was excited over is a bunch of money he's got in his house. He's about the richest man in town, and is a kind of banker too, and he's got several thousands of dollars of government money in his keeping. He can't get rid of it, for the railroad is busted up. He's afraid to let the Commanding Officer of the government troops know about it, for the simple reason that a lot of pay is already due him and his men, and they'd be liable to confiscate it and his own coin too. He claims that the rebel chief is an enemy of his and wouldn't hesitate to kill him and his whole family if he heard about the money and could get it. He can't let the money out of his house for the reason he's received word a federal officer is expected at any old time to get it, and if he didn't have it ready for instant delivery, he'd always be in bad with the authorities, and----"

"You have done enough talking, young man," interrupted First Sergeant Douglass, who overheard the latter part of Jones' discourse, "and I want to tell you, if ever I hear you or any other orderly disclosing, without authority, official matters which you may happen to overhear while on duty in a position of trust, I'll see that you get well and properly punished. You may not have thought of it in that light, but it's a sneaking, unmanly trick, and marines are supposed to be men, not sneaks."

Private Jones was honest enough to feel the humiliation of this rebuke, but that did not stop the tales he told from being quickly carried to every member of the crew.

Soon after, "all hands" was called. Rifles and ammunition issued to the sailors and word passed that the landing force would sleep under arms until further notice, after which recall sounded and the routine drills were resumed.

Much to the disappointment of the crew, no one was allowed ashore, and though the town did not offer much in the way of diversion or entertainment, it was a new country and a new people for the majority, and all were naturally curious.

On the steep slopes of the hill, rising abruptly from the water's edge, nestled the little town, consisting of one principal street following generally a contour line, while from it on either hand were cobbled lanes and narrow paths with no general symmetry or direction. Back of the town on a spur of the mountain stood the red-walled fort, a winding road leading to its entrance. Barefooted soldiers in red caps and blue denim coats and trousers and armed with nearly every make of antique rifle lined the walls of the fort or marched along the road. At frequent intervals strange calls sounded on high pitched bugles to which no one seemed to pay the slightest attention.

Night fell! A glorious rising moon spread its effulgent rays over a peaceful scene. From the little village on the hillside came the tinkle of guitars, the shouts of playing children. The shore lights twinkled cheerfully, while in a large building a dance was in progress. Added to the moon's brilliancy were the beams of the ship's search-lights constantly moving over woods and town, making objects clear cut and distinct but casting massive black shadows where house or hillock intervened.

"This is the bloodiest war I've ever heard about," said Henry in disgust at the peaceful turn of affairs. "I do wish they'd start something, don't you, Dick?"

Dick glanced about at the sleeping men, their rifles by their sides, canteens and haversacks and bayonets within easy reach, ready for any emergency, but instead of answering he emitted an unintelligible grunt, turned over on his side and was soon asleep.

For two nights peace and quiet. The insurrectos had withdrawn from the near-by hills, so it was reported, but were guarding all the roads and keeping fresh supplies from reaching the inhabitants.

On Wednesday afternoon liberty was granted a limited number of officers and men. Henry, being on duty, was unable to go ashore, so Dick found himself alone soon after his arrival on the beach.

A small hotel attracted most of the men with its one decrepit pool table, tinny piano and refreshment café. The town was a little garden spot, each yard filled with a profusion of flowers. Dick turned to the left at the main street and strolled along in the direction of the consulate. Passing the house, easily the finest residence in sight, he noticed the bright colors of the American flag hanging from the white pole, and on the spacious piazza three children, olive-skinned and dark-eyed, waved their hands in friendly greeting to the young marine. He addressed them in his halting Spanish, but they hung back bashfully, making no reply.

Señor Perez's residence was at the end of the well-kept street on the outskirts of the town. Dick, not noticing where the winding road to the fort branched off, continued into the country before he became aware that the road was little more than a wide trail, which had turned and twisted away from the bay. Occupied with his thoughts, and the tropical vegetation and strange birds on every hand, he had gone much further than was his intention.

He was about to retrace his steps when a woman's scream from around the bend ahead arrested him. Though no words were uttered it was distinctly a call for help, and without a second thought Dick ran towards the spot. Arriving at the bend of the road he saw a young woman in the grasp of two disreputable looking natives, while a few yards beyond a half dozen others with rifles slung over their shoulders were turning off the trail into the dense underbrush.

The leading man of those in the distance carried a struggling child, a girl, in his arms. From where he stood Dick noticed her face was covered with a dirty cloth which stifled any outcry. The two men holding the woman were so occupied in keeping her from breaking away in pursuit of the men with the child, and attempting to gag her, that they were unaware of Dick's timely approach. The fact that the ruffians did not see him favored the attack which the boy delivered silently and swiftly. One of the men was holding the woman's arms while the other, bending, endeavored to bind them behind her with a piece of rope. She twisted her supple body and kicked vigorously with her stout walking shoes.

As Dick reached them he swung his right fist with all his strength on the jaw of the standing man, knocking him senseless to the road. Grabbing the other about the waist he fairly lifted him off the ground and threw him heavily.

Like a cat the native was on his feet. Rushing at Dick with a savage cry he drew back his right arm, in which was a dangerous looking knife. His assailant was within a few feet of him when Dick launched his one hundred and sixty-five pounds of brawn and muscle in a low tackle which did credit to his football training at Bankley. Unaccustomed to such a method of attack, the native had no chance at all, and again he fell to the path, his head striking against a rock; the knife flew from his hand into the bushes, and he lay there motionless.

In another moment Dick was up, and taking the pieces of rope he found near by, he quickly tied both men securely, nor did he do the task at all gently. The man whom Dick had first struck was now groaning, for the terrific blow had fractured his jaw; as for the other, it was not certain in Dick's mind whether he was dead or not, for he had not moved since his second fall.

For the first time Dick looked at the woman whose summons for help he had so effectually answered. To his surprise she was lying in the road, her eyes closed and face deathly pale. What should he do? Was she dead? Had her assailants dealt her some fatal blow? Had he arrived too late to save her?

Kneeling at her side Dick looked anxiously into her face; he felt incompetent to cope with this phase of the situation. She was a comely woman about thirty years of age, her fair complexion and light hair proclaiming her of a northern race. As he watched, the color began slowly returning to the white cheeks. He saw her lips move and bending he caught the one word they uttered:

"Soledad!"

He was still bending over her when the eyelids quiveringly opened and drawing a deep sigh the blue eyes of the woman looked straight up into the dark eyes of the brown-skinned boy, whose straight black hair and aquiline features, now covered in dirt and dust, brought to her mind but one thought--the horrible men who had attacked her. She started to scream, but the unspeakable terror again crept over her and again she fainted.

Dick's mind was working with lightning rapidity. The name "Soledad" must be that of Señor Perez's daughter; this woman must be the new governess! Her two assailants, securely bound, were no longer a menace, but the child was in a dangerous predicament. The German woman would soon regain consciousness and be able to secure help--but Soledad, the little girl already in mortal fear of rebels, who for two years had suffered from a former revolution, what of her? If he returned for help her abductors would be far away by that time. If he set out in pursuit at once he might overtake them and--and what?

He was unarmed! What could he accomplish against so many? Six men had disappeared in the tangle of woods,--there might be more, and those he had seen were armed with rifles. He remembered that point distinctly.

How fast his brain worked!--the pros and cons flashing before his mind's eye with kaleidoscopic clearness, in all their varying positions. Would those who had gone wait for their two comrades?

In that thought was a glimmer of hope, for it might be they were even now waiting not far off. Could he find them? The trail, the country,--all were new to him!

His roving eyes swept the two men lying at the roadside. Here were weapons. He at least would not go unarmed. Rising, he went to the trussed-up men and calmly took from them their revolvers, holsters and ammunition belts. The man with a broken jaw was suffering, but with the stoicism of a brute rather than of a man. From him Dick also removed a two-edged dagger in its sheath, while the fellow glared at him silently. A moment in adjusting his weapons, another to find his campaign hat, a final inspection of the bound legs and arms of the natives, a last look at the woman, who was showing signs of returning consciousness, and he was running off down the road. Not a mad dash such as he made in his attack, but the long swinging stride of the cross-country athlete.

It seemed to Dick as though hours had elapsed, when in reality the minutes had been but few. In the stress of action, when brain and mind, flesh and bone, nerve and muscle, are working in perfect coördination even Time in his flight appears to stop and wait. But Dick's mind was not engaged in thoughts of this character as he turned from the trail and disappeared into the tropical jungle on his precarious errand of mercy.

Fräulein Stauche opened her eyes slowly. She almost feared to do so, for the last thing she remembered were the black eyes of a dirty ferocious native glaring into her own, his face so close she could feel his breath fanning her cheek. This time she saw nothing but the blue sky overhead. The sun, low on the western ridge, would soon sink, bringing a premature twilight hour to the little town nestling at the base of the lofty mountain. The glare, however, hurt her eyes and she closed them. It was easier to collect her thoughts thus. Why was she lying here under the open sky, and who had been the man staring at her when she looked but a second or two ago? Where was Soledad?

Soledad!

The name brought back with such startling poignancy the fearful tragedy through which she had lived that she struggled to her feet and looked about her in fear and trembling. She recalled how, with Soledad holding her hand, they had strolled along this path, when without warning two men sprang at her from the bushes and attempted to gag her, while others, how many she could not remember, grabbed her dainty little charge and ran along the path and disappeared in the thicket, leaving her fighting and struggling. She looked down the trail and caught sight of a man just turning where the others had turned.

What had they done with the child? What should she do? Fear was tugging at her heart and her knees shook with weakness. A movement at the roadside attracted her. She looked. Lying there were two men. They were now still, but the eyes of one were fastened on her. With a scream of terror, Fräulein Stauche turned and ran as fast as she could for the town behind her.

At last the consulate--and from the pole flew the stars and stripes in the evening breeze! Thank the good God that the gray ship was in the harbor. Help would soon be forthcoming, and as she struggled on she prayed it would not come too late.

When the officers reported their divisions at evening quarters on board the *Denver* that night another of the ship's force was among those missing. For Drummer Comstock had already been reported as absent upon the return of the liberty party at five-thirty, but now the Engineer Officer stated that Joe Choiniski had jumped ship.

"How do you think Choiniski got ashore?" asked the Captain of Mr. Ogden.

"The only solution I can offer is that during the noon hour, while the men were buying fruit from the bum-boats, Choiniski secreted himself aboard one of them. He was seen hanging around the port gangway at that hour in dungarees and Chief Master-at-Arms Fitch ordered him below."

"Did he obey the order?"

"Fitch does not know, sir. The Officer of the Deck called him at that second to drive away some bum-boatmen trying to tie up to the starboard gangway, and when he returned Choiniski was gone."

"That coal passer is a bad man, and I hope, now that he's gone, that we have seen the last of him; but, isn't it a strange coincidence that Drummer Comstock did not return on time? Do you attach any significance to that?"

"Oh, no, Captain, Comstock and Choiniski are not in the least friendly. They would not hob-nob together."

"That is not what I mean. I have heard that Choiniski threatened to get even with Comstock on account of the affair in Culebra. I was thinking that he might have made his threat good. I believe him capable of almost any act. I don't like his face."

"Here is Sergeant Douglass, sir; he may give us some information," said Mr. Ogden, and the Captain turned to the old marine.

"Sergeant, what have you heard regarding the actions of Drummer Comstock while on shore?"

"From inquiries, sir, I find he did not stay with the others, but went around town by himself. Some sailors were talking with him in front of the hotel, and they state that he started off for the fort. After he had gone some distance they also decided to visit the fort and followed him, but when they came to the road that leads up the hill they saw him still going along the main road in an easterly direction. They thought he acted queerly in not asking them to accompany him, for they were discussing the matter between them, and when they saw he didn't go towards the fort at all, they decided he must have some reason for not wanting them along. That was the last seen of the boy."

"Thank you, Sergeant, that is all. Let me know if you hear anything further."

"Aye, aye, sir," and Sergeant Douglass saluted and turned away.

"It's after six o'clock, sir, and if that is all for the present I will get ready for mess."

Captain Bentley was about to reply when the Gunner came hurriedly up the ladder and, spying Lieutenant Commander Ogden, he approached and saluted.

"Mr. Ogden, the chief gunner's mate reports to me that two Colt's forty-fives, and a dozen boxes of ammunition have disappeared from the armory since morning quarters. He put the revolvers away himself and locked the door--it is a snap lock--which was still as he left it when he went in the armory a while ago."

"Who has access to the armory, Mr. Nelson?" asked the Captain, and a dark frown appeared on his face. Too many inexplicable things were happening on board his ship this day to suit him, and he was becoming decidedly annoyed.

"I have the only key, sir, and I never allow anyone in the armory except the chief gunner's mate. Whenever he gets through his work there he always brings the key to me. Of course, Mr. Ogden has duplicate keys, as you know, sir."

"Does the chief gunner's mate permit anyone in there?"

"No, sir, I believe he obeys my order to the letter. A few days ago he asked and received permission to allow Drummer Comstock of the marines in there. The boy wanted to familiarize himself with the mechanism of the Colt's machine-gun."

"Hm-m-m-m! What do you think now, Mr. Ogden?" and Captain Bentley gazed scowlingly at the darkening shadows on the mountainside, and the lights appearing, one by one, in the houses ashore.

Even while he looked there came distinctly to his ears the loud:

Sh-h-h-s-h-h! like escaping steam as from the vicinity of the consulate a streak of fire shot into the air. Then came the sound of an explosion, while directly over the ship three green balls of fire cast a ghostly glare on the upturned faces of officers and men.

Señor Perez had called for aid!

CHAPTER XIII

CIRCUMSTANTIAL EVIDENCE

The three green balls of fire floated past the ship and slowly faded away in the heavens. Absolute silence reigned, while those on the *Denver's* deck watched with fascination their weird progress.

From the shore came no sign nor sound of disturbance. No calls, shouts, nor firing of guns. What, then, was the meaning of the rocket?

"It was fired from the consulate," said Captain Bentley. "My agreement with the consul was to send up a rocket in case he absolutely needed assistance, but he is such an excitable individual and his nerves are in such state that he is quite capable of committing any error of judgment."

"The shore looks peaceable enough," remarked Mr. Ogden. "Shall I have the search-lights turned on, sir?"

"Yes, and then I wish you to go ashore and investigate. Take a squad of marines with you and a bugler. If in your estimation an immediate landing is required, he can sound 'call to arms' from the consulate. It will save time. I seriously doubt if there is need of such drastic action."

The search-light beams lighted up the shore while the Captain was speaking and those officers who had binoculars scanned the town for evidences of excitement. A few people strolled about the streets turning their faces from the glare as the travelling rays momentarily flooded them with daytime brilliancy.

"Call away the steamer, Mr. Gardiner, and send word to Sergeant Douglass to have a squad of men and a trumpeter ready to get aboard when she comes alongside. I will go ashore in the same boat," and having given his orders Mr. Ogden disappeared below to get his sidearms.

Ensign Gardiner, Officer of the Deck, issued his orders promptly. In the marine compartment Douglass was besieged with requests from eager marines to be among those landed, but his announcement that Corporal Dorlan's squad was detailed for the duty blasted the hopes of all but the fortunate ones included. Henry Cabell, being the only music left in the guard, was also detailed, and a few minutes later Mr. Ogden followed the last of his guard into the steamer.

"Shove off, coxswain. Take your orders from Mr. Ogden," ordered Mr. Gardiner, and the little steamer started on its way to the landing, full speed ahead.

A little after five o'clock that afternoon Señora Perez awaited the return of the governess and little Soledad. The rebel forces had withdrawn; the American sailors were ashore, and no thought of danger entered her mind. From the high ground of the garden in front of the house she could now see the boats returning to the ship laden down with the liberty party. It was high time for Fräulein to be back.

A sound as of someone trying to lift the latch of the gate came to Señora's ears.

"They have come home," she thought as she turned to watch the entrance, but the next moment, with a cry of apprehension she was running to support the faltering form of the German governess.

"Where is Soledad? Where is my child?" she demanded in a shrill, strange voice.

But Fräulein Stauche was unable to answer. She had reached the limit of her endurance, and she fell into Señora Perez's arms, overcome and speechless.

With the help of servants she was carried into the house and restoratives given. Messengers were sent for the consul and a physician. In the meantime the distracted mother listened to the disconnected words and sentences which told her of her child. Finally the consul arrived and in turn was given the sad news. But all this took time, and nearly three hours had elapsed since Soledad was snatched from the keeping of Fräulein. Unhesitatingly the consul fired the signal which would bring the most efficient aid he could command, and while he watched its gracefully curving arc shooting out over the darkening waters, and the three green balls of fire slowly drift across the bay, he lost all hope of ever seeing his child, for he knew the rebel chief Gonzales whose forces held the approaches to the town and he knew nothing but evil of the man. Waiting there in the darkness he heard the bugle on board ship calling away the boats, bringing aid to his door. He saw the search-lights illuminate the shore line and then he paced from door to gate, back and forth waiting--waiting! No longer a fussy, ridiculous figure, for the despair which gripped his heart lent him a new dignity.

Soon the tramp of men on the macadam road! No native soldiers ever walked with that long swinging stride. He watched them pass beneath a glimmering street light at the corner, "two, four, six, eight," he counted, as the rifle barrels flashed by. What! No more than eight men, when hundreds were needed if ever they hoped to catch Gonzales! Yes, more than hundreds!

Then he saw two more Americans pass the light, one a naval officer in his white uniform. Ah, perhaps this little body was merely an advance guard!

Rushing to the gate, he met Lieutenant Commander Ogden and in the fewest possible words, brokenly related his pitiful story. Meanwhile Dorlan and his men entered the grounds and stood at ease, silently attentive.

"May I see Fräulein Stauche?" asked Mr. Ogden. "Perhaps she may remember more incidents now that she has recovered a little. Does she speak English?"

"Si, Señor[#] Ogden, she speaks four languages fluently. Come this way," and the Consul led the officer to the hysterical governess, and while the questions he asked her were being answered Dorlan stood by listening.

[#] Yes, sir, or master, or mister. Señora is lady, madam, etc. Niña means little girl and niño, little boy.

"Yes, two men first attacked her. No, they were not soldiers. On second thoughts she was positive one with whom she fought was dressed like the American soldiers from the ship. He was the one she remembered bending over her when she recovered consciousness, and now she recalled seeing him run down the road after the others with the child. Yes, he was armed with two revolvers. No, she did not understand why two natives were lying near her on the road--she only remembered seeing the eyes of one of them fastened on her and, becoming terrified, she fled. Not a word had been spoken, but the last man looked like a Spaniard. He was good looking but very dirty."

Mr. Ogden was at a loss as to what action he should take. It was out of the question to send a searching party into the country; in the night they could accomplish nothing. Leaving Dorlan and his men in charge he returned to make his report to Captain Bentley. The Consul had sent word to the Commandant at the fort, but that official said he could not order his men out on such an errand without permission of higher authority. More than likely his men would refuse to go in any case.

"The evidence against Drummer Comstock and Choiniski seems to be growing," said the Captain when Mr. Ogden had ceased speaking as they sat in the cabin, after the Executive's return.

"Yes, it is, startlingly so, for to-night Corporal Dorlan told me that every man on the ship knows the Consul has a large sum of money in his house. I supposed that fact was known only to you, the Consul and myself."

"How did it leak out?"

"Your orderly, Jones, repeated what he had overheard the first day Señor Perez came on board. Both the absentees were present and Choiniski even questioned Jones later regarding the talk. As for the Drummer, Fräulein Stauche describes him very accurately, dark eyes, black hair, dark skin,--you know how tanned he is--and 'dressed like soldiers from the ship.' Comstock claimed he was bound for the fort, and apparently was anxious to be alone, but we know he did not go up there. He was last seen on that very road, and shortly before the attack happened. Dorlan swears that the boy is innocent, and believes he was hurt and possibly is lying on the road wounded or else he has gone in pursuit of the men who abducted the child."

"It is a serious matter," said the Captain. "I dislike to hold a suspicion of the kind against the young marine, but the circumstances are certainly damaging, and there are some points you have overlooked."

"Something derogatory to the marine?"

"Yes. If you recall, he was allowed in the armory as a favor, and to-day two revolvers are missing from there; also the governess says the last man who disappeared had on two revolvers."

"Well, sir, it looks black indeed. If it is true then the rebel leader Gonzales is not the guilty party. But what is the object in taking the child?"

"Having possession of the Consul's daughter and knowing the Consul has a large amount of cash, the object is altogether too plain to admit of error in arriving at a conclusion;--hostage and ransom money, Mr. Ogden! It is Choiniski's idea, and Comstock's help in the matter will make the venture a success. I was cruising in the Mediterranean when the missionary, Miss Stone, was abducted in Turkey. The bandits of the Balkans and of Turkey resort often to this method of procuring funds. Joe Choiniski was born in Krajik, a small village hidden away in the wildest part of the Albanian Mountains. To him this is no horrible thing, as it is to us."

For a while there was silence in the little cabin. Then the Captain continued:

"By morning I think we may have some news. I have no fears for the child's life. She is too valuable alive. Her abductors want money and will find a way to have a message reach her father demanding payment. But nothing can be done to-night."

"One more thing, Captain. I have stated these facts about the young marine, not because I am convinced of his guilt, but because every point having bearing on the case should be weighed. Now, if he is not guilty or implicated, what has become of him? Corporal Dorlan wanted permission to go up the road to where the attack took place and look over the ground. He feels that young Comstock may be lying there in the road and unable to return. He is staunch in his belief in the boy, and if you have no objection I would like to send him on the errand. It could do no harm."

"Is there anyone ashore who can read signals?"

"Almost all the marines are good signalmen, and Trumpeter Cabell is an expert. He can read any kind of a message not in code."

"Very well, send the order, and have Dorlan report by signal immediately upon his return. But he is not to go off the trail nor further than the point mentioned. You say he has a flash-light, and it should be easy to discover traces in the dirt of the roadway."

Trumpeter Cabell felt the importance of his position when, a little later, he began spelling out the message, from the string of red and white lights, sent by Ardois[#] from the *Denver*. Corporal Dorlan took down each letter carefully, for he wanted to make no mistake in his instructions.

[#] "Ardois" lights are used for night signalling in the Navy.

"It's about time they was doin' somethin' regardin' that lad," he mumbled as he wet the stubby pencil in order to write more legibly. "Now, young feller, ye wigwag to the ship, when they throw the light on this balcony and can see yer, that I want 'em to keep that fool search-light away from this place. Every time they shine it over here it puts the whole lot of us in plain view to git shot up by any Spig in the neighborhood. Tell 'em you will signal with a lantern, and we don't want their bloomin' old light around here."

With this parting word the corporal started out on his reconnaissance along the road where the Fräulein had met with her adventure.

There was no moon, and soon the trail turned back from the bay. Here the darkness of the tropical night hung heavily about the little party. The old soldier took no chances in his work, and formed his three-man patrol in accordance with the rules of warfare.

One man marched about fifty yards ahead, the other the same distance in rear of Dorlan. This formation lessened the danger of a surprise, and increased the chances of at least one member of the patrol's escape, if attacked. Dorlan had brought his small flash-light with which to search the ground for clues of any import.

"I know that lad ain't mixed up with that rascal Joe Choiniski," mused Dorlan as he walked, "no matter what the First Lieutenant believes. It's more'n likely he's the very one what knocked out them two fellers what tackled the Dootch girl, and--ah! Here we are!" he exclaimed.

With a low peculiar whistle he halted his men and began a systematic search of the tracks in the dusty path.

"Here's where the Dootch girl fainted, and here's where the shoe marks show the scrimmage took place. These tracks were made by government issue shoes and were worn by a marine. The imprint of the strap of the leggin' is plain as the nose on yer face. Them's Dick Comstock's tracks; and it's as I says,--he's gone after them greasers for sure. Hello, what's this? The grass and bushes all bendin'. Ah, ye dirty Dago ye. I've got ye. Come back here, Smithers, and help untie these two fellers. We'll take 'em back and see what they've got to say for themselves. And I guess that's about all I can do this night, accordin' to me orders."

And back over the trail to the consulate went the patrol to deliver their two prisoners and make their report. But if the natives knew anything, they refused to talk, and the whereabouts of little Soledad and Drummer Comstock still remained an unsolved mystery.

CHAPTER XIV

DICK MAKES THE ACQUAINTANCE OF COLUMBUS

Lieutenant Commander Ogden's surmise as to the manner in which Joe Choiniski jumped ship was correct, but as to the theft of the revolvers, which he was inclined to fasten on Drummer Comstock, was not.

Just before the noon hour Choiniski, happening by the armory and finding the door ajar, entered, confiscated the weapons and ammunition and with them tucked inside his dungaree jumper left the place, snapping the lock after him; he was unseen by any of his shipmates.

Since the *Denver's* arrival off Sanchez, he had been bargaining with the bumboatmen to secrete him and take him ashore in one of their boats, but they would not risk the chance of discovery without payment, and having lost all his money by sentence of the court-martial, Choiniski was without funds, nor could he borrow any sum sufficient to tempt their cupidity. That noon, however, when he promised a Colt's forty-five together with cartridges in payment, the bargain was consummated.

Choiniski had visited the Samana Bay ports previously while attached to his former ship, and on one occasion he met the man Gonzales, a Spanish-negro stevedore in the employ of the German concern owning the one and only wharf. Gonzales was now in command of the rebel forces holding the roads leading into the town, and Joe felt sure his information regarding the large sum of money in the consulate would be a certain means of securing for him an established position with the rebel chief. His familiarity with the language and his experience, not only in the Navy but with the armed forces in the Balkans a few years before, was enough to make him at least second in command if he worked his wires properly in dealing with the rebels.

Within an hour after reaching the shore he was talking with Gonzales.

"And how much money do you say Señor Perez has in his house?" asked the general.

"Many thousands of dollars. I do not know the exact amount, but enough to keep us both comfortably for many years," answered Choiniski.

"How do you propose getting it?"

"It should be easy," said Joe. "To-night we will go to his house and demand it. The Consul will answer our summons. We shall prevent him from sending any message or signal to the ship. If he does not give us the money and if we cannot find it on searching the house, we will take his daughter as a hostage.

It is said he loves her more than anything else. Having her in our possession he will pay up promptly."

"Your idea is good, Señor. Now I must get my brother, Alfredo, to assist us. I do not trust these men with me on such work. They would want too much for their share. My brother is in command of an outpost on the Camino Real not far from the consulate. I will go to him at once. In the meantime, Señor, await my return. Adios!"

And off went the chief to consult with his brother, commanding a half dozen picked men in hiding on the road along which Soledad and the Fräulein, who was a stranger and who did not understand the danger, were even then strolling.

Gonzales had no intention of permitting anyone but himself to reap the benefit of the news confided to him by the deserter from the Yankee ship. Least of all did he intend that Choiniski should be a gainer thereby. The plan was excellent, but the sailor would never see a peso of that wealth stored in the house of Señor Perez.

Before leaving camp Gonzales gave orders to disarm the sailor and hold him a prisoner.

"We do not need his help," said he, after having outlined the plan to his brother. "How do I know that it is not all a clever scheme to catch me! Perhaps it is a spy who has come among us."

"Hush! Hermano mio!" said Alfredo, and he gazed up the road intently. "Ah! We are indeed fortunate, for here comes the Señorita Soledad and her duenna, along the trail. Good luck is with us! You will take the niña, while Juan Mendoza and I secure the woman. We will carry her into the hills with us and at nightfall set her free. She will be unable to find her way back until morning. You and the rest of my men will carry the child to camp and leave her. To-night we will make our attempt to get the money after the Yankee sailors sleep. Then, before they can do anything, we have the money and are gone."

This was agreed to and it was with great satisfaction that Alfredo, a little later, saw his brother, Fernando, disappear in the bush carrying the child and followed by his erstwhile soldiers. But the duenna was putting up such a desperate struggle that he was glad indeed Juan was there to aid him.

As the rascal pinned Fräulein's arms behind her, his black eyes sparkled with happy anticipation of the prosperous days of joyous living about to be his. He grew careless in his efforts to hold the governess, and in the one instant her mouth was freed she had called loudly for help. But this made little difference. No one dared to leave the town these days with General Gonzales' band of insurrectos holding the roads, and----

Then came the crashing blow of a hard fist on his jaw and for a time he knew nothing more. As for Juan, though taken by surprise and thrown heavily to the path, he was quick to attack on his own account, but with the result that has been told.

When Juan recovered his senses darkness had fallen. His chief, Alfredo, was endeavoring to untie the cords which bound him, but to no avail. They turned on their sides, and back to back, worked at the knots, each trying to assist the other. Then their quick ears heard footfalls of someone approaching from the town, and fearful of discovery they rolled over and over in the grass and shrubs, away from the trail, only to be discovered eventually by Dorlan and his men and marched back to the consulate as prisoners.

Corporal Dorlan's request regarding the searchlight had been observed and the consulate was in darkness when the reconnoitering party returned. It was then decided to hold the prisoners until morning before turning them over to the military authorities and by the time the final message to that effect was exchanged with the ship, "taps" had sounded over the quiet waters, and the crew settled down to a night's rest. However, many discussions were being carried on in an undertone regarding the circumstances connected with Dick Comstock's absence and Joe Choiniski's "jumping ship." In spite of Sergeant Douglass' warning another orderly had violated his confidential position and the news was common property throughout the cruiser. Most of Dick's ultimate friends were indignant at hearing the story, but the majority were inclined to regard his actions as suspicious and proclaimed him guilty.

How fortunate it was that the object of all this commotion was unaware of the nature of these rumors flying among his shipmates, for had he known of them his brain would not have been so free to grapple with the task he had set out to accomplish.

Soon after turning from the trail he was following at a discreet distance the six men carrying off little Soledad.

How should he go about getting the child? He must take no chances, because to do so might mean his own capture and but add to the child's troubles; so he carefully trailed along behind her abductors, waiting for some circumstance which would assist him in solving his problem.

That the men did not intend to wait for their two accomplices was evident, for they proceeded through the forest without a backward glance. All the time Dick was drawing nearer to them, but as he was forced to make his way warily, and often off the poor trail, he was seriously handicapped.

Finally the men with the child emerged from the woods into a clearing in which was situated the barrio[#] where Gonzales made his headquarters. A dozen or more houses and shacks along either side of the road afforded shelter for his troops, about one hundred in number. A few native women, and dirty, half-naked children could be seen, while the barking of several mangy canines filled the air.

[#] Barrio--Small collection of houses.

Beyond the houses on the far side of the road were a few scraggly bushes, and a thick grove of cocoanut trees filled the space to the shore of the Bay. Here some native boats were drawn up on the beach out of sight of the water, and in the grove small groups of rebel soldiers were engaged in various pursuits.

Perforce, Dick was obliged to stop on the edge of the woods and watch General Gonzales and his small band cross the clearing and enter the largest house on the far side of the road. Dick crouched down in a thick bed of ferns and studied the situation, keeping close tab on the incidents taking place before him and waiting for the darkness which would soon fall. That the rebels were carefully guarding the road was evidenced by the little groups of men, to be observed about one hundred yards from either end of the barrio, who halted all persons approaching.

Near Dick's refuge was a well which supplied the drinking water for the community, and frequent visits to this well were made by men, women and children.

It was nearly dusk when a small native boy came bounding out of the quarters of General Gonzales, and the General himself appeared in the dimly lighted doorway. That he had been chastising the urchin was evident from the way the boy rubbed his shoulders and from his loud lamentations as he stood at a safe distance and observed the rebel leader.

"Here you rascal, you! Be quiet, or I will beat you more. Go and bring me some fresh water at once, or you will be sorry your namesake ever discovered this island," and with the words Gonzales threw a battered pail at the boy.

"Come now, hurry, you imp of Satan;" with that the General entered the house and closed the door.

Painfully the boy picked up the pail and approached the well. Dick could hear his sobs as he drew near. Arriving at the well he made no attempt to draw the water but stood looking back in the direction of the house. Finally he shook his small hand in a gesture which Dick's knowledge of West Indian customs told him implied contempt and insult, and from the boy's rapid speech Dick heard enough to convince him that here was a possible ally, could he but win the native lad's confidence.

With a sibilant hiss Dick attracted the boy's attention, but though he looked about him in some fear he was unable to discover who called.

"Quien habla?"[#] he questioned, still looking about him.

[#] Who speaks?

"Un amigo: un Americano,"[#] answered Dick, and then before the boy had time to make an outcry he spoke again.

[#] A friend, an American.

"Do you want to make plenty of money, muchacho?"[#]

[#] Spanish for boy.

The boy had now located Dick's hiding-place and he approached warily.

"How can I make plenty of money?" he questioned in a dubious tone.

"If you will help me, I will see that you get it, and also I will see that the big man is punished for beating you."

The boy was by this time squatting down on his haunches within a few feet of Dick and even in the dusk, Dick could see the eyes flash with anger at the mention of the past incident.

"But what can you, an American, do against General Gonzales, and all his soldiers? Everyone here fears him! Even my father grovels at his feet, and my mother must do as he says. He will kill my father and my mother and me some day, I fear, when he becomes angered. He is a big chief. I am afraid to do aught against him."

"There will be no danger if you do as I will suggest and----"

At that moment the door of the General's house was thrown open, and again the figure of the chief was framed in the lighted doorway.

"Columbus! Columbus! Come here at once!" roared the harsh voice across the clearing.

"I must go, or he will send the soldiers for me. But I will return," said the lad, rising, and quickly filling the pail he ran back across the clearing.

CHAPTER XV

THE ESCAPE FROM THE BARRIO

In an incredibly short time Columbus was back, and this time he nursed a large bruise on the side of his head where the General's cane had fallen with no light force.

"If my father were able to fight he would kill that nigger," exclaimed the excited lad. "But my father was crippled in the last revolution. That general, he makes our house his own. He makes my mother to cook for him and to wash for him. We could not leave my father when the rebels occupied the barrio. We had to stay to look out for him. They eat our food and kill our pigs and chickens, and never pay. They----"

"Is your name Columbus?" inquired Dick in order to cut short the boy's tale of trials and tribulations.

"Si, Señor."

"Well, Columbus, here are two brand new Americano pesos for you, and there will be many more if you do as I tell you," and Dick passed over the silver coins.

"What must I do?"

"First of all tell me how many soldiers are in the barrio."

"Over one hundred, Señor."

"How far is it from here to Sanchez?"

"By the shore road it is nearly three kilometers. The shore road passes through the barrio," said the lad.

"Is the road guarded by more soldiers than the group of men I could see before dark on the outskirts of the town?"

"Oh, yes, Señor, they patrol the entire road every night. The big light from the ship does not frighten them."

"Can you see the ship from the beach back of your house, Columbus?"

"No, a point of land prevents that, but it is not far by boat,--a little over a kilometer."

"Who is in your house with the General?"

"The five soldiers who came with him this afternoon, my mother and father and a little girl the general stole from her people. I do not know her name.

She weeps all the time, but makes no noise. He has told her he will kill her if she tries to run away."

"Columbus, I want to get the little girl out of that house and return her to her father and her mother. If you help me they will pay you well."

"It is impossible, Señor. I overheard the General making plans to go to Sanchez and attack the house of her father to-night, and he gave his men orders to guard the child carefully. There are to be men both inside and outside the house all the time."

"Would your father and mother help us?"

"No, Señor, they could not afford to. They would fear to go contrary to General Gonzales' orders."

"At what hour does the General start for the town?"

"Very soon, for he expects to be there by ten o'clock, Señor."

"Are there any small boats on the beach?"

"Oh, yes, and the best canoe there is my own."

"Providing I get the little girl out of the house, will you go in the canoe with me to the American ship?"

"No, Señor, I am afraid; but I will place paddles in my canoe and I will do what else I can to assist you. My canoe is the last one on the beach nearest the town."

"Describe your house, Columbus. Where are the windows and doors?"

"That reminds me, Señor--after all, I can help you. If you approach our casa from the rear you will find a little cocina[#] which opens into the middle room. My father and mother occupy the room on the right as you enter from the cocina. My room was on the left, but it is now the General's, and the little girl is lying in there now, weeping. Long ago I loosened a board at the side near the cocina so that it will slide back, and I used it to go out when my parents believed me asleep. I will tell the child about you and the hole and she can escape that way. First I will put my paddles in the canoe, and then you can take her in it to your ship. Keep close to the shore until you are around the point, then go direct to the vessel. There are no shoals to fear. The only thing to be careful about is passing through the cocoanut grove. Avoid the hut, for soldiers are guarding a prisoner there also."

[#] Cocina--Kitchen.

"Another prisoner? A native?" questioned Dick.

"No, he is a sailor who ran away from your ship and came here shortly after noon to-day, and he told the General about the money and the little girl. But the General had him imprisoned, for he distrusts him and he had the sailor's pistol and ammunition seized."

"Did you hear the name of the sailor, Columbus?"

"Yes, Señor, his name is José. He is a dark man and very dirty, and wears peculiar blue clothes."

"Joe Choiniski, or I miss my guess!" exclaimed Dick as he looked towards the lights flickering through the grove on the far side of the road.

"Can you get me some meat, Columbus?" Dick asked, after a brief pause.

"Has the Señor hunger?"

"No, I don't wish it for myself, but there are many dogs in the barrio, and when they discover me they will betray me to the soldiers if I come near the houses. With the meat I could quiet them."

"Never fear, amigo mio; all the meat in this village would not be enough to satisfy the appetite of the dogs in the barrio nor keep them quiet. They are ever barking and fighting at night, so the soldiers would not think it strange, especially in the early part of the evening. If that is all, Señor, I will go, for the General may miss me. What time shall I tell the niña to be ready for you?"

"Tell her to wait for three knocks on the wall of her room from the side of the cocina, after the General leaves the house. Then she must slide back the board and I will be waiting for her in the cocina. Make her understand I am her friend and will take her back to her people. And, Columbus, here is all the money I have with me, but I will see that you are rewarded later on, if you carry out our plan," and Dick pressed all his remaining currency into the hands of the boy crouching by his side.

"Thank you, Señor, but I cannot take this money. I am a common peon and my people are poor, but they would not wish to accept money to help a little girl in distress," and Columbus bravely handed back the bills to Dick, though his fingers were itching to keep them.

He made his little speech with such an air of pride, however, that Dick did not insist and with a low whispered, "adios, amigo mio," the brown boy was swallowed up a moment later in the shadows and darkness.

Impatiently Dick waited in his refuge for the departure of General Gonzales on his proposed expedition. Finally becoming tired of such long inactivity he arose and boldly stepped out into and across the clearing. Dick reasoned that in the darkness of the night should he pass anyone inside the camp he would not be recognized nor suspected. He pulled his khaki shirt outside his trousers so as to appear more in keeping with the native soldiers' costume should he happen to meet anyone.

With rapid strides he was soon in the vicinity of the houses lining the near side of the road. The barking of a dog at his approach caused him a little nervousness, but he kept on, remembering what Columbus had told him. Another dog came sniffing and growling at his heels. He paused long enough to kick the canine and it scampered away with shrill yelps of pain and fright.

The following moments were the most thrilling of Dick's life. Turning, after delivering the kick which sent the cur scampering off in the darkness, he almost ran into a man.

"Get out of my way, you spawn," said a voice which he recognized as none other than that of General Gonzales. "Why are you on this side of the road, anyway, when I told you to guard my quarters? Go over there where you belong, and let the dogs bark as much as they please, but attend to your duties, or it will fare badly with you in the morning. Obey me, pronto!" and the rebel chief shoved Dick out into the wide street.

How grateful Dick was that no answers were required of him, otherwise he might have been discovered. He did not know now whether or not Gonzales was following after him, and he feared to turn and look. He could hear no footfalls. Now directly in front of him and not fifteen feet distant was the house where Soledad was held a prisoner. According to Columbus, and this was already verified by the remark of Gonzales, there was a sentry guarding the house, and somewhere in the shadows ahead that native soldier was walking. What if he was waiting to attack Dick on his nearer approach? Perhaps he had heard the chief talking to Dick on the opposite side of the road and was watching his movements with catlike eyes. Dick's ears detected no sound as he drew nearer the house. Now he was within a few feet of the walls. The next moment he dodged around the corner of the building, and just in the nick of time, for, as he did so, the front door was thrown open and the light from the interior streamed into the street. Flattening himself against the wall Dick peered around cautiously. Before the door stood Gonzales, while emerging from it were five men, presumably those who had accompanied their leader from the outpost on Camino Real.

"Everything is ready," announced the General. "Come, let us go. The others have already started, and we must not delay." The party moved off down the road in the direction of Sanchez, and once again quiet reigned in the immediate vicinity. Dick now knew the time for action had arrived. Forgetting for the moment that he had to deal with the sentinel who was supposed to be here on duty he was about to step out in the direction of the cocina when he observed the dim moving figure of a soldier coming from the rear of the house.

Slowly the soldier sauntered towards Dick until he arrived so near that the boy could have touched him. Here the man stopped. Dick's heart thumped so violently from the suspense that it almost seemed the soldier could not fail to hear it. The noise pounded in his own ears like the striking of a bass drum. It was so dark that he could not see what the sentry was doing. Perhaps the eyes of the native, more accustomed to darkness than Dick's own, were even then fastened on him and enjoying his discomfort, perhaps----

A rattling noise assailed Dick's ears. It was the sound made by safety matches shaken in a partially empty box. The sentry had seen him, but now was going to strike a light in order to discover his identity.

The match scraped along the box, but made no spark. At the second attempt the yellowish flame flared up. In its light the dark brown face of the soldier stood out boldly in the Stygian darkness. A white papered cigarette was between the fellow's lips and his dark eyes were bent solely on the flame, seeing nothing else. The flame wavered, then there was the sound of a dull blow, the light disappeared and the sentinel sank to the ground. Once again Dick Comstock's hard fist had found a victim, and once again he was binding and gagging a rebel soldier.

Dick used his own regulation belt to make fast his victim's arms, while the soldier's belt sufficed to secure his legs. Pulling the native's shirt over his head Dick stuffed part of it in his mouth and bound it there with a handkerchief. In the darkness it was difficult work, but he did the best he could, and after dragging the soldier to one side and under a bush, the drummer boy began to feel his way towards the cocina at the rear. A dim light, shining through the cracked walls of the center room, saved him from stumbling into a collection of pots and pans in the small lean-to, which Columbus had dignified by the name of kitchen. Creeping cautiously to the wall of the building under the lean-to, the lad rapped the boards three times, giving the signal agreed upon. Then he waited breathlessly for some response. Finally he heard the scraping of one board on another. The noise came from near the floor where he was waiting. Then he saw the white figure of little Soledad squirm through the opening. Quietly he assisted her to her feet and without a word, hand in hand, the two stole from the house and out into the grove in the direction of the bay.

They had gone about fifty feet when another figure suddenly confronted them, and again Dick's heart seemed to jump to his throat while his right hand sought the pistol hanging at his side.

"Silence, Señor, it is Columbus. I have come to help you find the canoe. Follow me, carefully, for we are near the house where the sailor is imprisoned," and on the little party went like flitting shadows through the grove.

Soon came the soft rustle of waves on the shore, and emerging from under the dense overhead foliage of the palms, objects were more distinguishable. They found the canoe, and in it the paddles which the faithful native boy had previously placed there. Dick took his place in the stern, the little girl tremblingly, but with no hesitation, sat in the bottom. Then with a whispered "buenas noches,"[#] Columbus shoved the frail craft from the sands out into the waters of the great bay, and with a happy heart Dick sent the canoe on its way with long powerful strokes.

[#] Buenas noches--Good-night.

CHAPTER XVI

THE ATTACK ON THE CONSULATE

Corporal Dorlan on making the rounds of his little force shortly after taps noticed the Ardois lights from the *Denver* were flashing regularly. Not being an adept signalman he sought Trumpeter Cabell, who was trying to snatch a little sleep on the back piazza of the consulate, and shook him into wakefulness.

"Come, me lad, shake a leg, for the ship is callin' of us, and I want ye to read the message."

"Be with you in a jiffy," said Henry, going to get the lantern, which he had already put to good use in the earlier part of the evening.

Soon he was acknowledging the call, and the message Corporal Dorlan noted down as Henry called off the letters caused the veteran many a chuckle of satisfaction. It was a long message, and immediately it was finished Dorlan and Henry shook hands over it in great glee.

"I knew that lad would turn the trick, and come out on top," remarked the older man as he entered the house in search of Señor Perez.

In the center of the building was a room, which, because of past revolutions, the Consul had prepared against the chance of stray bullets. It was but a makeshift affair, but it had served its purpose on many occasions, and during times of danger the family always occupied it. Around the walls of this compartment rows of iron-wood railroad ties were placed from the floor to ceiling and these tough native timbers could be counted upon to stop the leaden bullets used in the guns with which the opposing factions were generally armed. Corporal Dorlan's knock at the door of the "strong room," as it was called, was immediately answered by the Consul.

"'Tis the 'best of news I have for ye, sir," he said, and his face shone with delight. "Yer little daughter is safe and sound aboard the *Denver*. It seems that our drummer boy, Dick Comstock, followed them rascals what stole her, and he's just now got her away from 'em and is back on the ship. After ye give yer wife the good news I've got somethin' important to tell ye, and the quicker the sooner, sir." With that the thoughtful fellow closed the door and impatiently awaited the Consul's reappearance.

Soon the little man came out and, running up to Dorlan, he embraced the marine in true European fashion by kissing him on both cheeks, much to the old fellow's embarrassment.

"Your good tidings have made me the happiest man in the world, whereas, but a short time since, I was the most miserable," said the Consul, and he again threatened Dorlan with another exhibition of his enthusiasm, but this time the marine evaded it.

"That's all right, yer honor, but we can't be talkin' of that now. There's other doin's afoot this night, and with yer help we can do a neat stroke of work to cap the climax of this day's excitement."

Thereupon he outlined his plan, and an understanding having been reached Señor Perez returned to his wife, while Dorlan made mysterious visits to each member of his little force. He then distributed them to his satisfaction about the house and grounds. All the lights were extinguished except a low-burning lamp in the spacious hallway, and then he sat down to wait behind the closed front door, much as a cat sits before the mouse hole she knows will soon be the scene of some lively action.

Since the end of the message from the ship not a light other than the usual anchor lights could be discerned by the closest observer on the shore. Nor could activity of any kind be noted, but as a matter of fact khaki-clad marines were even then silently embarking in one of the cutters and under muffled oars were pulling towards the landing pier. And from the opposite side of the ship three boat-loads of bluejackets were as silently doing the same thing--but, pulling in the opposite direction, en route to a little barrio less than three kilometers down the coast.

General Fernando Gonzales at the head of his picket force of thirty men halted on the beach road and looked out over the waters at the ship. He heard the beautiful notes of the bugle sounding the soldiers and sailors good-night, and he saw the lights, which had been flickering at the masthead for so long, cease punctuating the darkness. With their cessation he felt reasonably certain that the crew had a feeling of security, and that they felt that everything ashore must be going well, for the big search-light was not shining as on previous nights. He did not understand the meaning of the red and white lights, nor know that they were just finishing a message regarding his whereabouts at that very moment. Such signals were unknown in the armies of San Domingo.

Already the people of Sanchez were closing their doors and windows; soon the streets would be deserted. Leaving his men concealed, General Gonzales ventured forth in the direction of the consulate for a little preliminary scouting. It was high time his brother and Juan Mendoza were at the rendezvous, but their non-arrival caused him no great uneasiness. The street before the Consul's home was also deserted, and he approached the place boldly. As he passed the gate the lights in the house were turned out,--the family of Señor Perez had retired. A few yards beyond the last few members of the Club were closing the door and leaving for their homes. He decided to wait no longer. Calling his men, he soon stationed them in the hedge and shrubbery surrounding the consulate, then with his chosen half dozen villains he approached the front entrance and mounting the broad piazza he knocked loudly. Finally the door opened a few inches and the face of Señor Perez appeared.

"Who are you, and what do you want at this hour of the night?" said the Consul in a voice he tried hard to control.

"I wish to talk with you, Señor, on a matter of great importance to us both. Let me in."

"Who are you?" again came in inquiry, though the father knew well that this was the man who had caused him so much heartache that day.

"I am General Fernando Gonzales, and if you do not admit me without further talk I will shoot you," and a long-barreled revolver was shoved ominously through the opening into the face of the consul, who fell back into the dimly lighted hall. In a moment the General and six followers rushed in, well pleased over the success of their operations thus far.

Was it a sudden draft of wind which closed the door so softly behind them? Gonzales never had time nor thought to inquire, for suddenly the large room became a blaze of light, and he found himself staring into the leveled muzzles of six gun barrels in the hands of Dorlan's men.

"Hands up, ye spalpeens!" called out the voice of the Corporal, and though not a man there understood his words they did understand the menace in the voice, and in a twinkling there were fourteen dirty brown and black hands held tremblingly aloft.

"HANDS UP!"

"HANDS UP!"

"Take them guns and knives, and throw them in the corner, me lad," now ordered Dorlan, and Henry began to disarm the rebels. It was then that the leader Gonzales, knowing what would be his fate if he were turned over to the government troops, made a break for liberty.

Although he put up his hands with the rest he still held in his right hand the revolver he had carried on entering. Now with a wild yell the negro half-breed fired one shot into the air, another in the general direction of the Consul, and as he dashed for a window near by he fired the remaining four shots at the marines lined up across the hall. On reaching the window he unhesitatingly jumped through the flimsy lattice work which guarded it, and was running across the lawn before the house.

The sudden attack of the negro so surprised most of the marines, who were not looking for any active resistance after the men had thrown up their hands, that there was an appreciable moment of inactivity which held back their fire.

But not so with Henry, for with the first shot of the rebel chief, the trumpeter had pulled his automatic from the holster, and as Gonzales jumped through the window he fired two shots.

One of those bullets found a resting place in the fleshy part of the native's leg. The impetus of Gonzales' rush carried him on, but now he stumbled and called upon his followers hidden in the bushes to come to his assistance. Again he stumbled, this time falling headlong into a flower bed. As he attempted to rise, a figure in khaki rose in front of him; there was the flash of a clubbed rifle, then the weapon descended with crushing force on the general's skull, and he sank to the ground. The days of General Fernando Gonzales as a rebel chief were ended.

From all sides came a fusillade of shots. The bullets tore their way through wooden walls or spattered on the tin roof of the building, but harmed no one. From the fort on the hill came the sound of high pitched bugles sounding the alarm, while flashes of light and the sound of guns showed the government troops were as usual wasting ammunition by firing at nothing in particular and everything in general.

Then a red star shot up from the main road a little to the west of the consulate; there came a rush of heavy shoes on the macadam, a rattle of accoutrements, and First Sergeant Douglass at the head of the remainder of the *Denver's* guard charged down the road. Again the search-light of the ship flooded the shore and then, without waiting to see what had befallen their leader, the rebels took to their heels and fled.

It was daylight before the excitement in the town subsided, but by then it was known that the hold of the rebels over the inhabitants was effectually broken. The General was dead, his brother, his lieutenant, Juan Mendoza, and the six others were turned over to the custody of the Federal troops. As for those rebels in camp at the barrio, they too had been dispersed, for when the landing party of sailors, guided by Dick, reached the shore near the barrio and demanded the surrender of the deserter Choiniski they fled incontinently, fearing an attack from the Americanos, which they did not relish.

When a search of the barrio and the hut in the grove was made it was found that Joe had either taken the opportunity to escape or the rebels had taken him with them into the hills, for the place was deserted. The only persons remaining behind were the native boy Columbus, his crippled father and his mother. On learning how well the urchin had assisted Dick, and how the rebels had treated the poor peons, a very substantial purse was collected by the kind-hearted men and presented to the lad's mother, and the landing party was then towed back to the ship.

It was Dick Comstock's privilege to escort little Soledad ashore at an hour shortly after sunrise, and though Señor Perez was too much overcome to thank the rescuer of his favorite, Dick felt fully rewarded just to witness that joyful reunion.

Reports now began coming in from all points that the revolution was toppling, and soon those who were still under arms were pleading to be allowed to surrender and go to their homes and former occupations. Orders also came for the *Denver* to leave Sanchez and proceed on a surveying trip near the border line dividing San Domingo and Haiti, and incidentally to watch for some smuggling reported to be carried on extensively in that vicinity.

The day of departure arrived. In the afternoon a shore boat came alongside carrying Señor Perez, his wife, children and the governess. Captain Bentley met the party at the gangway, and after a few words he gave orders that the crew be assembled aft. When all had gathered there in the shade of the awnings, Captain Bentley stepped forward and called for Richard Comstock of the United States Marine Corps to come to the mast. Then in behalf of the Consul, his family and the governess, the Captain presented the drummer boy with a beautiful gold wrist watch, appropriately engraved, which the grateful donors had ordered by cable from New York City and which the Clyde Liner had but that morning delivered.

Dick felt that he should make some reply, but for the life of him he was unable to utter a single word. Suddenly there was a patter of light feet on the white deck and to his relief Soledad rushed forward. As he bent to take the child's hand, she threw her arms around his neck and kissed him squarely on the lips. The look of amazement now on Dick's face was so great that the entire assembly roared with laughter, and Chief Master-at-Arms Fitch, regulations to the contrary notwithstanding, called out:

"Three cheers for our Drummer Boy and the girls he rescued."

They were given with a will, for now there was no longer doubt as to the loyalty, faithfulness or bravery of Richard Comstock.

CHAPTER XVII

A MAP-MAKING EXPEDITION

"I consider that we are the two luckiest youngsters in the service, Dick. What do you think about it?"

Henry looked about him at the surrounding country, a combination of river scenery, swamp land, tropical jungle and lush savannahs, with an appraising eye.

The two boys stood on the rickety landing near the Captain of the Port's house at the mouth of the Estero Balsa, a branch body of water communicating with Manzanillo Bay, where the *Denver* was anchored, and where certain members of her officers and crew were engaged in making a chart of the coast line, river deltas and numerous lagoons.

It was interesting work for those so engaged, and each day the various boats of the ship started at an early hour taking lines of soundings from one point to another, measuring angles, plotting positions, sketching in prominent features, or locating reefs and shoals. At night they combined their data, and with compass and rule worked over the smooth copy of the chart which would be sent to the Department at Washington when complete and eventually supplied to each ship of the Navy cruising in these waters.

Having received permission from the Navigating Officer, Dick often accompanied the chart makers on their expeditions, and, always eager to learn, he proved himself a valuable helper with compass or sextant, in taking angles, both vertical and horizontal, and working them out.

Also at night the *Denver's* boats were engaged in other and more exciting work. Owing to various causes there was a systematic smuggling going on between the two island republics. Small sailing vessels and motor launches were suspected of carrying contraband merchandise back and forth across the Bay at night, and organized bands of smugglers made the passage of the Massacre River from its mouth up to and beyond the San Domingan town of Dajabon, on its eastern bank, and the Haitian village of Ouanaminthe, directly opposite. The customs officers were doing their best, but they were too few in number to cope with the situation. In consequence money was being lost to both governments. The United States was administering the customs affairs of San Domingo, and the Navy had to be called in at times to aid in putting a stop to this illegal traffic.

The presence of the *Denver* had its salutary effect, and the smuggling by day in the boats had practically ceased, but at night activity was resumed. Consequently the ship's boats, which during the day were engaged in the aforesaid work of surveying, became at night a fleet of armed patrols with certain definite sectors to cover. Many exciting chases resulted in the overhauling, arrest, and, occasionally, resistance and escape of the venturesome smugglers.

The marines were often detailed for this night work in the patrol boats, and they enjoyed it, for there was always a chance of a lively little "scrap," and that is what marines enlist for--scrapping.

All articles coming across the border were supposed to be entered at Dajabon, and after customs dues were adjusted the goods were sent to other points along the only really passable road which led through Copey, a town at the headwaters of the Estero Balsa, thence to Monte Cristi or towns and cities of La Vega Real.

Somewhere in the dense jungle between Dajabon and the office of the Captain of the Port, where the two boys were now engaged in conversation, were trails unknown to the general public, and these trails the smugglers used for their purposes. As charts made by naval officers usually show but little of the interior terrain it was not the intention of Captain Bentley to include any roads on the map his officers were engaged in compiling. However, if Dick and Henry succeeded in getting information of value it was decided that their work should be incorporated with the rest. Both boys had studied surveying while at school, and early on the cruise they had secured a volume on Military Topography and spent many hours in acquiring a thorough knowledge of what was needed in a military map. First Sergeant Douglass, seeing how they desired to get ahead and only too glad to give them something to keep them out of mischief (for musics are generally conceded by all hands to be mischievous), allowed them to have a cavalry sketching case from his storeroom, and with this they became quite expert in making position-sketches and road-maps.

In response to Henry's question, Dick finally replied:

"Yes, I think we are lucky, but it's not going to be an easy task, Hank."

"Right you are, Dickie. This country is all swamps and jungle, with few trails really leading anywhere. I believe it is going to be a difficult proposition to cover the entire area between this place, Copey and Dajabon, in time to be back and meet the steamer in three days."

"Let's not count up the obstacles, though, Hank. We will meet them as they come in the best way we can. We are handicapped by being obliged to do the work secretly. Captain Bentley impressed that upon me. You know, since we were so lucky in the Culebra and Sanchez affairs he has come to regard us as older than we are and capable of a man's work, and with a man's reasoning powers and discretion. I'm not so sure of it myself; but it certainly is up to us to make good now that the opportunity has come our way."

"Tell me just how we happened to get here, Dick. I've been so busy getting things together since you sprung the surprise this morning that I've not had time to question you."

"Well, it was this way! Last night I was out in the steamer on patrol work. Mr. Gardiner was in command. About midnight one of the lookouts thought he spotted a motor boat moving in from the west. We gave chase, but as often happens it was a false alarm and the lookout was conjuring things from being so anxious to see something.

"Well, after it quieted down, Mr. Gardiner began talking about the chart, and how it would aid the ships to be stationed here later on in searching out smugglers. Then he said it was too bad the trails between the coast line, Dajabon and Copey couldn't be sketched in on the map, particularly as one of the ship's boats was to get the data of the Massacre River the following day. With that, and all the trails in between, the map would be of much greater value, he thought. The trouble was, they didn't have enough officers to do the additional work and get through in time, for we are expecting orders to leave here most any day now."

"I reckon you didn't let that opening get by you, Dick," Henry remarked.

"You just bet I didn't. I said that I thought you and I could do it if the Captain would allow us, and told him how much we'd like to try it."

"What did he say?"

"Well, he said, 'Maybe you could,' and he mentioned that First Sergeant Douglass had shown him one of the road maps we made together, last winter while at Culebra, and then the subject was dropped. But this morning Top told me the skipper wished to see me in the cabin at once, and when I reported Mr. Gardiner was in there, and the Captain told me what was wanted, and that I might go ashore and try my luck. He said I should have to go on what was ostensibly a hunting trip, and that I should probably get into trouble with the authorities if they discovered what I was up to."

"Did you ask if I might come along?"

"Of course! I told him we had worked together on road sketches and showed him that one we made of the road from Playa Brava to the old naval station. He seemed satisfied with the work, but then he began to doubt if it were wise to let two kids such as we are go on such an errand."

"He surely put enough restrictions on us," said Henry.

"Oh, not so many, Hank, and they are all wise provisions."

"But why is it necessary that we should return each night to this place? Why can't we stay where we happen to be when night comes, then continue our work next day right where we left off?"

"The Old Man wants to be sure we are all right. Each night I will make up a report and send it in to him, and also all our data up to that time, by the boat making the trip here on the high tide. Then, too, they are nearly through their work anyway, and orders for us to move on are daily expected. The next reason is, that by making our headquarters here we won't have to move our camping outfit or our rations, and this place is centrally located, so that each day we can cover new territory."

"I hadn't thought about all those things," said Henry thoughtfully, "but I reckon the Old Man is right, after all."

"Well, now that you are satisfied, let's get our gear up to the palatial hut assigned for our use by Señor el Capitan del Puerto, fix things shipshape, and make our plans for to-morrow."

This was done, and in the vacant, earthen-floored shack they unstrapped their cots, arranged their bedding, hung mosquito bunk-nets, and after building a fire, cooked their evening meal. It seemed to the two boys as though fried hen-fruit, baked spuds, crisped bacon, ship's punk and steaming java,[#] never tasted so delicious. Nor did the coffee make any difference to such healthy bodies and minds, when a little later they crawled under their white nets and blue-gray blankets, and went to sleep.

[#] Sailor and marine slang for fried eggs, baked potatoes, crisped bacon, ship's bread and steaming coffee.

Though advised against doing so by the native owner, they left both doors to their domicile wide open to admit the night breezes. In most tropical countries, the natives, of the poorer classes especially, close every door and window at night, so as to prevent the slightest breath of fresh air from striking them, and it is for this reason, undoubtedly, that during times of epidemic, the fatality among the natives in semi-civilized places is so great.

Sometime before dawn the boys were awakened by the sound of agonizing cries and the rush of many feet across the hard-packed floor of their hut. Almost at the same instant they sat up, and reached for their automatics. Then they listened, but all was silent, except for the creaking of night insects or the gentle stirring of the palm leaves on their thatched roof. Inside the room was inky darkness, nor was the light outside much brighter.

"Did you hear that, Hank?" questioned Dick, softly, not quite daring to make any further move until he knew where his companion might be and until he understood a little more of the situation.

"I reckon I heard it right enough, Dick; but what was it?"

"I haven't any idea. I heard a yell and someone running and suddenly found myself awake and sitting up."

"Same here, Dick, but I thought it was you chasing something or someone. It looks a little funny, doesn't it?"

"Keep quiet a minute, Hank; I believe they are still in here. I hear someone moving."

Silence followed the caution while they listened intently. Then came a deep-drawn sigh from the center of the hut, and the sound as of a heavy body being dragged across the floor.

"Who's there?" challenged Dick. "If you move again I'll fire."

Once again absolute silence, which was finally broken by a series of sharp staccato taps. Dick immediately recognized the private call Henry and he used in their practise at telegraphy and sound signalling. His companion was rapping on a match-box with some kind of an instrument. If the person or persons in the room understood English then any conversation would inform them of the action to be taken against them. Dick grinned delightedly to himself at Henry's quick way to secret and safe coöperation. As the light sounds shuttled back and forth it was evident to what a state of expertness these two young marines had drilled themselves.

"Look out, I will turn on my flash-light. Be ready to shoot. Do you understand?" came Henry's message.

"It is dangerous. Let me do it, and you shoot," cautioned Dick.

"No! You are the better shot. I think he is near the door, and if I flash the light you can get him better than I can. Stand by right after I sound 'preparatory.' Stand by!"

The safety catch on Dick's automatic hardly made a sound as he pushed it down with his thumb and peered into the darkness near the door. The weapon was already loaded, so that but a slight pressure on the trigger would bring its deafening response. Breathlessly he waited. The next moment came the rattle of the match-box as once again Henry struck it with sharp emphasis:

One rap--two short raps--one rap--one rap!

Then the room was lit by the electric torch from Henry's side of the hut. There was a wild rush of many feet, loud squeals filled the air, and out of the open doorway raced and scrambled an enormous razor-back pig with a litter of squealing, frantic piggies at her heels.

The sudden transition from the serious to the comical was so great that both Dick and Henry burst into a roar of hysterical laughter, and both made a solemn pact never to relate this part of their adventures to a living soul. After this, sleep being out of the question and the gray dawn already lightening the eastern horizon, they prepared their morning meal and made ready for an early start.

From previous tests each of the boys knew the exact stretch of ground covered in one of his strides[#] and Dick's stride being sixty inches, even though he was a six-footer, and five feet being a most convenient multiple, it was to be his duty to keep account of the distances between observation points or stations. For this purpose he carried an instrument used in checking off the number of coal bags hoisted on board during coaling ship, and with each step taken with his left foot he recorded it by pressing on the lever with his thumb. The tally was so small it could be carried unobserved in the palm of the hand. Besides the tally Dick carried a small pocket note-book, conveniently ruled, in which he entered his data and from which, on their return, they would be able to make a very comprehensive sketch of their travels.

[#] A pace is the distance between footsteps; a stride the distance between the spot where one foot strikes the ground and the next succeeding fall of the same foot; a stride is therefore the equivalent of two paces.

Henry was provided with a small prismatic compass by means of which he read the angles from each selected point to the next station. With these simple instruments they could accomplish their work and arouse no suspicion, at least in the minds of any ordinary native with whom they were liable to come in contact.

There was but one trail for them to follow from their point of departure, and it led to the town of Copey. To follow this trail the first day and plot in the cross trails between it and the Massacre River on the following days was their intention, and as the sun rose in a soft pink cloud of color, with shotguns under their arms, game bags over their shoulders, and the heavy Colt's forty-fives strapped to their right thighs, the young surveyors started out on their quest with an eagerness born of youth and enthusiasm.

CHAPTER XVIII

MEXICAN PETE AGAIN

The method followed by the two marines was very simple. Having selected a landmark some distance ahead of them on the trail, Henry, with the sight-leaves of his compass raised, would look through them towards the point and read the azimuth or angular direction with respect to the north and south line, or meridian. This angle was called the bearing of the point or station.

Starting at the Captain of the Port's house they named their point of departure "A," and sighted upon a distant tree, calling it station "B." A line drawn from "A" to "B" would form an angle with another line passing through station "A" and the north pole. This angle was read off in degrees on the compass-card from north going around in the same direction as the hands of a clock, and there would be two methods of recording it. They could state the whole angle as read from the compass, which would then be the true azimuth of station "B," or they could note the true bearing of the line A-B. The true bearing of a line is that angle less than ninety degrees which the line makes with the true meridian. The boys decided to use the true azimuth in their data.

Dick, having made the entry in his book, started marching towards "B," pressing on his tally register with every fall of his left foot. Reaching "B," the number of his strides were entered, a new sight taken, and the march resumed.

Where trails crossed or joined the route, their bearing was jotted down. Features of the country to one hundred yards either side of the trail were kept under observation; houses, corrals, streams, bridges and their nature, cultivated fields, swampland, all were noted carefully.

It was several hours before they met a native, though there was every appearance of the way being well travelled. At noon they halted in the shade of a clump of bamboo and ate their luncheon. There was nothing about them to indicate they were members of a famous military organization, because they had been supplied before leaving the ship with some "cit" clothes. Their canteens of water were carried in the game-bags, for good soldiers never drink water found in strange countries until it has first been boiled, and there was no time for work of that nature while engaged in their present task.

Overhead the sky was a brilliant azure. The sparkling beams of the noonday sun danced gaily with the shadows cast by the leafy foliage and a soft breeze whispered through the feathery leaves and hanging moss. Little lizards darted about in quest of insects, butterflies floated by on downy wing and the hum of bees seeking honey-laden blossoms added a drowsy note to the lazy hour.

"When should we reach Copey, Dick?" asked Henry, with an undisguised yawn.

"In about an hour, I guess. We have been going slowly, but it won't take long on the return trip. From now on we must be extremely careful. The country in front of us is more populated, and the trails joining this one are more numerous."

"Hullo--here are some people coming along the road," said Henry, sitting up; "sounds like a goodly party."

Soon after a considerable company came riding by, consisting of about twenty mounted men and boys, driving before them a number of burros and horses. Most of the party passed without noticing the two marines, but at the rear of the cavalcade was one man who permitted nothing to escape his roving eyes. Spying Dick and Henry, he rode up and inquired in Spanish as to their business.

"Buenos dias, amigos! I see you are hunting! What luck have you had?"

"Very poor luck," Dick replied, looking up at his interrogator but without deigning to rise. "And what did you hope to shoot along this trail, my friend?" inquired the native, looking searchingly at Dick.

"'Most anything--we heard that the ground doves were plentiful, but it has not proven so to-day."

"Where do you come from, stranger?" the horseman now asked. "I know you are Americans, but I have never seen you around this part of the country before, and I know every foreigner from Monte Cristi to the border."

"We are just passing through," said Dick, evading a direct answer.

"Ah! Then, of course, you are bound for Copey. I regret I cannot be there to offer you the hospitality of my home, humble though it is. I am Señor Don Antonio Lugo y Suarez, alcalde[#] of the town, and if you are to remain in this neighborhood for any length of time, it will----"

[#] Alcalde--Mayor.

"Thank you, Señor, but we are to be here but a short time, otherwise----" and Dick, now having risen, waved his hand in a gesture that was meant to indicate his regret.

"Nevertheless, I shall hope for the pleasure, Señors, and now I must hurry along to my friends. Adios, amigos!" and with a low bow, the alcalde put spurs to his steed and disappeared up the trail.

"That fellow is a slick one, Hank. He talks too much, and he's too suave to suit me. As for his expressions of regret and regard--it's all tommy-rot."

"He surely kept his eyes busy during his visit," drawled Henry.

"Well, there was nothing to satisfy his curiosity," said Dick, looking around to see if he was correct in his statement. "By jinks, Hank, if he put two and two together he might have cause to suspect. You know I didn't give him any satisfaction as to who we were, but as alcalde, he naturally would have heard of the *Denver* being busy around Manzanillo Bay, and so it's easy to connect us with the ship. But if he wanted proof of what we were doing, there is the evidence."

Henry immediately sat up to look where Dick pointed. On a small tree near by were hanging the two canteens of water with the black letters "U.S.M.C." stenciled on their sides, while on the ground beneath, the flap to one of the hunting-bags had fallen open, and there lay note-book, pencil, tally register, compass, and a rough sketch of the locality around the Bay, which Dick had brought along as a possible aid in their work.

"If Señor Don Antonio and-all-the-rest-of-his-name, was half as wise as he looked he knows pretty well, right now, what we are up to," added Dick grimly. "I wonder what his next move will be!"

The sound of a horse galloping along the trail came to them and then like a streak, horse and rider dashed by and along the way they were about to travel. The rider was spurring and beating his steed as he bent low in the saddle. If he saw the boys, he at least gave no sign.

"That fellow reminds me of something or someone," mused Dick, watching horse and rider disappear in a cloud of dust.

"The way he's beating his animal makes me think of the Mexican you horsewhipped in Culebra last winter," said Henry.

"By jinks, Hank, that's who he is, and no mistake. He was riding along with that outfit a while ago, and now the alcalde has sent him back on an errand. I'd bet an old hat that it won't help us any either; also I hope Mexican Pete doesn't see us, for we can hardly hope he won't remember us. And if he does, the jig is up."

"I've got an idea, too. If that is Mexican Pete, then he's in cahoots with the alcalde, and they are starting out on a smuggling expedition, and the alcalde is sending back word to prevent us from any possibility of getting information of it."

"That's more than likely correct, Hank, and we shall have an interesting report to send in to the Captain to-night. Well, we'd better be getting along, for I've a feeling the more we can accomplish to-day the better it will be in the end. If that outfit is a band of smugglers then it's up to us to discover their trail and see where it leads. It will be easy to find it, and we shall have accomplished our mission if we find even one of their routes."

"Let us go after them right now," suggested Henry.

"If we go back now, of course we can pick up their trail easily enough, but they have taken the precaution to send back word regarding us, and they surely have left some people to watch us if we attempt to follow them. On the other hand, we may never get another such favorable opportunity to finish up the road map to Copey, and as it will be a valuable addition to the chart for future reference, I guess we'd do well to complete it."

"Vamos,[#] then," said Henry, rising and starting off.

[#] Vamos--Let us go.

They worked more rapidly now, taking every precaution against arousing suspicion. The houses beside the road were more frequent, and often they had to guess at the azimuths from one station to another when curious natives were watching them. The pacing of the distances, though, was not interfered with, and they hoped to be able to check up questionable data on their return. Fortunately it was the siesta hour, and few men or women were abroad. Even the streets of the town, when they arrived, were fairly deserted.

The road on which they entered Copey continued through the town until it crossed the broad highway which lay between Dajabon and Monte Cristi. Arriving at this point and accosting a native lounger as to where they could procure refreshments, they found themselves surrounded with surprising rapidity, and the attitude of the men in the group was anything but friendly.

"There is a good cantina there on the corner, Señor," replied one of the men in answer to Dick's question.

"Thank you," said Dick, starting for the store; "and perhaps you will join us?" he added, believing it better to appear sociable even though he did not feel so.

The native accepted with alacrity. Inside the little building it was cool and dim and they ordered, at the proprietor's suggestion, "huevos fritos, pan tierno y mantequilla, y cafe con leche."[#]

[#] Eggs fried, fresh bread and butter, and coffee with milk.

During the preparation of the repast, Dick and Henry, taking their weapons with them, repaired to the yard in the rear of the cantina, where a small brown girl brought them fresh water, soap and towels. Dick, having finished his ablutions first, gave the diminutive maid a silver coin, over which her little fist closed greedily, and the next moment she was displaying it to her mother, who stood in the doorway of the cocina, and who smiled pleasantly at the donor.

"Your child is very pretty, Señora," said Dick.

"The Señor Americano is very kind to say so," replied the woman in her soft voice.

"And how do you know I am an American?" asked Dick.

"Hush!" almost whispered the woman, glancing cautiously back into the cantina. "Listen to me, Señor, your lives are in danger here. It is said you are spies sent here by the Americans, and everyone in the town knew of you before your arrival. You must never attempt to go to Dajabon. The alcalde here is very powerful, and his orders are law. The feeling is very bitter against all Americans. Some of your officers were stoned yesterday in Monte Cristi. Be careful! I can say no more!"

"And why do you tell us this, Señora?" asked Dick.

"Because I like the Americans. An American surgeon saved my child's life when she was ill last year. You, too, were kind to her. Hurry and finish your meal and leave at once. Watch out for trouble, as they will follow your movements. Do not let them suspect that you know anything. Be careful-- here comes my husband," and the woman hurriedly occupied herself with some household duties.

"Everything is prepared, gentlemen, and awaiting your pleasure," announced the owner of the cantina, and the boys followed him to their places at the table where their guest still awaited them.

During the meal conversation was confined to the subject of hunting, and it was noticeable how their guest and host agreed that it was a bad season for doves, that the birds never were numerous in the locality, and discouraged any further attempts at enjoying sport of that nature anywhere except along the coast, where snipe of all kinds abounded.

Many times the proprietor left them for the purpose of supplying numerous thirsty individuals who seemed to flock to his little bar, and all his customers seemed mightily interested in scrutinizing the party seated at the marble-topped table. Finally, after paying their bill, the boys bid good-bye to their host and, still accompanied by the native who had partaken of their bounty, they began their return trip over the road by which they had entered the town.

On reaching the outskirts of the village their self-appointed escort volunteered the information that if his friends were returning to the Captain of the Port's house at Estero Balsa he would be glad to serve them by showing them a short cut which was very easy to travel, but with many expressions of good-will they declined and, with relief, they saw the native turn back over the trail to town.

"Phew! But I'm glad that Spig has gone! I've been nearly bursting to talk over what that woman told us," said Henry. "Do you believe they are up to anything?"

"Did you see any of those men coming into the cantina while we were eating?" asked Dick, as he loosened the flap covering his automatic in the holster, and turned it back so that he could easily draw the pistol in case of need.

"No; my back was towards the door, and I thought it best not to appear too curious."

"If you'd seen them you'd not feel very easy over the matter, Hank, for one of them was none other than Mexican Pete; and he recognized us, too. He came sauntering in, and I noticed him start when he saw me sitting there. He didn't know I was looking at him; and later he kept his back turned all the time, but was giving us the once-over in the looking-glass behind the bar. I saw him at the head of a detachment of mounted men leaving town about fifteen minutes before we left."

"Do you reckon they expected us to take the short route and hoped to catch us on some blind trail?" asked Henry.

"Possibly. You see the country along the road is fairly open on either side, and a considerable body of men would have some difficulty in surprising us. But they can easily pick us off if they are good shots."

"I see you've unlimbered, and I reckon I'll do the same," said Henry, looking at Dick's pistol; "also I'm going to change my load in this pump-gun from bird to buck shot."

"Mine has been loaded with buck since we started this morning," said Dick. "If ever I had taken a crack at a wild pigeon and one of those slugs hit, there wouldn't have been enough feathers or bird left to satisfy the appetite of an Argentine ant."

The boys kept up a pretty rapid pace, and it was not long before they had left behind their noonday resting place and now were keeping careful watch of the trail in order to discover where the alcalde and his troop had turned from it. The marks of the horses on the road had not been disturbed, and about five miles from Copey the tracks plainly turned off to the left up a trail through the dense woods. It was certain that here was at least one clue to their credit which would be of value to the customs officials.

"Why did you hurry on by, Dick? We might have gone up that trail for a way. We've plenty of time."

"Yes, and we might never have come down it and returned to the ship with our information, Hank. That is why I told you not to stop nor act as if you'd noticed anything unusual. I saw something I didn't like when I squinted up that beautiful sylvan dell, and I believe we'd better do some tall hustling from now on."

"What did you see?"

"Well, it looked like a full-sized native jumping behind a tree. I believe they thought we might turn up that way, and were waiting for us. As it is, I'll feel a whole lot better when I can get around that turn ahead of us. I've an idea there is a gun pointing between my shoulder-blades this minute, and it doesn't feel a bit comfortable."

Unconsciously Henry turned his head to look back over the road; then with a shout of caution he started forward on the run.

"Beat it, Dick; Mexican Pete and his gang are after us!"

With the words came a scattering volley, and the yells of the natives in their rear, the sound of the leaden bullets tearing through the leaves and shrubs, helped the boys onward in their flight.

CHAPTER XIX

A BRAVE ACT AND A CLEVER RUSE

As the two marines dashed around the bend in the road they found before them an open plain with small clumps of low-lying shrubs here and there on its sun-baked, level surface. Three hundred yards to their right a thatched hut of mud stood at the edge of the mangroves which bordered the plain. Apparently deserted, it offered the only real shelter in sight, and this was shelter from observation only, in all probability, for its walls would offer little resistance to the shots of their enemies.

"Make for the shack, Hank," called Dick, and together they dashed across the firm ground. Before they reached their haven the bullets were again zip-zipping about them. Dick, in the lead, was within a few yards of the hut when he was arrested by a cry of distress from Henry. Turning, he saw his chum on his hands and knees about twenty yards in the rear, while from the direction of the bend an exultant yelling told him the natives were aware that one of the party was injured. Instantly Dick doubled on his tracks and was soon at Henry's side.

"Did they get you, Hank?" he inquired anxiously.

"Yes, in the right leg," answered the plucky boy, with a smile. "It knocked me down. Doesn't hurt much, but I can't seem to use my leg."

"I'll fix you all right," said Dick cheerily, though he felt far from happy, and bending while Henry sat up, he easily picked up his companion in the way he had been taught to use in carrying wounded men off the field. He took Henry's left leg under his own left arm, and made the injured boy bend over his left shoulder. Then, grasping Henry's left wrist with his right hand, Dick was up and again running towards the hut. The shooting kept up while Dick was bending over his chum, but when the natives saw him carrying away the fallen boy they redoubled their fire and their yells increased in proportion. Fortunately they were poor marksmen, and Dick reached the shack without further mishap. Here he deposited Henry on the dirt floor and reaching in his hunting-bag he brought forth a first-aid package. The wound was bleeding freely, and without hesitation Dick ripped the right trousers' leg from the knee downward with his knife (the same one he had taken from Gonzales at Sanchez) and then with an expert hand he bound the wound up firmly.

"I feel O.K. now, old chap, and you'd better squint outside and see what those rapscallions are up to."

"They've quit shooting and there is no one in sight," said Dick, who crawled to the empty doorway and looked out across the flats towards the bend.

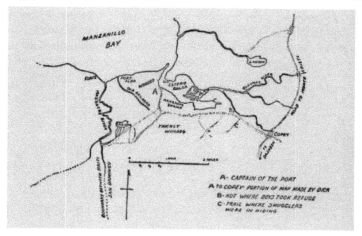

Map Showing Position of Hut in Which Boys Took Refuge

"Do you reckon they've decided to let us alone?"

"I don't know, Henry, but I'll know in a minute. I'm going out after our shotguns. We're pretty poor soldiers to leave our weapons lying all around the country," and Dick's grin was meant to convey the idea that the task he was about to undertake was not of much importance nor danger.

"Don't try it, Dick. Perhaps they are only waiting for us to show ourselves and then when we do they hope to pot us."

But Dick had rushed out of the doorway before Henry finished speaking. He zigzagged his way across the open space to about fifty yards, the point where he had rescued Henry, and with his reappearance another fusillade began. As Dick reached the spot he saw the two guns lying within a few feet of each other, and between them and the enemy was a small clump of green bush.

Back in the doorway Henry now sat watching with bated breath. He saw Dick stop in his mad rush, then he saw him throw up his hands in a wild gesture of despair and fall to the ground. That his brave friend was in great agony was evident to the helpless watcher. He saw Dick roll over and over, his arms and legs seeming to thresh the air. Finally the movements ceased and Dick lay stretched out like a log on the scorching hot plain. The tears rolled unheeded down Henry's cheeks, and then, hearing the loud victorious shouts of the natives as they streamed out from behind the shelter of the woods near the bend, and on across the plain, his lips pressed together and

- 149 -

his eyes grew cold and stern, for the brain behind was dominated by but one thought, the desire to avenge his comrade.

With grim determination he placed all the spare magazines for his pistol within easy reach and drew his heavy Colt's from the holster. Not a man should ever reach Dick's body if the steady hand and cool nerve of Henry Cabell could prevent.

On came the natives, and Mexican Pete was leading them. Even as they came they continued firing at the hut and in the direction of the still body lying behind the little bush where it had rolled in the last struggles. Henry, unheeding the pain in his leg, rolled into the doorway on his stomach and, resting both elbows on the floor, he squinted over the sights and took careful aim at the Mexican. He meant to make every shot count, and so he waited until the leader should be within seventy-five yards of him. So intense was he on judging the precise moment to open fire that he saw nothing but this one man whom he covered with his pistol.

As he looked he saw the Mexican throw up his arms, whirl about and run back towards cover. What caused this? Henry lowered his pistol, and now saw the rest of the gang wildly scattering, leaving two of their number lying on the plain. The next moment Henry was rubbing his eyes to see if he were awake. The body lying in the shelter of the bush had come to life. Dick Comstock was working his shotguns with lightning rapidity, and clouds of dust flew up from the plain as the buckshot sprayed about among the fleeing men. As the last one was lost in the distant cover Dick ceased his fire and came running, with both guns in his hands, for the hut.

"Say, boy, but didn't I fool 'em?" he joyfully shouted as he sprang through the doorway. "Did you see me get 'em, Hank?"

"Old boy, I thought they had gotten you. I reckon I was pretty much all in too, Dick, when I saw you go down, and I was just about to open up when you began on them. It was sure a good trick you played, but, Dick, be careful to let me know about it the next time or I'll die of heart failure. Did they get you at all?"

"Not once; but one of their darn slugs took off my cap, right enough, and right then the thought flashed through my mind to play the trick. Whew! It's some hot out there, and, Hank, do you still see those two chaps that fell? I wonder if they're hurt, or--or---- Gee! I feel kind of squeamish, now that it's over," and Dick sat down rather suddenly with his back against the wall.

"No, they are not dead, Dick, for one of them jumped up and limped off when your fire stopped, and the other is yelling for help right now. Besides, they deserve no better fate, and our death would have meant nothing to them in the way of regret, at least."

"I feel better, after what you've said, but for a moment the thought of killing a man was making me sort of sick at my stomach. I didn't feel that way when I was shooting at 'em, though," and Dick took a deep breath of relief, then rising he looked out at the scene of recent conflict. Out in the middle of the plain the wounded native still called for help, but if his comrades were within hearing they made no attempt to render any assistance.

"I reckon those buckshot sort of stung a bit," snickered Henry; but his snicker ended in a little painful gasp that he tried in vain to control.

"I've got to get you out of here, Hank, and in a hurry. There is no telling what they'll do next, and they'll be back as soon as the first fright wears off. I believe that path back of the hut will take us to a creek which flows into the Estero Balsa and which the officers plotted in on the chart last week when I was with them. Anyhow, it's worth trying. If you feel well enough suppose you keep an eye out on the plain while I reconnoiter in the rear."

"Good; I feel fine, Dick, so go along, and I'll keep them off, don't worry."

In ten minutes Dick returned with the news that his surmise was correct, and as luck would have it, a small boat with two men was even then coming up the narrow creek. Taking Henry on his shoulder once more, Dick carried him to the bank of the creek, arriving there as the boatmen reached a point opposite. At his hail the boat was soon nosing the bank, and the natives inquired what was wanted.

"My comrade just met with an accident, and I wish to take him to the Captain of the Port's house; will you row us there?"

The two fishermen at first demurred, but Dick settled the matter by taking hold of the gunwale and at the same time drawing his pistol. It was no time to parley; in a moment they saw the force of his remarks. Henry was placed carefully in the bottom of the boat, and soon they were speeding downstream.

Once during the passage the two boys looked at each other and winked knowingly, for from far upstream came the sound of numerous shots.

"Seems to be a lot of hunting in this country," said Dick aloud.

"Oh, yes, Señor, the doves are very plentiful this year," said one of the rowers.

Crossing the waters of the Estero, they drew up alongside the wharf, where they had landed less than twenty-four hours previously. One of the ship's boats was there, and the coxswain in charge hailed them.

"Hurry aboard, you leathernecks. I've all the stuff from your camp. The ship's under sailin' orders fer Nicaragua, where there's a hot little revolution goin' on. What's that, one of you hurt? Well, they shouldn't let boys carry guns anyway; they're all the time a-shootin' of themselves. Steady, lads! Handle him with care, and make a soft place fer him in the cockpit with them cushions. Shove off, for'rd! Full speed ahead! Say good-bye to this heck of an island, fellers; we're off this time, for sure!"

CHAPTER XX

"TO THE DITCH AT PANAMA"

"There goes the good old *Denver*, Mike. I guess she'll reach the fighting grounds before we do."

"Don't let that be for worryin' of ye, Dick, me lad," responded Corporal Dorlan. "We'll be havin' a bellyful of it, I'm thinkin', if all signs is correct. Nevertheless, she was one of the foinest little crafts I've ever served on, and they was a grand lot of Navy officers on her, too; but I'm glad to git back to the Corps again. I'm a marine, Dick, through and through, and though I get along with them Navy men well enough, I like to serve with me own kind best of all."

The old veteran and young drummer were standing on the wharf at Cristobal, at the Atlantic end of the ten-mile stretch of land across the Isthmus of Panama known as the Canal Zone, which by treaty with the Panamanian Government had come under perpetual control of the United States. Fading away in the dim distance was the ship which for many months had been Dick's official home. Diverted from her original orders, she had put in at Cristobal long enough to land all her marines, with the exception of Henry Cabell, who was still under the surgeon's care; and now she was bound for Bluefields, on the Mosquito Coast of Nicaragua. In order to fill existing vacancies in a regiment of marines hurrying to the scene of action on board the Naval Transport *Dixie*, which ship was just appearing above the distant horizon, the guard of the *Denver* had been unceremoniously "dumped on the beach," as the men put it.

There was no question that the revolution in progress, most active on the Pacific coast of Nicaragua, was a lively one. Marines were being assembled from all available points, even reducing the guard at Camp Elliott to a mere skeleton detachment. These men from the Zone were the first to leave for Nicaragua, and the army men stationed there had watched them depart with feelings of envy.

"Blame it all! Those marines are always getting into something. I'll bet I take on with that outfit the next time I sign up," more than one regular army "file" had been heard to say.

And that first lot of "soldiers of the sea" had already met with opposition. Even now they were somewhere between Corinto and the capital city, Managua. If they found the rails torn up, they repaired them; bridges burned, they built new ones temporarily. They were threatened with annihilation if they interfered, yet they continued with a dauntless, young and able leader at their head, relieving the fears of the foreigners in the interior and keeping the single line of railroad back to their base in fairly good order. Only this very audacity could assure the success of their undertaking, and also a possible misunderstanding on the part of Federals and Rebels as to which side "these interfering Yankees" were really there to help, though it was the bearers of the red rosettes who actively opposed their progress. American financial interests were jeopardized, and underlying all the fuss and furor were greater stakes than the general public realized.

Perhaps Drummer Richard Comstock and Trumpeter Cabell, in a talk before they separated that morning, were closer to the real reason for this strong force being despatched than were even the best informed officers of the expedition.

"I reckon a certain conversation you all overheard in Washington a year ago is bearing fruit," suggested Henry, looking up from his bunk in the sick bay where Dick had gone to visit him.

"It looks that way," Dick had replied.

"Well, if you run across a certain German and a three-fingered Limey,[#] Dick, you'll do well to keep an eye open. I sure wish I could go with you all, but we'll get together again before long; so good-bye, old boy, and good luck," and Henry turned to the wall to cover the emotion this separation caused him. Thus they had parted.

[#] "Limey"--British maritime regulations require the captain to issue regular rations of lime-juice as a preventative for scurvy. British ships and sailors are therefore known as "Lime-juicers," or in sailor slang, "Limeys."

Steadily the transport grew upon the vision of those awaiting her arrival. Finally, when she came alongside her berth, the place became a seething ant-hill of activity. Tons and tons of rations, tents, munitions, wireless outfits, buckets, clothing, field ranges, medical supplies, field artillery, and the thousand other things necessary for extensive operations were sent up out of the ship's holds and packed on freight cars, and soon trains of men and supplies were slowly creeping from under the railroad sheds, out past Monkey Hill, on and on, with ever-increasing speed, towards the Pacific terminus at Balboa.

Much to Dick's pleasure and Corporal Dorlan's satisfaction they found themselves detailed for duty with a company commanded by an old acquaintance, Captain Kenneth Henderson, formerly in charge of the Marine Detachment of the U.S.S. *Nantucket.*

"Well, Sergeant Dorlan, I'm glad to have you back under my command," said the Captain as he shook hands; "report to the First Sergeant at once, and tell him I said you are in charge of the working detail loading the cars." Then he turned to Dick. "Where have I seen you before, music? Your face looks familiar, but I can't place you."

"I met the Captain on the *Nantucket*, sir, if the Captain remembers the day we were upset by a motor boat and Dorlan rescued Tommy Turner."

"Now I know! You are Drummer Comstock. Your friend's uncle asked me to keep an eye on you in case I ran across you. How is it that you are a drummer? I understood you enlisted to get a commission."

"I hope to have my rank changed before long, sir, but at the time I enlisted they were taking only musics into the Corps."

"Does this young man know anything? Can we make a corporal out of him?" asked Captain Henderson, turning to Dorlan, who still stood at attention near by.

"Indeed he's a broth of a lad, sir, and knows more'n most of the corporals right now, but if the Captain will excuse me, I wanted to explain before goin' to the First Sergeant that I'm only a corporal meself, sir. Ye may disremember I was reduced in rank over a year ago."

"I remember it very well, Dorlan; but from to-day on you are again a sergeant. So get busy with that work of loading. As for you, music, I'll make you my orderly for the present. Go aboard, find my mess boy, Jackson, and get my luggage on that train. It is already packed. Then present my respects to the Colonel, and tell him my company is ready to move any time he sends me word."

Thus it was Dick found himself on board the first troop train to cross the Isthmus. He was well repaid now for the hours he had devoted to his graduation essay. At that time he had gone deeply into the subject and since then, while cruising in the West Indies, many times his previous reading and study had been of great help. The history of the Panama Canal was a favorite subject, and now he verified his book knowledge by actual experience. The sight of the vast area already flooded as a result of the nearly completed dam at Gatun, the names of Frijoles, Bas Obispo, Camp Elliott, Cucaracha, Pedro Miguel and Miraflores brought back to his mind afresh the disappointments of the French and the difficulties overcome by his country. At one place on the road a dirt train held them up for a short space of time, and from the car window he caught glimpses of the mighty Bucyrus steam shovels scooping up tons of earth and rock in their capacious maws with almost human intelligence. The new line they travelled passed to the east of Gold Hill, back of which was Culebra Cut, where the slipping, unstable earth caused so much delay, disappointment and expense by its dangerous slides. Every where were scenes of activity! Hundreds of cars and engines, empty trains, trains filled with excavated earth, trains of freight, passenger trains, workmen's trains, thousands of men, negroes from the South and the West Indies, Spaniards, Englishmen, Frenchmen, Chinese, Latin-Americans, full blooded Central American Indians, Hindoos from the Far East, all busy, all hustling, even in this tropic zone. They passed through little villages and settlements, each a reminder of the fabled "Spotless Town," with their excellent roads, splendid drainage, immaculate, screened buildings, stores, boarding-houses, hotels, public buildings and residences, all under the supervision of the Government. How proud the young drummer was to be a part of this big republic which did things on such a wonderful scale; that he served this country which flung to the breeze the Stars and Stripes: that he was even then on his way to help a misguided people, who, under the far-sighted provision of that Doctrine of President Monroe, now needed a helping hand to guide their ship of state over treacherous waters: that he was Richard Comstock, United States Marine.

All too soon the passage of that narrow neck of land was completed, and the train pulled in under the sheds of the Balboa wharves. Again the hustle and bustle, for close behind followed freight trains and more troops, and the work of unloading the cars and filling up waiting lighters was begun.

Men's hands, unaccustomed to the rough work, blistered and went raw, their backs ached, their muscles grew stiff and strained, the perspiration soaked their khaki clothing a dark brown color, but cheerfully they stuck to their task. And truly it was Herculean, for after being placed aboard the lighters the stores were towed alongside a great gray battleship lying far out in the harbor, where they again had to be transferred aboard and stored away.

The companies worked in two-hour shifts, one battalion being detailed at each of the transfer points. They arrived at Cristobal at noon, and a little after midnight the work ashore had been completed. Captain Henderson's company was one of those detailed for work on the Balboa wharves, and shortly before ten o'clock he started in a motor car for the city of Panama, taking his newly appointed orderly with him. About the time the relief shift was to go on they returned, laden down with sandwiches of all kinds and several big freezers of ice-cream with which to regale officers and men. The cooks in the meantime had made gallons of hot coffee, and when mess-call sounded, never was food and drink more welcome than to those dirty, grimy, sweat-laden marines, who, seated on box or barrel, gun carriage or packing case, in the glare of many cargo lights, munched and drank to repletion. Then "carry on" was sounded, and with cheerful shouts and renewed vigor they tackled their task.

By six o'clock the next morning the big ship slowly swung her bows out towards the ocean of Balboa, the mighty Pacific, and laid her course for Corinto, Nicaragua's principal seaport on the west coast.

Then it was that Dick Comstock realized he was tired--good and tired, but there could be no rest for the weary. Every man must first know to which boat he was assigned in case of "abandon ship," what he was supposed to do in case of fire, where he was to berth; then there were roll calls and cleaning ship and stowing away the stores on deck, and it was dark once more before the willing workers finally found the time and the place to catch a little sleep. But it was all worth while when the Colonel Commanding sent around to each company his official word of praise: "No body of men could better their record, and he doubted if any could equal it," so read the memorandum. And Dick, curled up in an unoccupied corner on deck, fell asleep, while ringing in his ears was that well-known stanza of the Marines' Hymn which a group of still energetic Leathernecks were softly singing somewhere up near the bridge:

"From the pest hole of Cavite

To the ditch at Panama,

They're always very needy

Of marines, that's what we are,

We're the watch dogs of a pile of coal

Or we build a magazine,

Though our duties are so numerous,

Who would not be a Marine?"

CHAPTER XXI

THE MARINES HAVE LANDED

"That's a fine-looking engine," said Dick, three days later, as he gazed, with a derisive laugh, at the locomotive backing onto the wharf at Corinto to couple up with a train of laden flat cars ready to start on the precarious journey to support the battalion of marines somewhere along the line, but just where no one rightly knew.

And indeed it was an engine of a type quite new to most of the marines perched on every available sticking-place amid the boxes, barrels and bales with which the train was laden. A care-free, jovial lot of huskies they were, taking this back-breaking work as a mere matter of course. They were marines, so it was their just due to be chased from one corner of the world to the other; and if it had not been so, they would have said disgustedly that they "might as well be in the Army." The world moved and the marines moved with it; they themselves were sometimes inclined to think they moved it.

"The only place I ever saw an engine of that type was on those blue three-cent stamps the United States put out for the centennial celebration many years ago," remarked a junior officer, seated near Dick on the floor of the car, with his feet swinging idly over the side.

"You are not much of a philatelist, Mr. Mercer," said Captain Henderson, who happened by, "or you would have known of other postage stamps with an engraving of the wood-burning type of engine on their face. This country we are now in uses a series of them over on the Mosquito Coast, and Honduras has another series. But I see we are about to start. Pass the word to fix bayonets: no rifles to be loaded without command. Each man must understand this affair is being handled with kid gloves, and they must not precipitate things by any hasty action on their part. Remember, too, that we are here to keep order, and unless interfered with we will go about our business quietly. To us, at the present time, all Nicaraguans are our friends until they prove otherwise. Treat both parties alike until you get orders to the contrary. Those men wearing red rosettes and ribbons are 'agin the government'; they are rebels; so be careful of your every act."

The engine with its enormous bell-topped stack by now had bumped into position and with a jerk and wrench and creaking of wheels the journey was begun.

All along the route could be seen small bands of men. Some carried rifles, but the majority were armed with long knives, called machetes. Many sported uniforms, but most were attired in ordinary clothing, the little red badges identifying them with the insurgent forces.

Hour after hour they clattered and bumped along the fearful road-bed. Forward! Bump, stop! Bump, ahead! Stop! Little by little, mile after mile, they progressed. Here the rails were slippery, and with shovel in hand the men jumped off the cars and covered them with dirt so that the wheezy engine could once more proceed. At a town named Quezalgaque, just as darkness fell, the engine ran out of water. A bucket line was formed down the steep river embankment at this spot and under the glare of flaming torches the men worked filling the boiler till the Navy Machinist in charge of the engine stated the gauge was "full up." Then forward once more with the cheers of the detachment of Uncle Sam's sailors, stationed here to guard the bridge, ringing in their ears.

The night was so black that it was difficult to see one's hand before one's face and when, after about five miles more of bumping and thumping had been covered, the train again halted, word passed from the head of the train for no one under any circumstances to leave the cars. There seemed to be a mysterious something in the air, as of a dense crowd of humanity pressing in from all sides, yet there was no sound, other than the puffing of the wood-burner at the head of the train.

"Wonder what makes this place so spooky like?" whispered Dick to Dorlan, who sat beside him filling his old corn-cob pipe preparatory to lighting up; "I have a feeling that if I put my hand out I'd touch some human being; and yet I can't see a thing in this blackness."

Dorlan did not reply, but the light from his match made a small glare in the surrounding night. Small as it was the men in his immediate vicinity were startled at what it disclosed. A sea of faces, a forest of armed men, crowded up to the very edge of the track on all sides.

"Whew! Did you see them?" whispered a man near Dick. "Every beggar in sight has a gun, and here we are right in the middle of 'em, and we didn't know it."

There was a restless movement on the part of the marines. Those who had been drowsing awakened, to grip more firmly the rifle which, since darkness, no longer held the knife-like bayonet. One man quietly opened the bolt of his rifle and nervously fingered a clip of cartridges in his belt.

"Easy, men!" came the caution down the length of the train, and the slight flutter of nerves calmed to steadiness. But the tension was there, and only the excellent discipline held them in check, for these rebels were too close for comfort. Then followed the slow ringing of the locomotive's bell, brakes were released and the train moved on, crossed a high trestle bridge, and again halted.

"Pile out, everybody! Throw our company stores off the cars at once and stow them alongside the track. Get some lanterns working, men. On the jump, now!" and Captain Henderson strode along the embankment shining his flash-light and encouraging his men to do good work.

Lights flickered along the train. Stores were tossed off in quick order, camp sites selected, police parties immediately prepared latrines, and the guard was posted. Then, the immediate requirements being attended to, the men rolled up in their blankets on the hard earth to get such sleep as they could.

"Who were all those hombres[#] surrounding us before we crossed the big bridge, Sergeant?" asked Dick, pulling his knapsack into a more comfortable position beneath his head.

[#] Hombres--Men.

"They was the chief army of the rebels in these parts," replied Dorlan. "When we stopped back there we were right in the middle of the biggest town in Nicaragua, and the one where all the trouble starts. The people of Leon are always ready to revolute with the hope of makin' it the capital instead of Managua, and bein' on the only railroad from the capital city to the seaport, Corinto, they're in a foine place to control things. The nearest Federal troops are at a place called La Paz, about twenty-three kilometers from here."

"How long is a kilometer, Sergeant?" questioned one of the men.

"It's about five-eighths of a mile, so La Paz would be about fourteen miles south of here. From there on the Federal troops hold the railroad to the southern outskirts of Managua, and as this line goes on to Granada, I figure it's up to us to do considerable of work yet, for they say that we'll never get through the rebel lines beyond the capital without a fight. However, so far things seem to be goin' pretty slick."

"Do you know how many troops there are in Leon, Sergeant?"

"About two or three thousand, so they say, and they didn't want us to pass through there to-night, but finally consented. The Adjutant told me the leaders were pretty ugly about it, but as you see they finally gave in, and here we are."

"Now we are here what are we going to do?" inquired Dick.

"This battalion's goin' to camp right here and watch these fellers in Leon; the rest of them behind us will go on through when they come up and help the outfit that's ahead. All the telegraph and telephone lines are down between here and La Paz Centro. The rebs have cut 'em, and we can't get word of what's goin' on up ahead; but we'll know by to-morrow night. Now, quit yer askin' of questions. It's three o'clock in the mornin', and reveille's set for five A.M. Ye always want to get all the sleep ye can on campaign, for ye can't never tell what's a-goin' to be happenin' the next minute. Good-night, boys," and Sergeant Dorlan rolled over, his snores soon announcing he had followed his own excellent advice, but it was a long time before Dick's eyes closed in slumber, and it seemed as though the notes of reveille awakened him even before he had succeeded in getting the time-quoted "forty winks."

"I can't get 'em up! I can't get 'em up!

I can't get 'em up in the morning!

I can't get 'em up! I can't get 'em up!

I can't get 'em up at all!

The private's worse than the corporal,

The corporal's worse than the sergeant,

The sergeant's worse than the Captain,

And the Captain's worst of all."

*   *   *   *   *   *   *   *   *

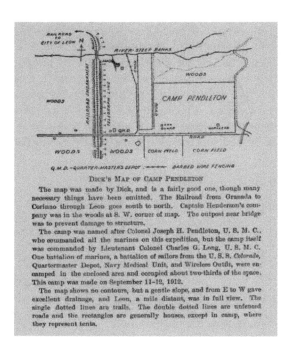

DICK'S MAP OF CAMP PENDLETON

The map was made by Dick, and is a fairly good one, though many
necessary things have been omitted. The Railroad from Granada to
Corinno through Leon goes south to north. Captain Henderson's company was in the woods at S. W. corner of map. The outpost near bridge
was to prevent damage to structure.

The camp was named after Colonel Joseph H. Pendleton, U. S. M. C.,
who commanded all the marines on this expedition, but the camp itself
was commanded by Lieutenant Colonel Charles G. Long, U. S. M. C.
One battalion of marines, a battalion of sailors from the U. S. S. Colorado,
Quartermaster Depot, Navy Medical Unit, and Wireless Outfit, were encamped in the enclosed area and occupied about two-thirds of the space.
This camp was made on September 11-12, 1912.

The map shows no contours, but a gentle slope, and from E to W gave
excellent drainage, and Leon, a mile distant, was in full view. The
single dotted lines are trails. The double dotted lines are unfenced
roads and the rectangles are generally houses, except in camp, where
they represent tents.

Dick's Map of Camp Pendleton

DICK'S MAP OF CAMP PENDLETON

The map was made by Dick, and is a fairly good one, though many necessary things have been omitted. The Railroad from Granada to Corinno through Leon goes south to north. Captain Henderson's company was in the woods at S.W. corner of map. The outpost near bridge was to prevent damage to structure.

The camp was named after Colonel Joseph H. Pendleton, U.S.M.C., who commanded all the marines on this expedition, but the camp itself was commanded by Lieutenant Colonel Charles G. Long, U.S.M.C. One battalion of marines, a battalion of sailors from the U.S.S. *Colorado*, Quartermaster Depot, Navy Medical Unit, and Wireless Outfit, were encamped in the enclosed area and occupied about two-thirds of the space. This camp was made on September 11-12, 1912.

The map shows no contours, but a gentle slope, and from E to W gave excellent drainage, and Leon, a mile distant, was in full view. The single dotted lines are trails. The double dotted lines are unfenced roads and the rectangles are generally houses, except in camp, where they represent tents.

*　*　*　*　*　*　*　*　*

"Come on, ye lazy bones, roll out of yer hammicks," called Dorlan cheerily, "and if ye foller that path down by the shack acrost the road ye'll reach the river and a good place to wash, only don't go too far down-stream, as there's a bunch o' buzzards cleanin' up some dead men, and the sight ain't extry fine on an empty stummick."

It was not long before Dick had finished his ablutions, and as he had avoided the buzzard's feast he felt quite capable of doing justice to the breakfast the mess cooks prepared.

The day was spent in fixing up the camp, preparing it for defense, reconnaissance work, and sorting stores. That the rebel general felt kindly towards the Americans might have been implied from the fact that he sent two beeves to the Colonel Commanding, with his compliments, but these were returned with expressions of thanks, as the Colonel did not feel he could accept the gift. Many parties of rebel soldiers passed the camp during the day and curiously watched the soldiers from the great Northern Republic at their varied occupations. Other days followed, some filled with flurries of excitement, some slow and monotonous. The rest of the regiment passed on towards the capital and a battalion of sailors came to augment the force, and for the time they were ashore, absorbed the Marine Corps spirit, "hook, line and dipsey."

One day a rebel "armored" train came puffing along from Leon, where they kept it carefully locked up in the station shed, and proceeded towards La Paz, with red flags streaming and a poor edition of Joan d'Arc astride the cow-catcher brandishing a big machete and cheering on the deluded soldiers.

"Viva Luis Mena! Viva Leon!"[#] they shouted to the marines, and waving their guns wildly, passed on.

[#] "Hurrah for Louis Mena! Hurrah for Leon!"--Mena was the rebel candidate for presidential honors and after the battle of Coyotepe he was taken under guard by the marines to Corinto and deported.

"They are off for a fight," hazarded the onlookers, but it was only a foraging party out for wood and fresh beef which they confiscated as they found it. One of the flat cars was arranged with sand bags, and over the parapet thus formed a Hotchkiss machine-gun menacingly stuck its baleful snout. This rebel train was an eye-sore to the American officers; for as long as General Rivas, who commanded at Leon, had this train and locomotive locked up in the station, so long it was sure to be a menace. The marines were in Nicaragua primarily to keep open the railroad, which was American-owned, and orders now came from the Admiral commanding the forces afloat and ashore to demand the surrender of the train. This Rivas refused, feeling confident that the few Yankees encamped across the river were neither strong enough nor brave enough to attempt to force him, and should they do so then it was quite certain they were no longer impartial. One Sunday morning in September, to his astonishment, three trains filled with marines and sailors pulled into the sidings at Leon. The attitude of the officers and men on this train was such that Rivas considered surrender the better part of valor, though at one time it looked as though his enraged men would precipitate a bloody struggle. Anyway, the train was taken out from its shed; the rebels were permitted to remove their gun, and amid the curses and execrations of the multitude gathered at the station, it was towed back to the American camp.

As for Richard Comstock, he found the life exciting and full of adventure. Following his application, he had had his rank changed to that of a private, and accompanied Sergeant Dorlan, who had been appointed special messenger to carry despatches, up and down the line. The situation was getting more critical every day. Then came orders to send all the field artillery from Leon to Managua, and on the train that took them went Dorlan and Dick, bearing special despatches to the Admiral who had gone on to the capital city for a conference. The rebels near the Leon camp looked gloomily upon this move. A few days before a train bearing marines, on passing through Masaya, a city south of Managua, had been fired upon, some men being killed and wounded on both sides.

Now it was apparent that the Yankees were going to assist the Federal troops. What would be the outcome? Would they attempt to attack the rebels at Barrancas and Coyotepe? If they did they could never take those positions. No troops had ever yet wrested those strongholds from the soldiers defending them. It had never been done in the history of the republic and its many wars. Secretly General Rivas despatched bodies of mounted men to augment the rebels in the vicinity of the threatened points.

When the artillery train stopped for watering the engine at La Paz, hundreds of Federal troops met it with a band at their head and cheering vociferously:

"Viva los Americanos! Viva los Federales!" they shouted till their throats were hoarse.

"Let's get off and buy some fruit, Sergeant," said Dick, who was riding on the engine with his companion.

"You go along, Dick, but hurry back, as I heard the engineer say we'll be pullin' out o' here in a jiffy."

Climbing down from his seat, Dick elbowed his way through the crowd till he came to a fruit stand at the far side of the station platform. After selecting some oranges and mangoes he was hurrying back when the broad shoulders, red neck and blond, bristly hair of a foreigner standing at the edge of the crowd drew his attention. Beside him was a tall man whose tanned face could not hide the fact that he too was a stranger from another land. Under the brim of the taller man's hat was a white spot of hair over and behind one ear, and the left hand, as he raised it, showed half the middle finger missing.

"The German and the Englishman!"

Dick almost said the words aloud in his excitement over the discovery. Both men were watching the crowd in front of them with great interest, and conversing in rather loud tones in order to make themselves heard above the din made by the enthusiastic soldiers cheering the train. Unobserved, Dick stopped directly behind them.

"Just our blooming bad luck to have them go through during daylight, after we have been waiting for this very move for several days," said the Englishman in a drawling voice.

"I never expected they would make the move by day, or I should have made better arrangements. If it were dark, as we expected it would be, we could pull off the same kind of game we worked in Masaya when Butler's Battalion went through there. I had to do that trick against General Zeladon's wishes. If he had consented to let me work it as I wished that train-load of marines never would have lived to get through as they did. I had to make it appear an unpremeditated affair, and as a result not half the people joined in the fight. A single defeat of these Yankees to the credit of the rebels, and the whole country would have joined us, Mena would have been president without a doubt, and our plans would be well under way towards consummation."

"You made a mistake, though, Mein Herr. You should never have made it appear that the rebels began the shooting. Our policy is to lead these Americans to believe that the Federal troops are against their interference."

"Bah! You don't know what you are talking about," said the German in the same arrogant way of speaking that Dick remembered so well.

"Well, don't let us get ratty over it; you know, old top, we have other things to think about. Now if we might delay this train in some way it would still be possible to work the game here."

"No chance at all! Not a chance!" exclaimed the big man impatiently, "but it would have been a fine opportunity to turn the tables had it only been dark. Our men here would have been enough to make them believe the whole outfit of Federals were shooting them up, and in the excitement the marines would have returned the fire, and the fight would have become general."

"Will the other trick work?" the Englishman now asked. "Will those papers implicating Chamorra come into the Americans' hands in a perfectly natural way?"

"Yes, and it is our last hope, outside of actual defeat of this Yankee rabble by the rebels, and I believe that is a possibility. These men are nothing but play soldiers. What do they know about war? And as for taking Coyotepe away from Zeladon and his men, bah! they can never do it! They will have to declare war first, and get down their miserable army. That will delay them long enough for us to defeat the Federals, and Mena and his men will be in supreme power. Hello, the train is off. Donder und Blitzen! How I wish it were night!" and the speaker stamped in wrath upon the gravel of the roadway.

So interested was Dick in the conversation of these two men which for a second time had been overheard by him that he had failed to note the train was moving away. To his consternation he saw now that he could not catch it because of the crowd between him and the last car, which was passing as he looked over the sea of heads. Running to the telegraph office where, owing to many previous visits with Dorlan, he was well known, he dictated a wire to be sent on to Nagarote, the next stopping place along the line, explaining briefly that he had missed the train. Then he turned to the operator, and before the man knew what was happening had divested that surprised individual of his coat.

"Quick, Frederico, loan me your coat and hat," he said. "Take charge of my canteen and haversack till I return. Oh, yes, I'll borrow your necktie too," he added, stripping it off the neck of the open-mouthed native, and after pulling off his leggins and putting on the things he had commandeered, he sped out through the doorway in pursuit of the two men whose rapid strides were even then carrying them towards the center of the town.

CHAPTER XXII

DICK IS LEFT BEHIND

As Dick ran from the telegraph office and looked about him in search of the two foreigners, he saw them disappearing around a street corner a few hundred yards away, but when he arrived at the same spot they were nowhere in sight. He dashed up the long street scouring each crossing for a sight of them, but in vain. The town was practically deserted. Most of the smaller houses were open and vacant. The stores and larger dwellings were closed and locked. The inhabitants had vacated when the Federal forces occupied the town some weeks before. La Paz was in too great a danger of changing hands again to make it comfortable as a place of habitation.

Small patrols of Federal soldiers sauntered about, but the majority had returned to the entrenchments which surrounded the town on all sides. Even women and children were noticeable by their absence, for the families of the Latin-American soldiers as a rule accompany their fighting men into the field, living with them on the firing line. Often the women themselves join in the fray, armed with machetes, and are most savage and blood-thirsty opponents.

Failing to discover the whereabouts of the German and the Englishman, Dick was at first at a loss as to his next step. Then he recalled having met at the station a few days before Colonel Solorzano Diaz, nephew to the president of Nicaragua,, and second officer in command at La Paz. Undoubtedly this officer could give him information of the two he sought, as it was improbable they could be inside the Federal lines and not be known to him.

"Is Colonel Diaz in La Paz?" asked Dick of a group of soldiers standing on a corner.

"Yes, Señor, he is at his headquarters."

"Take me to him at once! I have important news for him!" demanded Dick.

The young soldier who had answered his query now volunteered to act as guide, and after a ten minutes' walk they came to the Colonel's tent, erected near a battery of field guns. The smart, military-looking orderly on duty there halted them and after inquiring their business, he ushered them into the Colonel's presence.

"You say you are an American and have important news for me?" asked the handsome young Colonel, immaculately attired in a splendidly fitting uniform.

"I have, Colonel, and will be glad to tell you what I know if I may see you alone."

"First, explain how you come to be within our lines. Your arrival has never been reported to me, señor."

"I met the Colonel three days ago when I delivered a letter from the Commanding Officer at Camp Pendleton. I am a marine, Señor."

"Why are you dressed as you are, if such is the case?" and the officer looked Dick over with suspicion in his eyes.

Briefly Dick gave his explanation, but before Diaz would consent to hear the rest of his disclosures the orderly was directed to telephone Frederico at the station to verify the statements.

Colonel Diaz was a graduate of an excellent military school in the United States, and his command was remarkable for training and discipline, and though Dick fussed over the delay, he nevertheless admired the native officer for his caution.

Dick now saw that he had erred in not telegraphing to have the train held at Nagarote until he could explain by wire to the marine officer in command all the facts in order to permit that officer to govern his future movements to better advantage. While thinking of this, Colonel Diaz entered the tent, having gone out in order to talk to Frederico in person.

"You are Private Comstock, guard for Sergeant Dorlan, special messenger for the American forces?" he stated in a questioning manner.

"I am."

"I will hear what you have to say. Step outside, orderly, and take the guard who brought this man here with you." Then turning to Dick, he said in a most agreeable tone, "Be seated, Señor, and proceed."

Dick now told of his two meetings with the German and Englishman, and of the conversation he had so fortunately overheard on each occasion.

"Do you mean to say, Señor, that these two gentlemen, Señors Schumann and Heffingwell, are the men you heard engaged thus?" asked Diaz in amazement.

"If those are the names of the German and the Englishman I have described, yes," answered Dick positively.

The black eyes of the officer flashed ominously, and a deep flush mantled the smooth olive complexion.

"They will pay dearly for this, Señor. Those two men have had many concessions from my uncle, the president, in the past. They have been in Nicaragua for some years, and now I understand why they were ever busy in travelling about on various pleas. Sometimes it was to investigate the mines, at others to visit the coffee plantations of Diriamba or the rubber industry of the midlands. But this is not action! Orderly," and the clear voice rang with decision, "find out at once if Señors Schumann and Heffingwell have passed the outposts; if not they are to be brought here immediately."

During the time they waited for the report Colonel Diaz paced up and down the tent in deep thought, puffing great clouds of smoke from his cigarette.

"The Captain commanding the outposts, sir, states the two foreigners and escort of fifteen cavalrymen crossed the southern outpost fully ten minutes ago. Their passes were in due form and signed by yourself, sir."

"Yes, I gave them permission to leave at any time that suited their convenience, and provided an escort for their protection--the same men who accompanied them in here two days ago with a pass through our lines from General Pollito."

"Probably rebels in federal uniform," suggested Dick, "and the ones they depended upon to start the fracas at the station had the train arrived after nightfall."

"Yes, uniforms these days consist of little more than a ribbon to be changed as it suits the fancy or the convenience, but the question is, what should be done in the matter? It is evident they can do nothing to harm the train. The road, which nearly parallels the track from here to Managua, is in no shape for fast going. I inspected these men the day they arrived here. Their horses were worn out and poor at best. Even the lay-up they have enjoyed would not put them in condition. I will acknowledge there have been times a man on a good horse could leave here and arrive at the capital ahead of the train, but never unless it was held up by carelessness on the part of the native engineers. Nearing Managua the train has to descend some tortuous grades in the hills and the wagon road is more direct and gives the horseman the advantage during the last few kilometers."

"What do you propose to do, Colonel?" asked Dick. "Could you not send your men out after them and bring them back?"

"I cannot spare the men. We are too few here already, and at any moment we are expecting an attack. Also I have no absolute proof of their perfidy which would justify me in taking such drastic measures. They are under the protection of my superiors, and though I believe your story, unfortunately I am not the only one who would need to be convinced. The best that I can do is to telegraph my suspicions to all points and have them watched carefully from now on."

A scraping on the canvas at the front of the tent attracted Colonel Diaz's attention.

"Come in," he called, and then as his orderly appeared he added, "What is it you wish?"

"A telephone message from the station states that the telegraph wires between here and Nagarote have been cut, sir," reported the soldier, and at a nod from his superior he withdrew.

"They are at it again," said Diaz quietly; "no sooner do we send out and repair it than the line is cut at another point."

For a few seconds the officer and the young marine sat lost in thought. That some disaster threatened the train bearing the battery of field guns and the marines had become a conviction in Dick's mind. He could not forget the Englishman's question, "Will the trick work?" and the German's reply in the affirmative. Dick felt sure that this "trick" was to occur before Managua was reached, and this being so, what could be done to prevent it? Could it be prevented? It was certain that he could not count on help from Colonel Diaz, and now, adding to the difficulty, the wires were down.

Glancing through the tent opening Dick saw beneath a tree, held by a uniformed orderly, two spirited horses, saddled and bridled. The sight at once suggested action to the mind of the worried boy. Anything was better than this inactivity. Furthermore, Dick knew that if he stayed on here at La Paz he should never witness the stirring events which were bound to follow the arrival of the artillery at Managua. Here was a means of going forward and joining his companions. Possibly too he might learn something of advantage by following the route taken by Schumann and his band. It was worth trying.

"Colonel Diaz, may I borrow horses from you and a guide? I wish to proceed to Managua at once."

"Do you ride--ride well, I mean?"

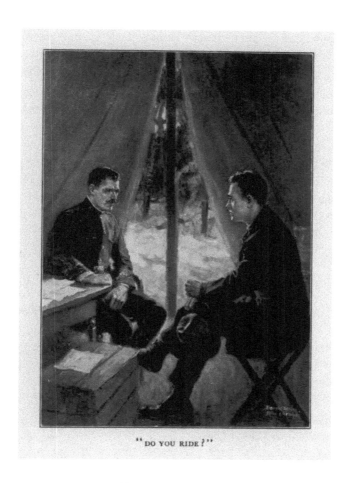

"DO YOU RIDE?"

"DO YOU RIDE?"

"Yes," replied Dick.

"It is sixty-three kilometers by rail, and about fifty-eight by road to Managua, señor. It is possible even to cut that distance with a man who is thoroughly acquainted with the country. A good horseman, well mounted, should reach there before dark."

"May I have the horses and a guide, Colonel?" and this time Dick looked enviously at the horses outside. Following the glance Diaz now espied the impatiently waiting animals.

"Ah! And did you mean my horses? Well, Señor, they are the only two horses in this camp capable of making the journey," and he said it with a pardonable touch of pride. "Those are not native ponies. They are thoroughbreds. I love them as a father would his sons, and----" he hesitated.

"I will give them good care," said Dick, who, to tell the truth, had no idea that the Colonel would entrust two such animals in his keeping when he had asked for horses, but now he thought possibly this would be the outcome of his request, and thought he understood why Diaz made his involuntary pause.

"That is not the only consideration, Señor Comstock. Those two horses are almost as well known as their master. You would be in constant danger of attack along the way, and seeing you, an American Marine, riding my horse, every rebel you encountered would do his best to stop you. They would not hesitate to shoot in case they could not capture you otherwise. Besides, those whom you seek are between you and your destination and they would surely hold you up. No, the chances are against you ten to one."

"Were they a thousand to one, Colonel, I would wish to make the attempt."

A smile of understanding lit the face of the officer and, rising, he gripped Dick's hand with warmth.

"I understand! It is the call of duty--of patriotism--and for you my heart holds naught but admiration, and my hand withholds nothing. You may take my horses, Señor, and may the good God who watches over brave men watch over you on your ride to the assistance of your fellow countrymen."

Colonel Diaz now called the orderly who brought the horses to the tent door, and turning again to Dick, he said:

"Tomas is an old servant in my household, Señor. He will accompany you and be under your orders. This paper will pass you through any of the Federal lines. Again, Señor, I wish you luck. Adios!"

Less than five minutes later Dick, mounted on the powerful black horse and followed by Tomas Casanave, a full-blooded Indian, was swinging along beside the railroad on a path which his guide informed him would save nearly a kilometer at the start.

At the first pond of water they came to, Dick ordered a halt. Dismounting and ordering Tomas to do likewise, he gathered up a quantity of mud and began smearing it over the velvety coat of the animal he rode, over his clothes and shoes, even putting some on his face.

"And why does the Señor do this?" asked Tomas, looking on in amazement at the proceeding.

"The Colonel told me his horses are known from here to Managua by every rebel along the line, but they are well known because they are always so well groomed, for one thing."

"I care for the Colonel's horses, Señor," said Tomas, simply, but with much pride in his voice.

"By spreading this mud over the horses," continued Dick, "it may help deceive persons whom we meet. Now, Tomas, turn those saddle cloths, smear mud on the trappings and harness, and tie your coat in a roll back of your saddle. Also hide your carbine and its boot where you will be able to find it on your return, and last, but by no means least, remove that blue band from your sombrero."

Tomas followed Dick's advice, and by the time he had finished no one would suspect either of them of belonging to any military organization. In fact the Tramps' Union, if there be one, would have disowned them.

"In case we are held up you are to answer all questions. I will tie this handkerchief about my neck, and you may state I am ill and we are hurrying to Managua to consult a doctor about my throat, which pains me and prevents me from speaking. Now, Tomas, we have lost time enough. You take the lead and I will follow. Save every minute, but also remember these horses must carry us to the end of the journey."

Springing into the saddle they instantly broke into the long lope which was to be their gait for the coming hours.

When told of the task before him by Colonel Diaz, Tomas had been anything but pleased at the prospect. He knew the danger of running the gauntlet of rebel bands infesting the country between La Paz and the capital city, and he was filled with apprehension. Dick's preparations won his admiration, and the boy's knowledge of Spanish was another agreeable surprise. He began to believe they might win through, rebels or not.

That the foreigners, who had a half hour's start, were following the same road, was soon discovered by the Indian. Accustomed to reading signs of the trail he interpreted them for Dick's benefit. Once he dismounted just before crossing a small stream which trailed across the road and carefully examined the ground on the far side near the water's edge.

"They passed here less than ten minutes ago, Señor," he said as he remounted and splashed across the brook. "I can tell this by the water which dripped from their horses, and the degree of moisture still remaining."

On they went to the accompaniment of the thud of the well-shod hoofs, the creak of leather, the jangle of bit and spur. Tomas was still watching the road, when without apparent reason he stopped.

"What is the trouble?" asked Dick, reining in the black charger on arriving abreast of his companion, but before answering the native looked about him cautiously.

"I have lost their trail, Señor. They have left the road."

"Which way did they turn, Tomas?"

"I cannot tell without going back, but I believe to the right."

"Is there any cross trail or road?"

"No, and there is no reason that I know for them to leave the road."

"Why do you suppose they have done so?"

"Quien sabe?"[#] answered Tomas, giving his shoulders a shrug which carried as much meaning as his words. "Possibly they are in hiding and watching us to ascertain if they are being followed. If so, it would not be wise to retrace our steps in case it is your desire to learn what became of them. But now that we are evidently beyond them, I think we are fortunate, and would suggest we proceed at once on our way. So far we have been unusually lucky, having met with no rebels."

[#] Quien sabe--Who knows?

That there was wisdom in the Indian's words could not be denied, but Dick felt a distinct sense of disappointment as he looked about him in the vain hope of seeing something of those they had been following so closely. About a half mile to the west an almost bare hill stuck its summit high into the glaring blue sky. Its slopes were cone shaped and fringed with a short stubby growth. In spite of disappointment, it was impossible to see the beautiful symmetry of the hill without admiring it, and as Dick watched, a cloud of smoke burst forth from its apex. Knowing the volcanic nature of the country he was nevertheless surprised at the sight, as Mount Momotombo, rising from the waters of Lake Managua, was the only active volcano in this immediate neighborhood.

"Is that small hill an active volcano, Tomas?" he asked.

The native looked long and searchingly at the smoking hilltop. At first his face expressed fear and amazement, followed in turn by a look of question, and then of understanding.

"No, no, Señor, it is not a volcano. It is a signal. Someone is sending smoke signals."

"Smoke signals? What do they mean?"

"They may mean anything. It is a method used by my people long ago and often resorted to by the natives of Nicaragua. If you notice the smoke is interrupted; sometimes long columns, sometimes short clouds or puffs."

"Are you able to read the message?"

"No! one has to know the code, Señor."

"If I had field glasses, it would be possible to see who is sending the message," said Dick, straining his eyes to discover if he could detect any movement on the hill.

"There are binoculars in the saddle-bags belonging to Colonel Diaz," exclaimed the native.

Dick placed his hand in the bag, which in the haste of departure from La Paz had not been removed, and brought forth a powerful pair of prismatic glasses. Adjusting them to his eyes, the cone-like hill appeared to be almost within reach of his hand. On the hilltop, more or less screened by the scrubby growth, were a number of men standing about a fire which gave forth a thick volume of smoke. Two of the men were moving a blanket back and forth over the fire, which caused the smoke to rise in irregular clouds. Half-way down the hill he saw about twenty horses with a few mounted men tending them.

Again he searched the hill. He was convinced these men made up the band whose trail they had followed from La Paz, and if he could discover the two foreigners his suspicions would be verified. As he watched he saw a man pointing to the southward. The others now turned their heads to look, and then from the shade of a boulder, he clearly saw both Schumann and Heffingwell arise and reaching for their binoculars, focus on the distant point.

"It is our party, Tomas," said Dick; "they are all looking to the south and evidently pleased at what they see there."

"That indicates their signal is answered," replied Tomas.

"It must be so, Tomas, for they are scattering their fire, and some are trailing down the hill. All have left now, except the two foreigners. They are apparently reading a paper between them, though I cannot quite make out what it is. Yes, it was a paper, for the German rolled it up and threw it on the ground near the rock on which they had been sitting."

"The message or the code, Señor," stated Tomas; "if we had it----"

"We shall have it, for I am going to get it. It is too good an opportunity to let pass, and even though it were nothing, I should not feel I had done my best if I left here without it."

"We are in plain view from the hill, Señor. If we remain here longer we may be detected."

"Never fear, they won't get us, but we must take to cover until they pass, and then secure the paper."

"As the Señor wishes; but having let them precede us again we may have difficulty in passing them in turn and reaching Managua in safety."

"We must take the chance," replied Dick, with no thought of wavering, and after replacing the glasses he led the way deep into a rough tangle of high trees and dense undergrowth at the roadside. Here they awaited impatiently the reappearance of the horsemen.

Soon the clatter of hoofs and the shouts of men greeted their ears, and they came galloping up the road.

"Seem to be in a big hurry, all of a sudden," mused Dick as he peeped through the green branches at their approach.

With the completion of his thought the blood in his veins seemed to congeal, for the black horse which he rode, hearing the oncoming troop, pricked his ears, and then before Dick had time to grab the quivering nostrils to prevent it a loud ear-splitting neigh filled the silent wood with its tell-tale message.

CHAPTER XXIII

DICK MAKES A FLYING LEAP

Too late the boy's firm fingers closed upon the nose of the black horse, and fearing a repetition of the alarm Dick pinched for dear life, meanwhile peering apprehensively through the surrounding mass of green foliage. To his mystification the road was clear of any living soul.

Turning anxiously to question the Indian, he caught him in the midst of choking back an amused chuckle. Not understanding the situation, and believing the guide was suffering from a stroke of apoplexy, Dick began to pound him vigorously on the back.

"Bastante, bastante![#] I am not choking," exclaimed Tomas as soon as he was able to stop his fit of laughter. "Pardon me, my friend; I expected your horse to send out his challenge, but I knew those in the road would never hear it. They were too noisy themselves. In consequence, I could not refrain from a little enjoyment at your expense."

[#] Bastante--Spanish for "enough."

"You mean to say they did not hear at all this black fog-horn-fourteen-inch-double-barreled-siren-and-brass-band all rolled into one? Why! It was enough to awaken the dead. Boy! but it sure made me sweat," and Dick wiped the beads of perspiration from his forehead.

"They heard nothing, Señor, and at the rate they were going they are well on their way by now."

"Then, Tomas, let us make haste to get that paper," and without further words they turned their horses' heads in the direction of the cone-like hill. On arriving at the point where those before them had left their horses Dick, dismounting and leaving Tomas in charge, climbed the remaining distance alone.

At the top of the hill he saw the dying remnants of the scattered fire, and then with a glad cry he sprang forward to pick up a crumpled ball of paper lying dangerously close to a glowing ember.

Seating himself he smoothed out the sheets. Upon one was a rude sketch in ink; the other was filled with writing in Spanish. Feverishly he translated it aloud.

"Señor: Everything is prepared, and when I see your smoke signals I will know the exact hour to spring my surprise. The rock is in position to roll on the track at the curve marked X, where the arrow points. Crushed beneath it, as if accidentally by his own carelessness, will be the body of a Federalista, a close friend of the President. In his pockets will be found the papers proving conclusively that the Federals planned to wreck the American train. Even the money paid for the work will be in the dead man's pocket, untouched. If the train arrives at the spot in the night, our scheme cannot fail. If by day, and it should be discovered in time to prevent a bad accident, the proof will be there anyway, and the northern meddlers must then believe Diaz and his adherents are implicated. Viva el Republic! Viva Mena!

"CANDIDO.

"P.S. My men have driven away those peons who fill the tender with fuel at the wood pile south of Mateare, and that will cause more delay."

Having finished the letter, Dick studied the map, but it was so inaccurate and he was so little acquainted with the country that he gleaned no real information from it. He believed that the curves depicted represented the tortuous stretch of rail a few kilometers north of Managua. There the road turned and twisted through a group of hills, and in many places the sides of the cuts were lined with rocks of great size and weight. Often these had been loosed in the past, either by natural causes or otherwise, and, falling into the right of way, caused many serious accidents. Perhaps Tomas would be able to recognize the spot, and Dick ran down the hill to question the waiting soldier.

"Here, Tomas, read this aloud to me," he demanded, thrusting the letter into the guide's hands. The reading proved that Dick's opportunities for learning the Spanish tongue had been used to good advantage.

*   *   *   *   *   *   *   *   *

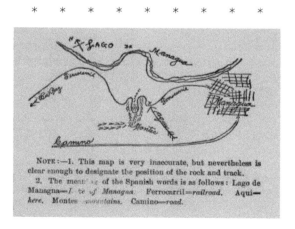

NOTE:—1. This map is very inaccurate, but nevertheless is clear enough to designate the position of the rock and track.
2. The meaning of the Spanish words is as follows: Lago de Managua—*Lake of Managua.* Ferrocarril=*railroad.* Aqui—*here.* Montes *mountains.* Camino=*road.*

Map Showing Position of Rock and Track

NOTE:--1. This map is very inaccurate, but nevertheless is clear enough to designate the position of the rock and track.

2. The meaning of the Spanish words is as follows: Lago de Managua=*Lake of Managua*. Ferrocarril=*railroad*. Aqui--*here*. Montes=*mountains*. Camino=*road*.

*   *   *   *   *   *   *   *   *

"I know the exact place, Señor," said Tomas, and his features reflected Dick's own excitement. "It is one hour's hard riding from here, and Señor, look! There is the train pulling away from the filling station now. You may know it to be so because of the trail of black smoke. We can never reach the spot before the train. We are too late, and soon it will be dark and we cannot then ride as fast."

"We must make the trial," said Dick, mounting his restive steed. "Come, lead the way. Do not spare the horses now," and with the Indian in advance they were soon clattering down the hill at breakneck speed. On reaching the road the Indian, bending low in the saddle, for the first time touched his horse with the spur, and the splendid animal responded to the unaccustomed punishment as if shot from a catapult.

Side by side the two sped along the roadway towards their distant goal. Again the rails and track ran parallel and Tomas, taking advantage of his knowledge of short cuts, turned from the highway and led the chase along the narrow trail beside the tracks, never once stopping the fearful speed of his mount.

Suddenly from behind them came the long wailing whistle of a locomotive. Glancing over his shoulder Dick saw a few hundred yards behind a fast approaching train. This could not be the troop train, he was sure. Once more he heard the whistle warning him to get clear of the track.

"Tomas," he called, but the Indian gave no sign of having heard his cry.

Another look behind showed the train rushing on with no slackening of speed. Still Tomas continued in his mad flight. Dick tried to swerve his horse from the trail beside the track, fearing that when the train overtook them the animal might become frightened and dash against the side of the train; but now the black horse was infected with the fighting spirit, and so long as the bay horse in the lead was ahead just so long would he keep up the heart-breaking run. Dick could feel the powerful muscles beneath him working with the smoothness of well-oiled machinery, and in spite of the enormous strides with which they covered the ground, he hardly rose from his saddle, so perfect was the action.

Then to Dick came a new thought. Unless the train ahead was delayed he never could hope to reach the danger point in time to warn the troops. He knew his attempt was futile, so why continue! This train now thundering along so close behind might catch up with and stop the artillery train. But how could he let those on board know of the danger? To attempt to flag the train was useless now. Had he thought of it before it might have been possible, but it was not very likely, under the most favorable conditions, that they would stop on the signal of two lone and unrecognized horsemen alongside the track. Should he attempt to interfere with its progress, the chances were that the train guard--men from his own corps, possibly his own company, would shoot him as a suspiciously acting native: "shoot first and inquire after," was a fundamental principle in these treacherous revolutionists.

His mind, naturally active in summing up situations in their true light in times of stress, and quick to formulate his plans, saw only one way left open to him. He must board the moving train. He must make the leap from his saddle in some way, grasp hand-guard, brake, door, window or sash, and hang there until those on the train could pull him to safety.

Even as he made his resolve the engine, foot by foot, was gliding ahead of him. From the cab window the engineer, a sailor from one of the ships of the Navy, watched with deepest interest what he believed was a vain race between two "loco Spigs"[#] and the train, and turning to his grimy fireman he ordered him to keep up the steam pressure at all costs and "Durn the expense."

[#] Loco--Spanish for "foolish."

That the horses could keep up their terrific speed for any length of time was out of the question. The Indian's horse appeared to have taken matters in his own hands and was running away, though Tomas was now doing his best to hold in the excited brute.

Now the tender and the first car had passed Dick. Another quick glance from the corner of his eye and he saw there were but three more cars in the train, and when his eye returned to the narrow trail he saw it gradually drawing away from the rails. Unless it returned beside the track within the next few rods his last opportunity would be gone.

On the train every window was filled with excited faces watching this uneven race between God-made and man-made power, but they tried to encourage the riders with shouts and yells and much waving of hats and hands. Dick heard and saw the "rooters," but beneath his cap there was no change of expression; his face was white and stern with a bulldog tenacity of purpose.

Now the second car had drawn past him, and the middle of the third car drew opposite the straining horse. Would the trail never get nearer? Must he in a last desperate endeavor pull with all his might on the left rein and cross the rough ground in order to bring the laboring animal against the side of the cars? If he did it meant almost certain destruction.

Now the fourth car appeared, nosing forward on his flank, yet he dared not take his eye from the trail. Must he leave it and make the dash across the rough uneven space? He would wait just a few strides more. Then once again he found the narrow path converging towards the tracks. Already Tomas was racing beside the car, ten feet in advance. Would the black horse be equal to the effort? With a wild yell the boy dug the spurs into the flanks of the steed, and with a gasp of surprise the horse bounded forward as never before. For a second the painted side of the clattering coach was like a dull smear on Dick's blurred vision--then he leaned far out in his saddle to his left, his clutching fingers slid along the beveled edges of the car's wooden frame, they gripped the iron hand-rail at the rear end of the platform, the next moment he was pulled from his saddle, his feet struck the steps and with a last, final effort he fell breathless on the floor, held in safety by the strong hands of two astonished train guards.

"Well, I'll be jiggered, if it ain't Dick Comstock," exclaimed Private Jones, late of the *Denver's* guard. "I ain't seen you since we separated at Colon. Say, Dick, what in the dickens are you doing here, and where did you come from? I sure am some glad to see you."

"Wait a minute; let him get his breath before you take it all away again by making him answer your questions," said the other marine, assisting Dick to his feet, and looking at this sudden arrival with unfeigned admiration. "My word, Bo, but you beat any movie picture hero I ever seen. By the way, your friend back there doesn't seem to know what's become of you."

"I'm thinking he must believe the Angel Gabriel come along and took you up in his chariot," said Jones, whose knowledge of Biblical characters and their history was fragmentary.

Far down the track Tomas could be seen halted in the middle of the rails scratching his head while he gazed after the train in evident perplexity.

"I guess he'll figure it out. He's a wise old Indian," said Dick; then the reason for his being on the train struck him with its full significance, and, "Who's in charge of the train?" he asked.

"Why, Dick, our old friend, Sergeant Bruckner. He's up forward on the engine. Why? What's up?"

But Dick did not stop to answer. Roughly pushing his way through the crowd of natives gathered at the end of the car to see what manner of man it was who rode hair-breadth races with railroad trains, he ran through the remaining coaches to the front end of the train, climbed over the tender, now nearly empty of wood, and finding the sergeant, he told him what he had done and what there was still to do.

"You say the artillery train left the vood station about tventy minutes ago?" asked Bruckner, reverting to his v-habit in his excitement.

"Yes, and they will necessarily have to go slowly. It is getting dark, and I believe we can catch them before too late."

"But ve also have to stop and refill with vood, and as ve von't find any men there to do the vork for us, it's going to be a very slow business."

"Slow? Why, if necessary, we'll make every passenger on this train lend a hand, willingly or otherwise," said Dick.

"Well, here we are," called the engineer who, though keeping his eye on the rails ahead, was an eager listener. "Come, all hands, get everyone on the job, and I'll lend a hand myself."

Never was wood hustled into a tender of the Ferrocarril de Nicaragua so fast as it was that October evening, and when the fireman finally announced that he had sufficient, the ear-splitting whistle had barely died away before the old wood burner was surging on into the gathering darkness, her headlight streaming on the lines of shining rails ahead, making them appear like two bars of yellow gold stretching on into infinity.

"If there are any ties out, fishplates gone or spikes driven between the rails this night we're goners," said the fireman to Dick as the two worked, throwing log after log into the capacious maw of the engine, where the draft seemed quickly to turn them into a mass of dark red cinders which streamed out of the great stack and left a glowing trail as of a comet's tail following them through the night.

"I've been with old man Strong, the engineer, every trip he's made, and I never seen him light out like this. I almost believe we're making forty-five miles, and mebbe more than that, especially on the down grades. Wow! Man dear, but he took that curve on two wheels, and it's a wonder we stayed on the track when he struck the reverse. What's his idea of pullin' the whistle every two seconds, anyhow?"

"He's started sounding the 'S.O.S.' calls," said Dick, "hoping the train ahead will hear us and wait to see what's up."

"How many miles have we got left to catch 'em?"

"I don't know," answered Dick, as for a moment he ceased his labors, and holding to the rail at the side of the cab peered ahead along the parallel lines of light; "it can't be much more, for we are in the hills now, and on the down grade. If we are to do any good at all it must be soon."

The next moment there was a long weird shriek of the whistle, then the grinding of brake-shoes on the wheels as the signal for the train guards to man the wheel brakes followed in staccato blasts. Groaning, straining, shaking, screeching, bumping and thumping, the train slackened its speed, crawled for a few yards, and then with one last resounding rattle it stopped, and there, but a few short yards ahead, waiting to discover the reason for the wild signals for help they had picked up, stood the officers and men of the artillery train, safe and unharmed.

Owing to a "hot-box" they had been forced to stop and repair at a station called Brasiles. While there they discovered that the lines of wire either side of the station had been cut and later, hearing the wild whistling of the engine in their rear as they proceeded cautiously on their way, and believing rightly that the signal was meant for them, it was decided best to await the arrival of the news before going further.

It was Richard Comstock who, a little later from the seat above the cow-catcher of the leading train, gave a shout of satisfaction. Rounding the last abrupt curve in the hills before descending to the straight road-bed of the plain, he espied a great mass of rock thrown directly across the rails. Had the train been other than creeping along through the cuts and defiles a serious accident would have followed undoubtedly.

Slowly the train drew up to the dangerous obstacle, and then, true to the contents of the letter which Dick had delivered into the hands of the Marine Officer in charge, they found crushed beneath the mass of rock the body of a man in whose pockets was the letter and the money, which, if the truth had not been known, might have changed the pages of Nicaragua's history.

CHAPTER XXIV

THE SITUATION WELL IN HAND

Zoom! Whiz-z-z, and then a distant bursting cloud of cottony white smoke high in the blue sky over the hill called Coyotepe. Soon the waiting ear heard the sharp explosion of that seemingly soft fluffy cotton-ball, which in reality carried death in its wake, for with the bursting came hundreds of tiny bits of steel and bullets seeking out the enemy behind their entrenchments. And through the day and the night following the sound of the field guns prepared the way for the attacking marines, sailors and Federal troops the next morning.

At the first break of day two battalions of United States Marines began their advance. In reserve, a battalion of sailors, as yet untried in land warfare, fretted and fussed at their position behind the actual firing line, and some even rolled in the yellow mud till their white suits were the color of marine khaki and then, rifle in hand, sneaked away from their command and joined their brothers in arms. As for the Nicaraguans, supposed to attack but not relishing the job, they delayed and delayed, only too happy to let Colonel Pendleton and his command assume the task of attempting to drive Zeladon and his insurrectos from Coyotepe and Barrancas. Deep down in their hearts they felt that what no Nicaraguan army had yet accomplished could never be carried to a successful issue by these few pale-faced Americans from the North.

No! It seemed that those who held these two hills which commanded the road and railroad, north and south, could never be driven from them. Yet, little by little, step by step, up the rocky, slippery slopes, struggled the thin brown lines of marines. On through briar and bush; over jagged cliff or bullet-strewn open space; on and ever on. Through prepared traps of barbed wire; cutting, slashing, firing, sweating, swearing, always upward, till finally in one mad, glad, glorious, soul-stirring, blood-thrilling rush, they mounted the earthworks on the hilltop's crest, in spite of rocks, in spite of cannon, in spite of rifle, in spite of machine-gun fire, and there at bayonet's point engaged in hand-to-hand conflict with enraged men and wild Amazonian women who wielded bloody machetes with fanatical frenzy.

With those who shared in the glory of that conquest was Richard Comstock, his breath coming in short, labored gasps; the rifle he held, taken from a fallen comrade far down the slope, still burning hot, and the knife-like blade of the bayonet shining brightly in the early morning sunlight.

And the marines accomplished this supposedly impossible task in less than forty minutes from the beginning of their advance. Is it any wonder that the natives of the countries where the fighters visit and uphold the glory of the stars and stripes, honor and respect them, individually and collectively?

After the pursuit of the fleeing rebels the Federal troops, encouraged by the unbelievable success of their allies, attacked, took and sacked the town of Masaya in true native style, which always involves useless destruction and uncalled-for brutality.

The "handwriting on the wall" was now unmistakable and when later in the day some of the victorious troops and the battery of field guns were entrained and started for Leon, the rebels in that city gave up all hope of ever putting their candidate into office.

Carrying despatches on the first train north went Sergeant Dorlan and his guard, Dick Comstock, and in those despatches was a very complimentary letter to Dick's immediate commanding officer which told of his timely warning and the manner of its accomplishment.

Barrancas and Coyotepe were taken on October fourth, and on the sixth long lines of marines and sailors were seen leaving Camp Pendleton. That the rebels had agreed to surrender and lay down their arms without a fight was very much doubted, and Lieutenant Colonel Long, who had charge of the coming occupation, was going to enter the town in force and take no chances of a possible ambush.

Immediately after reveille the first troops had quietly reënforced the company already on duty at the railroad station. This was done without incident, and then on three sides of the city the forces began their advance. The rebel troops, knowing that their leaders, Generals Rivas and Osorio, had fled, had spent the night in drinking and debauchery. As the main column debauched into the principal street and the excited, inflamed wearers of the red cockades saw the stars and stripes of the United States flaunting in the breeze, they resorted to their usual street fighting tactics.

Street by street the marines advanced. Every inch of the way was disputed and the bullets whizzed and cracked, sang and stung; taking their tally of wounded and dead.

"Dick, me lad, I'd give me old pipe, I would, to be able to be on ahead with the advance instead of here with the colors, much as I love 'em," announced Dorlan as he stood in the shelter of an overhanging roof and watched the windows of a pretentious building on his right.

Reaching a street corner or alley a little later it was found that the natives had resorted to their brutal, inhuman tactics in dealing even with civilized troops. A sailor, stripped of his clothing and mutilated, was lying in the roadway.

Perhaps he had lost his section and wandering here trying to locate it, was set upon by the cruel natives.

"Ah! a sight like that makes the very blood in me bile," said Mike, shaking his fist in the direction of the dodging opponents far up the street; "if I knew the feller what did that to the poor flatfoot,[#] I'd be a brute meself and tear him to pieces with me bare hands."

[#] "Flatfoot"--Marine Corps slang for a sailor.

"Look out, Dorlan," yelled Dick, and falling flat on the rough cobble stones in the middle of the street he emptied a clip of cartridges into a doorway which that moment was flung open, and from which a half dozen rifle barrels were pointing from behind a rough barricade. But he did not stop the volley of shots which followed, and the heavy leaden slugs splashed, pattered, and flattened all about the little color guard. They rained against the walls of the buildings on either hand, gouging out great chunks of mortar and plaster to a depth of several inches, and one bullet, partly spent, struck Dick in the shoulder, penetrated to the bone and lodged there.

"I guess I'm hit, old pal," he said weakly to Mike, after they had silenced the fighters behind the barricade and had gone on for a couple of blocks. "I thought it was only a scratch, but the blood's running down my back, and---" but just then it seemed as though a great thunder-storm was descending upon the city; the sky grew black and the darkness came so swiftly that he could not see where to step, and with a sob he fell into the arms of his faithful friend.

"After all, it is not much more than a scratch; it is lack of sleep and nourishment during the last few days," said the surgeon, handing Dick a piece of lead he had recently removed from the boy's wound, "but I have recommended that you be sent back to Corinto, where you can receive proper attention on board ship."

"But is the fighting all over?" asked Dick weakly.

"Surest thing you know, my boy, for 'the marines have landed and have the situation well in hand,' as the papers always say," answered the surgeon smiling.

"Thanks for the Navy's bringing us here," added Dick with a wan smile, and then he dropped off into a much needed peaceful sleep.

Two days later as he lay on his white bunk in the sick bay of the U.S.S. *Buffalo*, steaming southward to Panama, and the wonderful hospital at Ancon, a letter was handed him. On opening it he found a document appointing him a corporal in the United States Marine Corps. Also enclosed was a very complimentary letter from the Commanding Officer of Marines ashore, thanking him for his excellent work during the exciting days of the campaign, and at the end he read with satisfaction that, owing to his information, a certain German and his accomplice had been arrested by the Government authorities and were on their way to the coast, where they were to be deported, and forbidden ever to return.

Lightning Source UK Ltd.
Milton Keynes UK
UKHW010743271222
414464UK00004B/346